BLESSED FURY

ANGELS OF FATE - BOOK 1

C.S. WILDE

Join the Wildlings at www.cswilde.com to keep up to date with the latest on C.S. Wilde and participate in amazing giveaways.

To the people who know it's impossible
and still do it anyway.

~

"Tell me, Ava, why do you think you're here?"
the Angel of Death

~

AVA

The stench of stale beer and sweat invaded Ava's nostrils as she moved toward the bar. A football game played on the screen behind the counter, but none of the three men populating the pub paid any attention to it.

The air inside was musty, old, and it only worsened as she approached the end of the room.

She passed by the first man, who sat in a booth on the left. He stared at nothing in particular, with a cry stuck midway in his throat and a half-empty jug of beer clutched in his hand. The bad lighting drenched half of him in shadows, making it seem like darkness was swallowing him.

He didn't notice Ava because she had masked her presence before entering. She wasn't exactly invisible. Humans could see her if they focused hard enough, but they rarely did.

Ava made a mental note to check up on that poor soul if she had the chance, her Guardian instincts urging her to help. He was clearly suffering, but she was here for a reason, and the reason was not that man. So she went back to the task at hand.

The wooden floor creaked as she approached the bar. The bartender, an old man with white hair and a face marred by deep wrinkles, cleaned a dirty glass from behind the counter.

She wasn't here for him, either.

The last man sat hunched at the edge of the counter. Well, he wasn't exactly a man. According to his file, he was a Selfless, an angel whose memories had been wiped out so he could be reborn as a human—standard procedure, considering centuries of memories could overload a human brain.

She stopped by his side and sat on the red padded stool to his left. The seat's ripped leather grazed the white fabric of her bodysuit, scratching her thighs.

The man was hunched over, so she couldn't see much of him except for his strong build and dark hair. He took a long gulp of his drink and didn't acknowledge her presence for a while.

So she waited.

"Archie isn't dead yet," he finally said, his voice rough like a cement wall.

"I do belie—"

"He's not dead," the man repeated, his attention solely on what was left of his whiskey.

She took a deep breath. "I know, Liam." She used her Guardian voice, the calm, soothing tone to which she had grown accustomed. It was how she talked to her charges, how every guardian angel spoke, actually. Using the same serene tone.

Liam turned to Ava, his brow furrowed and his lips twisted, and for a moment too quick to count, she lost her breath. Ava had seen his photo on file, but the live version of him was brutally handsome. Liam was a cool wind on a summer morning and a thunder waiting to crack. His features were all sharp angles and fierce lines, but his eyes … Ava had never seen eyes like those. Rough emeralds cut with razor-sharp precision, almost like crystalline water, if water were green.

"Don't call me by my name," he spoke through gritted teeth. "You don't *know* me."

"You're right, and I apologize." She patted her thighs as if she were fixing the apron of an invisible dress. "I only read your file, but I'd like to get to know you, Liam."

"You're a Guardian," he scoffed and took a sip of his drink.

"I am," she said, ignoring the contempt in his tone. "However, the word the Messenger used when he assigned you as my charge was 'temporary partner.'"

"You're not my partner," he barked through tight lips. "Archie is."

"I'm not here to replace Archibald, Liam."

He glared at her, certainly because she had used Archibald's name *and* his. This seemed to be a sensitive matter to her new charge, so she calmly added, "I can't replace your partner. No one can." Ava extended her hand to him. "I'm Ava, by the way. And I'm here to help."

He studied her from head to toe, almost as if he were seeing her for the first time. The fury in his eyes waned a little, giving way to something softer.

Ava blushed and looked down, focusing on the long curls of her strawberry-blonde hair that cascaded over her Guardian bodysuit. Her tresses almost reached the white linen kilt tied around her waist.

Instead of shaking her waiting hand, Liam turned back to his glass and finished his drink. "No hard feelings, Ava, but how's a fucking Guardian supposed to help me? Especially one who looks like some damsel in distress?"

"I do not—" She stopped herself. Ava knew better than to argue with a new charge. She was here to offer help, not cause friction.

Liam waved to the bartender, who quickly approached and poured him more whiskey. The side-glance the old man gave him silently called Liam crazy for speaking to himself. It must be odd for him, seeing a man muttering to empty space, but if Ava revealed herself, it would raise questions the bartender wasn't prepared to have.

She studied Liam. Ava's charges were often lost and angry, like the Selfless beside her. It took a lot of understanding and patience to help them. *But would it be enough?*

The Selfless had a reputation for being tough, especially considering their line of work. Assigned to precincts, they kept vampires and werewolves in check, and occasionally the lower-grade demon too. Being strong was less of a choice and more of a necessity for them.

Getting through to Liam wasn't going to be easy.

"I understand this is unorthodox," she said.

Guardians like Ava spread the love of the Gods; they never inflicted pain. Considering the Selfless' line of work, another Selfless, or at least a warrior angel, might've been a better choice for a partner.

But Ava never questioned her orders, especially if they came directly from the Messenger.

"I suppose," she continued, "that the Messenger sent me here because a Guardian might offer you great solace through difficult times. Perhaps this is exactly what you need."

Liam slammed his glass on the counter and leaned toward her like a bull about to charge. His breath hit her skin, but the scent of alcohol wasn't as pungent as she expected.

"I don't need solace. I need answers," he said, baring his teeth. "And Archie will be fine."

The bell above the door jingled as a tall, slim figure entered the pub. He wore a black fedora, along with a black shirt and pants. *A man clothed in shadows.* His cheeks were sunken, his pale skin covered in green veins, but the worst were his eyes—pitch-black orbs that held no hint of white.

The bartender and the man at the booth didn't notice the demon, which meant the creature, much like Ava, had masked its presence.

The demon glanced sideways at Ava and Liam as it strolled across the pub, but when it spotted the melancholic man in the red-padded booth, it shot him a sharp-toothed grin. The demon tipped its hat off to them and walked to the man.

The creature sat across from the poor soul and whispered words Ava couldn't understand. Shadows flowed from its lips, dancing in the air before they wrapped around the man's face. The man let out a whimper or two before bursting in loud sobs.

Ava immediately stood, but Liam grabbed her arm. "This is the real world, princess." He nodded to the demon. "Obsessors are way too low on the food chain. Not worth the hassle."

She wanted to slap Liam, first because of the condescending way he had called her princess, and second, because technically she was also "way too low on the food chain."

Instead of using unnecessary violence, Ava swallowed her outrage and let the love of the Gods flood through her. "Guardians bring solace and comfort to our charges. Those things …" She pointed to the demon, trying to steady her shaky hands. Apparently, the need for violence was still there, pushing to get out. "They destroy what we do."

"Ava, let it go," he ordered more than said.

She probably should've obeyed the experienced Selfless who had done this his entire life, but Ava's purpose was to help all creatures of the Gods regardless of the *hassle*.

She jerked her arm free and walked to the demon. "Be

gone, foul creature," she ordered, slamming both hands on her waist.

There, that should be enough to scare it.

The demon laughed. "What a pretty little angel you are." It licked its dark lips with a wine colored tongue. "I'd like to have fun with you."

She balled her fists and stepped closer to the sobbing man. She whispered in his ear all the love the Gods had for him, her words glittering wisps of light that soaked into the man's skin. Slowly, he stopped crying, and a hint of a smile brushed his lips.

The demon slammed its veiny hands on the table. "He's not yours!"

Ava didn't flinch, didn't step back, even though every part of her urged her to do so. "Leave," she ordered with a tone weaker than she had intended.

Liam walked to the booth and lifted the side of his black leather jacket, revealing a bulky holy gun placed in a shoulder holster. Just below the gun, attached to the black belt that circled his waist, was a sheathed longsword.

The sword's silver hilt was carved into a wolf's face, its eyes two blue gems, and the cross-guard formed wolf claws. The weapon sent tingles through Ava's essence, which meant the blade had been blessed.

A Selfless could use an array of weapons, such as holy guns, sun daggers, sometimes even bows and arrows, but a blessed sword? That was reserved for ascended angels only—certainly not for lower angels like Ava or a Selfless like Liam. Still, she was glad to see a blessed weapon, especially in a moment like this.

"Do we have a problem here?" Liam asked the demon, one dark eyebrow raised.

The crying man shot Liam a confused stare as he wiped tears from his cheeks. "Are you talking to me?"

The poor soul had no idea what was happening, given Ava and the demon still masked their essences.

The demon glared at Liam, completely ignoring the sword and the gun. "He's mine." Its voice turned into a mix of baritones and screeches, as if several people were speaking, yelling, chanting at the same time. "Mine, mine, mine!"

Liam rolled his clear green eyes at Ava. "Look what you've done, princess."

The demon seized in his seat, vomiting black blobs that stank of sulfur. The blobs quickly covered all of its body, eating at skin and bone, melting the demon's flesh into a puddle.

Four dark figures rose from the black goo, thorny shadows with shiny yellow eyes and sharp teeth.

It wasn't just one demon. It was several.

They placed themselves between the back of the pub and the door, blocking the exit.

The sound of shattered glass came from behind Ava and Liam. The bartender was gaping and breathing erratically, his mouth half open in an upcoming scream that never came. The man in the booth looked equally terrified. The demons weren't bothering to mask their essences anymore.

The crying man scrambled out of the booth and ran toward the bar, since there was no way he could reach the door without passing by the demons.

"Soon darkness will spread," one of the creatures said with a high-pitched tune.

"—and your precious Order will fall," another continued with a low baritone.

"Same old bullshit." Liam withdrew a sun dagger from his belt and handed it to Ava. "This will be fun." He unsheathed his sword, and it gleamed faintly against the darkness of the bar. He acquired a defensive stance. "Can Guardians fight?"

Not really, but the demons didn't wait for her answer.

They bolted at them, crawling on the walls like spiders made of shadows. Two demons focused on Ava, and two focused on Liam. Their thorny spider legs drummed a fast-paced *tick, tick, tick* on the wooden walls.

Ava gathered her holy essence atop her skin, creating an invisible shield over her body, but she wouldn't be able to maintain it for long. Her heart banged against her ribcage, and a cold sweat bloomed on her forehead.

Confronting the demons had been a big mistake. She hadn't fought with swords or daggers since her initiation, a hundred years ago, and even then, she had only learned the basics.

Soon those creatures would rip her throat open with their spiky claws, and there wasn't much she could do to put up a fight.

The Order prepared me for this, she thought, trying to remember her first lessons.

Ava balanced her stance and took a defensive position. She closed her eyes and locked her fear somewhere deep within her. *Tick, tick, tick ...* When she opened her eyes, the first demon was jumping at her, followed by the second. Without thinking, she drew a circle in the air with the dagger Liam had given her.

A dark lump that used to be the first creature's arm fell on the floor, oozing black liquid.

Yes!

The creature stopped and stared at its fallen arm, then at its befuddled companion. Both demons opened their jaws like pythons ready to engulf their prey, their furious shrieks piercing through Ava's ears. She hardened her shield right before the demons leapt at her with a vengeance.

"It's gonna get messy!" Liam's voice came from her left, and then a blue blast burst the first demon's head into a thousand pieces. Splatters of black blood rained down on her, sliding down the invisible shield that layered her skin.

The inky remains of the demon thumped on the floor.

The second demon stopped and stepped back, almost as if it couldn't believe its companion was dead. Then it shrieked in anger before jumping at her, its clawed hands aimed at Ava, but the angle ... it was too high. The demon wasn't jumping *toward* her, it was jumping *over* her.

And it landed behind the bar. Where the two humans were hiding.

Heavens, no!

To her left, a demon shrieked as Liam split it in half with his sword. Liam wielded the blade in his right hand and the holy gun in the left. And just like that, with only *one* hand, *one* blow, he'd cut a demon in two.

The two sides of the creature fell apart as easily as warm bread slices caving to gravity.

The second demon ran for the door, but Liam lifted his holy gun and closed one eye. A blue blast shot from the muzzle, and the demon's head exploded. The headless body fell on its thorny knees.

When Ava turned back to the bar, the crying man stood there with his arms crossed. His eyes were completely rolled over, his skin a sickening mix of white flesh and green veins.

"We'll dessstroy the humans you love ssso much, Guardian," the man said, his voice a continuous hiss.

A bitter sensation flooded her mouth. The man hadn't been her charge, and yet, Ava felt as if she'd failed him.

"We have a problem," she muttered.

Liam stepped by her side and shrugged. "I call it a normal day at the office."

He sheathed his blade and placed the holy gun in his holster. He then pulled a tiny golden necklace from his neck which held a pendant that formed a triangle within a circle—the symbol of the Gods.

How hadn't she noticed that necklace before?

"I do hate exorcisms," he grunted.

The possessed man walked away from the bar and licked his lips, almost as if challenging him to make the first move. Liam jumped at him, but the demon sent a swarm of buzzing darkness in his direction.

The Selfless swatted at the darkness, grunting something between annoyance and exasperation. Ava could barely see him through the buzzing pitch black.

The demon strolled slowly toward Liam, ready to strike a deathly blow while he was distracted.

In all the madness, Ava had dropped her sun dagger. She had only one option left, so she let her essence flood her from inside, tendrils of light that coated her neurons and connected with her thoughts. She stretched her hand toward a table, and with her mind, she flung it toward the possessed man. It wouldn't hurt him, since the possessed bore a great deal of strength, but at least it would distract the demon.

The damned thing bent his spine in a ninety-degree angle at the last minute. The wooden surface passed by the man's nose, missing it by an inch.

"Heavens," Ava grunted to herself, her head pounding.

Telekinesis wasn't inherent to Guardians. Only Erudites mastered the skill, and using it was painful. Ava's bones felt like they were rusting, and she had to focus not to fall on the floor.

The man's neck craned unnaturally to the left. He stared at her with a mad smile. "Interesting ..."

While the demon focused on her, Liam stalked behind him like a panther—how he had gotten rid of the shadows, she didn't know. He punched the man's spine straight before locking him in a stronghold, then slammed the pendant on the creature's forehead.

Smoke hissed from the man's skin, and the demon shrieked in pain. He cursed Liam in a thousand ancient languages, but the Selfless held on.

"The Gods are with you, and you're with the Gods," he began to chant. The possessed man writhed and screamed, clawing at Liam's arms to no avail.

Heavens, Liam was remarkably strong for a human, even if Selfless. To simply hold a possessed one so easily ...

Liam continued chanting the exorcism until black smoke burst from the man's throat. He quickly snatched his holy gun and shot at the cloud of smoke hanging in the air. Horrible shrieks filled the space around them as the smoke turned into burning ashes.

The sad man fell limp to the floor, and Liam immediately felt his pulse. He nodded at Ava. The man would be all right.

She rushed to the bar and soothed the bartender with her words, asking him kindly if he would step closer to the unconscious man. The bartender smiled and agreed.

"Are all Guardians so eloquent?" Liam asked with an amused grin as he fixed the pendant around his neck.

"We simply suggest." She shrugged. "Humans can choose whether they'll follow my words."

They rarely opposed, though.

Once the men were lying on the floor side by side, she touched their foreheads. She couldn't erase memories like Erudites, angels who mastered telepathy and telekinesis, but she could make the men's memories fuzzy.

Ava's head pounded from the effort. Her telepathic abilities were minimal, but she kept going, smudging the memories as much as she could. Her bones ached, and when her skull seemed to puncture the wall of her brain, she figured this would have to be enough.

"What will they believe when they wake up?" Liam asked.

"Nothing precisely. Just a blur of images."

He looked around the pub, then at the thorny, pitch-black bodies spread across the floor. "I wonder what story they'll come up with to explain all this."

Ava felt the surge of quiet, a tsunami made of void, rushing to shore.

Death's arrival.

"It won't matter," a calm voice said from behind her. "Humans tend to ignore what they cannot explain. I doubt the cleanup teams will even bother with this one."

Ava turned around to see a woman standing at the entrance of the pub. She wore a sleeveless gown made of night and shifting stars, as if her dress was a window opening to the galaxy. Unlike common folklore, the woman didn't look like a skeleton. Far from it. Her peachy skin was flawless, her red lips full, and honey-colored waves cascaded down her chest. Her all-white eyes shone on the edges.

"It's time," the Angel of Death said.

2

AVA

*L*iam was a tall, strong man that towered over Ava, but here, in this hospital room, standing by his fallen partner's side, he looked ... smaller.

"You'll be okay, Archie." He laid a gentle hand on the man's brow.

The Angel of Death leaned against the hospital's faded blue wall, not far from Ava. She crossed her arms and watched the man lying on the hospital bed. "It won't be long now."

Archibald's skin was filled with swollen purple blotches. There were so many of them, Ava could barely discern his features. Gauze was wrapped over half of his head, weaving through gray tufts of hair. Both his feet and arms were encased in thick plaster with metallic needles that pierced the surface.

A cold shiver trickled down Ava's spine. Whoever did this to Archibald had wanted him to suffer.

Liam squeezed Archibald's shoulder. His furious green eyes glistened, but he held back the tears. "Soon you'll become one of *them*," he glanced at Ava and pressed his lips in a line, "but I know you'll still be one of us."

"*Them?*" the Angel of Death asked with an enigmatic grin. "We're all angels, Liam. You simply can't remember your past as one of us."

Ava opened her mouth to say that the Angel of Death wasn't exactly "one of us," but she stopped herself. The Angel of Death was one of the Powers, an angel so high in the hierarchy that she surpassed the Seraphs who helped the Gods rule the Heavens.

There were only two Powers, one on the light side and one on the dark, brother and sister born from an agreement between the Gods and the Devils. Very likely the first angels ever born.

"If we're on the same team," Liam grunted, focusing on his fallen partner, "why didn't the big guys send a second-tier to heal Archie? After all his years of service, that's the least they could do."

Something inside Ava synched with Liam's words.

When an angel died, they got no second chances, no eternity or rebirth. They simply disappeared into the ether. But a Selfless was technically human, and therefore, could make *the choice* all over again. They could be brought back as the angel they used to be or be reborn as a Selfless.

The high angels, however, preferred they choose the first, which was why they often let the Selfless die.

Ava didn't agree with this. It was a cruel decision, and it went against her Guardian instincts to protect and aid. She respected the decision of the three high angels, however. After all, the will of the Messenger, the Throne, and the Sword was the will of the Gods.

According to Archibald's file, he'd chosen to be reborn as a Selfless for two consecutive lifetimes. Ava couldn't help but smile at the defiance.

Now the brave man lay there, nearing his death, bruised and mangled beyond repair. It didn't seem fair to her.

Ava wished she could whisper the soothing words of the Gods to Liam and to Archibald, but that would probably infuriate her new partner.

"I can try to ease Archibald's pain," she said quietly as she approached Liam.

Only an ascended angel could save Archie's life, but Ava could make the remaining minutes of his existence bearable.

Her new partner snorted. "Big deal." He sniffed, then shook his head. "I'm sorry. I ..."

"He isn't feeling pain right now," the Angel of Death said.

Liam pressed his lips in a sad smile that broke Ava's heart. She needed to help him, but she had no idea how, which was a first. Ava had always thought she was a decent Guardian; she put her charges first, and she knew exactly how to make them feel better. Not knowing how to help Liam cracked something in her chest.

"Tell me what you need," she asked as she gently squeezed his hand.

"Bring him back?" he begged, his tone weak, a far cry from the fearless man she had met at the pub.

Ava had never wished to ascend before. She was perfectly fine being a Guardian, a lower angel akin to a harmless kitten, but now she wished she could ascend to Dominion more than anything.

Would it even matter, though? Without the permission of the high angels, she'd be useless, even if ascended.

An idea struck Ava all of a sudden, and giddy happiness raised her spirits. "The Messenger and I, we ..." She cleared her throat, and her cheeks flushed. "We have a good relationship. I could ask him to make Archibald your partner after his death, you know, when he turns back into an angel. I'm sure if we tell Archibald, he will choose to be reinstated instead of being reborn all over again."

The Angel of Death scoffed, but Ava ignored her.

"Sure, it's unusual," she continued, her fingers interlaced with Liam's. "But the Messenger assigned me to you, and I'm an angel. Why wouldn't he assign you to Archibald?"

Liam stared at her, his mouth open. Finally he blinked and muttered, "Thank you, Ava."

"Archibald was an ascended angel, dear," the Angel of Death said. "You're a third-tier, a lower angel at the bottom of the hierarchy, alongside him." She nodded to Liam. "It's very unlikely the Messenger will pair an ascended to a Selfless."

"Well, we can at least try."

The Angel of Death rolled her blank eyes. "Guardians and your unending urge to help others …"

The realization she still held Liam's hand slammed against Ava at once. Heat flushed to her cheeks and she let him go discretely, but he didn't seem to notice.

A nurse with purple scrubs passed by the open door and looked inside the room. She couldn't see Ava or the Angel of Death, because they masked their presence. After a century being a Guardian, rendering herself invisible to humans was more of an instinct than a thought.

The nurse observed the dying man for a moment before her attention drifted to Liam.

"He's strong," she told him, but anyone could see Archibald wasn't going to make the night. Machines were performing most of his bodily functions, and his heart monitor beeped once every ten seconds.

"He is," Liam said without turning to her, his focus solely on Archibald.

"If you need counselling," the woman said with a hidden

grin as she eyed him up and down, "I'd be glad to point you in the right direction."

Ava saw red, which was a rare occurrence to her poised, Guardian self. That nurse oozed desire when Liam needed compassion. Without meaning to, Ava's hands balled into fists.

The Angel of Death leaned her head left and peered at her. "Something you care to share?"

"That woman …" Ava cleared her throat as she watched the nurse leave. She shouldn't speak badly about humans; they were on this Earth to learn. Her anger slowly dimmed, and her knuckles relaxed. "Never mind."

The Angel of Death smiled as if she knew something Ava didn't. Then she took a deep breath and closed her eyes. "It's nice when it's in the quiet of their homes or in the hospital. Right now, I'm present in hearings for thousands of souls. Some happen in dark alleys, some underwater, some with too much blood, and some in a gripping cold, like yours, Ava." The Angel of Death shrugged nonchalantly. "It's nice when they pass in the warmth of a bed."

"It was quite cold that day," Ava muttered, her stomach churning.

She hated remembering her death. She wasn't certain about what had killed her, either the cold or the strike to her head. Perhaps both.

Liam ignored their exchange. The pain in the way he looked at the dying man was a heart-stopping sensation that pricked at Ava's heart. Ava loved being a Guardian, but in occasions like this, she wished she could've been a Warrior or an Erudite instead.

"Why did you choose to become a Selfless?" she asked Liam, hoping this would take his mind elsewhere.

"I can't exactly remember, princess." He gave her a grin that bordered on playful.

Ava counted this as a victory. If calling her by that silly nickname helped, then he could call her *princess* for as long as he wanted.

"All I know is that Archie found me on the streets, and he took care of me." Liam smiled to himself. "It was easy becoming a Selfless after that, becoming like *him*. Archie always said that the Selfless were the truest of angels, because we chose to have our faith tested by being reborn as humans." Liam knocked on Archibald's chest softly and smiled. "I know he'll be different as an angel, but he'll still be Archie, and we'll keep making the Gods proud." He turned to her. "I really appreciate you putting in a word with the Messenger."

A man with long blond hair that fell on his shoulders in straight lines materialized in the room. His skin was pearly white, and the only thing he had in common with lower demons was his black, beady eyes.

"It's time," the Demon of Death said, his graveled voice booming throughout the room.

The Angel of Death nodded. "The hearing shall commence."

From the profusion of gauze around his face, Archibald pried his light gray eyes open and blinked, as if centering himself. He couldn't move his neck, but his eyes turned to Liam.

"Hey, kid," he said through tight lips, his voice rough, drawled.

From what Ava could see of his face, Archibald tried to smile, but winced in pain instead.

Liam laid a hand on his shoulder. "Hey, old man."

The Angel and Demon of Death stood on opposite sides of the bed, and Archibald watched them intently. Nothing in his expression denoted any emotion, his features a cold, gripping blank. Finally, he glanced at Ava, who stood at the end of the bed. He frowned, almost as if he were trying to remember where he knew her from, but he soon turned his attention back to Liam.

"This time, you better choose to become an angel, old man," Liam said. "You'll keep being my partner, I promise. We found a way."

Well, nothing was certain, but Ava wouldn't correct Liam in a moment like this.

Normal humans had no choice upon their deaths; they were simply reborn until the time they were ready for the final destination—the Heavens or the Hells. Their essence spoke to them, like an answer to a question they had never heard.

Some humans though, the ones who were ready, could become angels, like Ava once did.

Or demons.

Those who chose neither side were cursed by the Gods and the Devils to become vampires or werewolves, forever walking in between light and dark.

These hearings were never a surprise when it came to the Selfless, though. Their choices were either rebirth or being reinstated as an angel.

"Archibald Theodore Brennan," The Angel and Demon of Death spoke in unison. "As it is told, as it is said, the Selfless are granted a choice at their time of death. Like the humans they swore to protect, like the flesh and bone they chose to become. Be reborn as a human, an angel, or a demon. If you refuse, be cursed to the in-between. The Gods and the Devils require your decision."

Archibald's focus never left Liam. Tears strolled down his bruised cheeks, dampening the gauze.

Liam gave a soft knock on Archibald's shoulder. "We'll be back in the streets in no time, *Archangel Archie.*" The dying man let out a dim chuckle, and Liam took his hand. "Those blood-suckers and hells-hounds will run screaming when they see us."

"The light and the dark require your decision," the Angel and Demon of Death repeated.

"Kid, you be strong now, okay?" Archie's voice faltered, but he swallowed dryly and turned to the Angel of Death. "I choose to become a demon."

3

AVA

*L*iam let go of Archibald and stepped back. "Archie, what have you done?"

But Archibald's eyes had closed, and his heart monitor flat lined with a high-pitched whine that hurt to hear.

Ava gaped at the dead man, words hooked on the walls of her throat.

Why would a servant of the Gods choose the darkness? Was this even possible?

Liam turned to the Angel of Death. "You can't allow that. He's clearly not thinking right. He's an angel for Gods' sake! He can't become a demon." He turned to Archibald and shook his limp shoulders. "Tell her, Archie. Tell her!"

But Archibald didn't move. He was dead, soon to be reborn as a demon.

"Archie, please," Liam croaked. His desperation slipped into Ava's skin and squeezed her chest. Guardians could sense how others felt, which could be both a blessing and a curse. Right now, it was definitely a curse.

"There must be something we can do," she asked the

Angel of Death, but the woman dressed in nebulas and stars merely shook her head.

"There was darkness in him, so he qualified," the Demon of Death explained with a certain glee. "There's darkness everywhere, if you look well enough." At this he winked at Ava.

He touched Archibald's forehead with the tip of his long fingers, and a shadow swam over Archibald's skin. "The body has been blessed."

"You mean damned," Ava snapped.

The Demon of Death shrugged. "Depends on the point of view."

Ava knew what waited for Archibald. Blessed or damned, their sacraments were fairly the same.

Before she'd woken as an angel, her dead body had stayed in a stasis. She could hear the scream of little boy Charlie when he found her, and the wails of her sobbing mother as she clutched to Ava's frozen corpse.

Archibald could probably hear Liam right now, and it must kill him not being able to explain or to help the boy he raised. Ava remembered how gut-wrenching it'd been, to know her loved ones were in pain and to be powerless against it.

"He's not becoming one of those things." Liam's face turned red. "We've always done the work of the Gods, we've always remained faithful. This is how we're rewarded?"

Ava's stomach dropped as she remembered the lower demons from the pub. She hadn't known what hierarchy Archibald had occupied as an angel, but she knew that as a demon he would be starting from the bottom. After all, he had been human before, a Selfless, but a human nonetheless. Darkness would consume him in the way of a hurricane, hard and at once, just like the glory of the Gods had filled her. High on darkness, he would become a lower demon, perhaps one worse than the Obsessors she'd faced.

"There's nothing you can do, Liam." The Angel of Death stared at him with a blank expression. "He made his choice."

Liam opened his mouth to argue, but then his jaw tensed and he took a deep breath. His furious gaze focused on the floor now.

The Angel of Death turned to Ava. "You can ask the Messenger for help, although I can tell you it'll be pointless. You may be his favorite, but he's the Messenger of the Gods and this was *his* will."

"She can try," Liam snapped, then turned to Ava, his begging gaze breaking through her. "Right?"

How could Ava not grant him this?

The Messenger would refuse to help, she was certain, but Liam was her new charge. If there was any chance to help him, she'd take it without thinking twice. So she bowed to the Angel of Death. "I trust you will grant us passage?"

As far as Ava knew, only the Powers could teleport. None of the other angels could, except for the Throne, and even then, she could only teleport herself.

The Angel of Death rolled her eyes. "You know I can't interfere. I only allowed both of you to be present during this hearing because you begged for it."

Liam frowned at Ava. "You did?"

"She thought this would help bring you some closure." The Angel of Death narrowed her eyes at her. "Clearly, she was wrong."

Ava shrugged, ignoring her remark. "Sending us to the Order will hardly interfere with whatever cosmic rules you abide by. And if it does, you won't be able to transport us in the first place, correct?"

The Powers couldn't meddle in matters of Earth, Heavens, or Hells. They were allowed to reap souls and present them with the choice, but they weren't allowed to influence the material plane in any way.

The Angel of Death blew air through her lips. "I'll try."

Ava walked to Liam and took his hand. His skin was rough but so very warm. She hadn't noticed it the first time she'd wrapped her fingers around his.

Liam didn't oppose their proximity. His green eyes were trapped on hers, silently asking her to lead the way.

"Concentrate on the Order, dear," the Angel of Death said. "Also, hold tight."

Ava nodded and closed her eyes, ignoring the captivating man by her side.

She envisioned white marbled halls decorated with golden details and a small sun hanging from the ceiling. Then the floor beneath her vanished, and she fell into a void.

Her head spun, and she clutched Liam's hand tighter. Nausea took over just as her feet touched the ground again.

Heavens, she would never ask the Angel of Death to teleport her again. *Ever.*

When Ava opened her eyes, she and Liam were standing in the entrance hall to the Order of Light, close to a revolving door made of gold.

Ava's heart was still racing, her mind fuzzy. She swayed left—surely a side effect of teleportation—but before she knew it, strong arms had wrapped around her.

She looked up and straight into searching eyes that burned her from inside.

"You all right, princess?" Liam asked.

Heavens, his chest and arms might as well be made of concrete. *Smooth, tempting concrete.*

Ava blinked. "I'm fine, thank you." She steadied her feet and freed herself from his grip. "You look surprisingly well for your first teleportation."

Liam shrugged. "It was like a rollercoaster. I used to love those when I was a kid."

As they moved forward, Ava observed the gargantuan entrance hall that resembled a white marbled cathedral, with its domed roof and pointy arches for windows. Golden vines crept from the floor upward, standing out against the white. A golden sphere hung from the ceiling, light swirling inside it like lava in slow motion. *A small sun.* It drenched the entire place in daylight, even though it was night outside the massive arched windows.

She never got tired of strolling amidst these walls. Her home, her peace.

Giant statues of the three Gods were engraved on the wall opposite to the entrance. The God of Knowledge and Logic, father of all Erudites and Virtues, stood with old books in his grip and a kind smile on his old, wrinkled face. The Goddess of Life and Love, mother of all Guardians and Dominions, stood stoically in a flowing dress that seemed to bend stone into fabric. And the God of War and Resilience, father of all Warriors and Archangels, stood with a sword in his hand and pride swelling in his marbled chest.

Three Gods, three high angels who represented each.

It had been the Messenger, leader of all Dominions and Guardians, who had assigned Ava to Liam. And it'd been him who had denied aid to Archibald, which was ironic, considering their goddess represented love and life.

Ava bowed slightly to the Gods. Liam scoffed from behind her, probably because he was angry at them.

I'll help restore your faith, she silently promised him.

Third-tier angels such as Ava crowded the hall. Erudites, followers of the God of Knowledge, paced with books or electronic pads tight on their grips. Their light-gray kilts matched with their light-gray bodysuits, denoting their place in the hierarchy. It was the norm that the color of a lower angel's bodysuit matched with the color of their kilt.

Guardians, followers of the Goddess of life and love, walked with the standard white bodysuit that covered almost all of their skin from the neck down, and the same white linen kilts and boots Ava wore—although some females preferred to use high-heels. Ava couldn't fathom why.

There were also Warriors, followers of the God of War, walking with black bodysuits and obsidian linen kilts, carrying all kinds of weapons in the belts wrapped across their bodies.

Ava spotted only one ascended angel across the hall—an Archangel—which was rare given they didn't spend much time in the lower levels of the Order. Archangels, Virtues, and Dominions occupied the upper floors of the skyscraper, and because they had wings, they could come and go as they pleased, making the entrance hall pointless.

The Archangel stood near the help desk, waiting for the clerk. His folded, moss-colored wings turned white at the bottom, and contrasted with his full black bodysuit and wine-colored kilt.

He carried a sheathed sword and a holy gun at his waist— the guns were loaded with blessed bullets to kill vampires or werewolves, the so-called In-Betweens. Holy guns could also kill weaker demons, like the ones at the pub. *Or even a lower angel.*

Liam nodded to the Archangel. "I could take on a snobby second-tier in a flash," he said with a mischievous grin, something inside him eager for a fight.

The Archangel seemed to hear him, because he turned to Liam and looked down at him as if he were a bug or a worm.

This was odd. Second-tiers should love humans even more than third-tiers like Ava. They shouldn't glare at them with contempt. Besides, Liam was a fellow angel; he simply wore a human shell.

Liam saluted the Archangel mockingly and tapped the sword hanging around his waist. When the Archangel spotted the weapon, fury swirled behind his eyes and his wings spread wide in a predatory manner.

Ava shook her head at Liam. "I understand you're experiencing a storm of emotions right now, but looking for a fight won't solve anything."

"It'll be fun, though." His attention remained trapped on the approaching Archangel. "One thing is true, princess: when you guys ascend, you become monumental assholes." This he said point-blank at the incoming Archangel, fully knowing he could hear them.

Contrary to his own belief, Liam couldn't take a second-tier. In fact, the bulk of Selfless work consisted of hunting down misbehaving In-Betweens. Facing demons, even weak ones like the Obsessors from the pub, was a rarity. A Selfless couldn't face a second-tier demon—or angel—and live to tell the tale.

The Archangel stomped toward them with murder in his eyes. The military branch of angels was prone to brutality, but surely the Archangel wouldn't harm a fellow child of the Order ... *would he?*

Liam licked his lips and rested a hand over his sword, waiting for the right moment to unsheathe it. Ava realized this was heading toward a disaster, and whispered, "You can't possibly be considering—"

"If he attacks first, I sure fucking am," he said through gritted teeth, his attention fixed on the Archangel.

He was steps away from them now, and just as he started unsheathing his sword, someone stepped between them.

Ava could only spot majestic blue and green wings, like the sea on a sunny day. The booming voice said to the

Archangel, "Sithrael, were you about to attack one of your brothers?"

"He's wielding an Archangel's sword," Sithrael grunted.

"And?"

The Archangel stammered a reply, but no words came out.

Ava stepped to the side to see a beautiful Archangel with brown eyes and curly hair the color of limes. He emanated peace and calm, which was not a common trait among warrior angels of any tier.

She knew who he was, of course. A hero who had killed more demons in his days than any other.

Sithrael bowed his head. "Forgive me, Gabriel."

Gabriel laid a hand on his shoulder. "You're young. You will learn." He nodded to the end of the room. "Pray for forgiveness to the Gods. Then train for four hours and when you're done, you shall be responsible for kitchen duties tonight."

"B-but ..."

Gabriel merely raised one eyebrow at the Archangel, and it was enough. Sithrael turned to Liam and said, "I deeply apologize for my behavior. I ask for your forgiveness."

Liam watched him intently, and for a split-second, Ava thought he'd say no. He rolled his eyes and grumbled, "You have it."

The Archangel bowed to Liam and left.

Gabriel turned to them and placed a hand over his heart. "My apologies. They tend to be a little reckless when they've recently ascended." His attention lingered on Liam, his essence overflowing with the love and grace of the Gods. Then he focused on Ava. "I believe we haven't met. I'm Gabriel."

"It's an honor to meet you," she said with a shy bow.

He nodded to her, then to Liam. "I've heard of you, of course. How's the Selfless life, my brother?"

"I don't have brothers," Liam said, his tone colder than a winter's night.

Gabriel smiled, then laid a heavy hand on Liam's shoulder. "You will *always* be my brother." With that, he left.

Liam watched him go with a puzzled expression.

"Do you know him?" Ava asked.

He shrugged. "I can't remember."

4

AVA

The elevator's interior was all white marble with creeping silver vines on the corners, almost an exact copy of the hallway.

Ava pressed the silver button on the panel and said, "Take me to the Messenger's office."

As the elevator went up, she observed the green arrow that appeared on the screen above the doors. An awkward silence filled the space between her and Liam. Surprisingly, he was the one who broke it.

"So, Erudites are gifted with telepathy and telekinesis, Warriors with strength and speed, and you Guardians only get empathy and weak shields, right?" Liam shoved his hands in his jeans pockets. "Sounds like a bad deal, princess."

She rolled her eyes. "I beg to differ."

"Why don't you all just ascend? Second-tiers have your powers on steroids. And they can heal others, which would've come in handy when …" He didn't finish the sentence. He didn't have to.

"It's not that simple," she said quietly.

Liam frowned as he studied his boots. "So when you

become a Dominion, you'll be able to heal, create strong shields, and ... empathize with others on a 'deep spiritual level'?" He drew invisible quotes with his fingers.

"More like pressing emotions onto someone, like love and care—"

"—pain and despair?"

Ava bit her bottom lip. "That too, though a Dominion would never do such a despicable thing. No angel would."

"First time for everything, princess." He whistled and glanced around the elevator. "We learned about hierarchies during training, but being here feels strange."

"You've never been to the Order?"

"No." He leaned against the marbled wall of the elevator. "The Selfless are an entire different department. We work in precincts."

"Yes, but we're all angels."

He chortled. "Who patrols the streets? Who risks their lives every day?" He shrugged. "And who sits here on their asses doing nothing?"

Ava gasped. "Excuse me! Angels do a lot of work." She pointed at him and then herself. "Case in point. Guardians and Dominions help humans with their emotions, from establishing political treaties to helping an overwhelmed stay-at-home mother who feels like she's drowning." Ava felt her face flush, but the words kept shooting from her lips. "Erudites and Virtues are busy with research and technological advancements that could be taught to humans. Cars and tablets? You're welcome!" She crossed her arms. "Archangels and Warriors, even the Selfless, they—"

"—protect everyone. 'The Arm of the Order,' isn't it?"

She nodded.

Liam scratched his chin lightly, as if he were considering her words. "That doesn't change one simple truth."

"Which is?"

"The Selfless are expendable."

"You're not," Ava muttered, hating the fact he was right.

"Don't get me wrong, princess. I'm fine with sacrificing myself. As humans, if we die we can always come back, whereas you guys are gone for good." He smirked and didn't look at her as he said, "It's just … sometimes it feels like the Gods don't care about us."

"That's sacrilege." She narrowed her eyes at him. "For an angel, you're not very devoted."

"I take that as a compliment." Liam gave her a lopsided grin. "By the way, you don't look threatening at all when you pout."

Ava had no idea she was pouting. She immediately pressed her lips in a line and cleared her throat, trying to ignore the rush of blood that sprang to her cheeks. "That Archangel seemed less than pleased about your sword." She nodded at the weapon.

"He's just sour that a Selfless is using an Archangel's sword. They think I'm not worthy. Like I said, arrogant bastards, princess."

Again that nickname.

She let out an exasperated breath but controlled her nerves. For now, at least.

The elevator doors opened to a long, white marbled corridor lined with frosted glass doors with no doorknobs. Golden plaques attached to each door showed a number. *235, 236, 237* … Ava knew the one she needed.

"The Order's budget is certainly a lot higher than ours," Liam muttered as they went.

Ava stopped by number 245 and knocked.

"Enter," the Messenger's soothing voice rang from inside.

They did. The office's walls were light blue, the marbled floor white. A spherical chandelier, similar to the one from the hall, hung from the ceiling. Fresh night air ventured softly through the open arched window, making the taffeta curtains flutter, but inside the room it was as clear as day.

The Messenger sat behind a white marbled desk located near the window. Golden cracks snaked across the surface, as if someone had dropped the table then glued it back together with molten gold.

He signed some papers and didn't acknowledge Ava or Liam in any way. His light silver wings were coiled behind his back in the way of a hawk balancing on a tree. Under the room's light, they shimmered softly.

The Messenger might be centuries old, but he didn't look a day past thirty. His long silver hair was tied in a low ponytail with a few loose strands framing the sides of his face. When his intense blue eyes met Ava's, she couldn't help but skip a breath.

He gave her a dashing smile as he stood from his chair. The Messenger's silver bodysuit—a shade or two darker than his hair— hugged him in all the right places. His silk kilt had more intricate patterns than Ava's, but the color was the same white.

Soon enough, the Messenger trapped her in a heart-warming hug that felt like a bright sunny morning. His wings wrapped around them, closing him and Ava in a cocoon of feathers.

"Welcome back," he said.

"It's good to be back, Ezra," she countered, not knowing where to look—at the drop-dead gorgeous man before her or his glistening feathers.

He smiled softly. "How's the mission I gave you?"

"'The mission,'" Liam said from outside the cocoon of feathers, "is waiting right here."

Ezra's lips twitched in annoyance, but he let go of Ava. His wings folded behind him once again.

She turned to Liam, her cheeks feeling overly warm. "This is Liam, the new charge you assigned me."

Ezra observed her new partner, his clear blue eyes measuring Liam. His grin, before so wide and warm, shrunk into a dim smirk. "My sympathies for your lost partner." He put his hands behind his back. "You blame me for his death, do you not?"

"I do," Liam said through gritted teeth. "Why didn't you heal Archie, or at least send a second-tier to help? A Dominion, Archangel, or a Virtue, I really wouldn't care as long as they *saved* him."

"It was not the Gods' will," Ezra said. "Archibald was more valuable back in the Order."

"Well you *failed*." His voice broke at the end.

Ezra frowned at him as if Liam had said something foolish. "Our will *is* the Gods' will. If Archibald had something against our decision, then he's the one to blame for his own fate."

Ava feared that her new partner would punch the Messenger, but instead, Liam balled his fists as his chest heaved up and down. Ezra stared back at him with a hint of defiance.

Two beasts waiting to collide.

She quickly stepped between them. "This is precisely what we were hoping to discuss with you, Ezra."

He raised his hand and shook his head. "Ava, you're my best Guardian, but even you can't ask me to intervene. Archibald Brennan made his choice."

"Meaning you don't give a shit," Liam snapped.

"I do, more than you can imagine." Ezra's words were coated with sorrow. Such decisions must be difficult for a man who had once been a Guardian himself. Ezra cared about all creatures of the Gods unconditionally; it was why he was the Messenger. "We need angels to join the fight against the darkness," he continued. "To lose a powerful one such as Archibald to the other side is ... unfortunate."

Liam frowned, perhaps shocked at the Messenger's sort-of compliment to Archibald.

Ezra turned to Ava. "The loss of his partner is testing Liam's faith. You must guide him through this difficult time. It's imperative that he keeps fighting on the Gods' behalf."

"I'm standing right here, you fuckface," Liam said. "You can address me directly."

Ava gasped. No one had ever called the Messenger a *fuckface*, but Ezra took no offense in Liam's words.

He put a hand on his chest and bowed to Liam. "I apologize for excluding you."

Ava smiled at Ezra's kind gesture. He had once been a Guardian, just like her, then a Dominion, and now, he helped run the Order. He was the kindest, wisest angel she knew—the most powerful too. The glory of the Gods pulsed inside him, and Ava wished that one day she would also stand that close to the Gods.

"I will guide him," Ava said. "You have my word, Ezra. I will make you proud."

Ezra cupped her cheek and kissed her forehead, and when he withdrew, the imprint of his warm lips lingered on her skin.

He'd always treated Ava with kindness, and he'd always believed in her. She knew reporting directly to Ezra had been a stroke of luck, and she was truly grateful for it—usually Guardians reported to Dominions, who then reported to the Messenger. But Ezra had seen something in Ava, something she didn't know. And she hoped one day she would finally understand what it was.

Ezra went to his desk and pulled a white belt tied to a sheathed sword. He wrapped it around Ava's waist, his fingers brushing her hip ever so slightly.

Once he was done, he said, "If you're to follow Liam on his missions until he heals, you'll need to protect yourself."

"B-but," she glared at the sword on her belt, "I'm not a Warrior."

"The forces of evil grow with each passing day. You might have to face them, especially if you accompany a Selfless." Ezra lifted her chin with his finger. "You'll do fine, Ava. You do not know your strength, but I see it every day." Ezra turned to Liam and nodded to his Archangel's sword. "I assume you earned that?"

Liam patted the sword, a silent message daring Ezra to take it from him. "I sure did."

"Then show her how to battle," he said, a plea in his tone. "And protect her from evil. Ava is the kindest, purest angel I've ever met, and I'm *old*, Selfless." His thumb brushed the line of her jaw. "She's very important to me."

Ava flushed. *Important to him?*

She was a mere Guardian, and Ezra was the strongest of the three high angels. Sure, she spent a lot of time with him, and rumors in the Order said they were doing *things* that they weren't. Not that Ava would oppose doing such *things* with him. In fact, the mere thought of being important to Ezra made her smile in the way of a silly schoolgirl.

Liam narrowed his eyes at her, catching Ava off guard. She quickly acquired a more serious expression, but it was too late.

"Fine," Liam said. "I'll show your *girlfriend* how to protect herself. It's not like I have a choice."

"I'm not his—"

Right then, Ezra gently cupped her cheeks and kissed her. Not on her forehead or her cheek, like he used to.

On her lips.

Ava glared at him and then at Liam, who watched them with flared nostrils. She couldn't help but wonder if Ezra had kissed her because he liked her, or if he had done it to mark some territory she wasn't aware of.

Whatever his reasons, Ezra's lips were soft, gentle, much like himself, and Ava wished he wouldn't stop. Her eyes closed as she took him in. She had imagined this moment a thousand times over, and yet it was different than her wildest expectations. Not better or worse, simply … different.

He released her slowly, achingly, and smiled. "Complete your mission, Ava."

She cleared her throat. "Ezra—"

"I apologize for my lack of decorum, but I've wanted to do this for a long time now. I was hoping you did too."

She gaped at him, her heart beating against her ribcage as her mouth opened and closed without a sound, until she finally managed, "I did." Ava took a deep, recomposing breath. "This was quite sudden, though."

They'd had chances. Their past had been filled with them, moments were Ava hoped he'd kiss her, *needed* him to kiss her, only to find the comforting embrace of a friend.

So what had changed?

She caught her attention drifting to Liam.

"Once your mission is completed, we will speak about it, I promise." Ezra's voice was a sensual whisper, and her focus returned to him. He peered through Ava, seeing something beyond skin and bone, that thing she couldn't see herself. "I have faith in you. Do you have faith in me?"

"Yes," she answered without hesitation. "Always."

She did not agree with the plan of the Gods, especially the part where she'd have to wield a sword, and she didn't understand why Ezra had bluntly kissed her either—enjoyable as it was. But she wouldn't question him or them. If this was the Gods' path, then that's the path she would take.

"I'll make the Gods proud." She glanced back at Liam. "We both will."

"Good." Ezra nodded at her, then turned to Liam, all formal and proper. "Report back to your precinct."

Liam's brows knitted and his mouth twisted in a bitter way. "I need to find out who killed Archie."

"Knowing won't bring him back. You need to move on." He nodded at Ava. "She will help you with that."

Liam stepped forward, a scowl on his face and punches on his fists. "Well, then fuck yo—"

Ezra swirled his hand, and an invisible shield pushed them out of his office, bringing them to the corridor.

The door snapped closed before them.

5

AVA

*E*zra's sword was stunning. The ivory handle was engraved with a lion, and its white-gold blade emitted a faint glow. The sword felt warm in Ava's hands, a sign it had been blessed, probably by Ezra himself.

"So the Messenger can kiss his subordinates whenever he feels like it?" Liam asked, arms crossed as the elevator went down.

"Not exactly." Ava brushed her lips with her finger and smiled. "We've always been close, but never in that manner."

Ezra had helped Ava during her first years as an angel, and it didn't take long for her to become the best Guardian in the Order under his guidance. The Messenger gave her his words, his friendship, his time—nearly all of him.

Nearly.

When Ezra told Ava she would report to him directly, the two high angels who ran the Order with him—the Sword and the Throne—had been furious. Hierarchy was a vital part of the organization, and Ezra had burned it to embers. There was a defying wilderness in the way he'd handled the situation, something bordering on rebellious amusement. Ava often wondered if he had chosen her on purpose.

A part of her liked that Ezra had used her to defy a system which deemed one angel better than another. The part that knew his decision went against the Order's rules—the rules of the Gods themselves—not so much.

"This is never going to work." Liam rubbed the bridge of his nose. "The Messenger assigned you as my partner so you can talk me out of finding Archie's murderer."

Ava frowned. "If finding Archie's killer brings you closure, then that's what I'll help you do."

He stared at her wide-eyed, his mouth hanging open. "You will?" He blinked. "Won't that piss off your boyfriend?"

Ava rolled her eyes and lifted her index finger. "First, he's not my *boyfriend*." The words faltered on her tongue. Ava's friend Justine had once told her that if she ever wished to "get laid," she should snap her fingers and Ezra would be there. But Ava had never acted on whatever buzzed in the air between them, and neither had he. *Until now.* She cleared her throat. "Second, Ezra said I should help you heal, and I believe that encompasses anything that will help you move on. If finding Archie's murderer and arresting them is what it takes, then so be it." She raised an eyebrow at him. "As long as you promise to let the Throne handle their trial."

Liam rolled his eyes. "Promise."

Ava didn't believe him, not one bit. Revenge was a dark path, one that Liam was bound to take. This could push him into the darkness, but Ava still had time to persuade her new charge. Being a Guardian was about slow, persistent work.

"I also need to understand why Archie damned himself," Liam added.

"If you wish, yes. Anything to bring you closure, apart from ending lives."

Liam observed Ava with a hint of amusement. "Call me intrigued, princess."

They reached the ground floor and walked toward the revolving door when a familiar voice came from behind them, cutting through the busy hall. "Ava!"

She turned to see Justine approaching. Her friend walked the way a breeze moves. Her flowing light-gray kilt was clipped with golden pins at her waist to showcase her curves —a job already made perfect by her silver bodysuit. Her straight, dark-brown hair cascaded over her chest, highlighting the V neckline of her suit.

Ava smiled to herself. Erudites didn't care about appearances, nor did they approve of deep cleavages, but Justine had always loved to break protocol.

"It's so good to see you, my friend," Ava said, trapping Justine in a hug.

Love and care emanated from Justine's core as she hugged Ava back. "Likewise. It's been forever! Let's go for drinks, and don't you dare order something non-alcoholic this time."

Ava gave her a shy smile. "I'd love to, but I'm on duty."

Only then did Justine notice Liam. "What a fabulous *duty*, my dear." Her friend eyed him up and down before giving Liam the back of her hand to kiss. "Enchanté."

Liam frowned at Justine's hand and shook it awkwardly. Ava held a giggle.

"This is Liam, my new charge," she told Justine. "I mean, *partner*."

Her flirtatious manner vanished, replaced by sheer horror. "Partner? As in *Selfless* partner?"

"Obviously," Liam grumbled.

"No, no, no!" Justine shook her head and grabbed Ava's arm with strength. "You're not a warrior angel or a second-tier. You'll die out there! We don't get second chances, remember? No Heavens for us."

Back when Justine was alive, she'd been one of Ava's charges. Her friend had a wild but kind soul—the very reason Justine became an angel upon her death. Ava loved her for it, but it was strange having Justine worry about her and not the other way around.

"I'll be fine," Ava said, mostly to appease her friend. "Every angel learns basic self-defense on initiation day, and I still remember a thing or two."

This wasn't enough for Justine, whose eyes had begun to glisten. "Your initiation was a hundred years ago, Ava."

"I have a good memory." She winked at her. Then she remembered the pub and how she had slashed the demon's arm. *A stroke of luck.* Some lessons were definitely in order. "Liam will remind me on how to use this." She tapped Ezra's sword. "He's a skilled soldier of the Gods. You have nothing to fear, my friend, and neither do I," she lied.

Justine still looked at Ava as if she had been given a death sentence. "You fool. You'd lose your life for your precious charges. It's one thing to run past In-Betweens on the streets while you're on duty; it's something else to actually confront them! You'll have to fight vampires and werewolves, perhaps even the occasional lower demon. Oh, Heavens ..." She inhaled sharply.

Liam leaned closer to them. "Ava is helping me. We Selfless tend to appreciate that. I'll take care of her with my life." He put a hand on his chest and bowed. "Trust me. She'll be fine."

Justine gave him a hesitant nod. "You better keep your promise, Selfless." She then nudged Ava's ribs with her elbow, her usual playfulness returning to her. "Heard that? He'll take *good care* of you."

Ava blushed. "Justine!"

"Fine, sorry." Justine caressed Ava's blonde curls. "If you need anything, you tell me, okay?"

"Actually …" Ava looked side to side and lowered her tone. "Could you find any information in the records about Liam's partner and his death? His name was Archibald Theodore Brennan."

Justine shrugged. "I will certainly try. The fact you're whispering means no one should know I'm looking into this?"

Ava nodded.

"Consider it done." Justine gave her a sly smile. "But it'll cost you that beautiful golden dress you wore to last year's ball."

"It's yours," Ava said with a smile. "In fact, I'll pick it up right now if you'll wait for me."

"Of course."

Ava went to the open elevator and pushed the button. "Take me to Ava Lightway's quarters."

Lightway. This was her angelic surname given to her after her death. *Lightway.* A soft, harmless name for a soft, harmless angel. She glanced down at the sword on her hips and sensed this might change.

The button blipped red, and a robotic tone followed. *"Quarters closed until mission completion."*

She glared at the screen. Her quarters were never blocked during a mission.

Ezra's words echoed in her mind. *"You must guide him through this, Ava."*

Had he meant she should be with Liam at all times? That she wouldn't be able to return to her quarters at night? This wasn't normal protocol, but then again, nothing about this mission was normal.

Blasted demons of Hells, she cursed in her mind, but then

felt terrible about it. She would pray for forgiveness later tonight.

Ava walked out and toward Liam and Justine.

He waited with crossed arms, standing out amidst all the white and gold with his black leather jacket, dark jeans, and tanned skin.

Justine, who stood to his left, observed the tower of a man beside her. Her voice rang in Ava's mind. *"He's so hot. Please have sex with him."*

"Justine!"

She giggled. *"My dear, look at the size of those biceps."*

Liam's arms did bulge beneath his black leather jacket, but only slightly. He wasn't too muscular, and he wasn't too skinny either. Simply a harmonious combination of perfectly shaped parts.

Justine lifted an eyebrow as if she had heard Ava's thoughts. Which she probably did. *"Let me guess. They closed your quarters?"*

"They did."

She shrugged. *"I heard they do that sometimes. I suppose the Order needs your complete devotion to this mission."*

"I gave my complete devotion with my other charges. This is simply pointless." Ava let out a tired sigh. *"But it's the Gods' will."*

"So it is."

As soon as Ava reached them, Justine laid a hand on her shoulder. "Don't worry. I'll pick the lock when no one's looking, and I'll bring you a fresh uniform." She tapped her chin and winked at Ava. "While taking that gorgeous dress, of course."

Ava put a hand over her heart and bowed slightly to Justine. "I wouldn't expect it any other way."

Liam watched them as if their exchange was boring to him. He turned to Justine. "When you find some information, go to the Nine Five. It's my precinct. Ask for Liam Striker."

Justine nodded, then kissed Ava's cheek. "Be careful out there." She grabbed Ava's hands and pressed them close to her heart. "You might have a sword, but you're no second-tier. Don't try and be brave, okay?"

Ava gave her a comforting smile. "I promise."

Justine turned to Liam with a scowl. "If she ever gets hurt, pretty boy, I'll chase you down to the Hells myself."

Liam bowed slightly at her. "Oui, madame."

She raised her eyebrows at Ava and smiled. "Isn't your *partner* full of surprises?"

And with that, she left.

"Your friend really likes you," Liam said as they headed toward the revolving door.

Ava grinned to herself. "I like her too."

Once they reached the exit, he turned his back to her. "Well, thanks for showing me the way out. If you'll excuse me, princess, I've had a long day."

"Hmm." Ava scratched the back of her neck. "Can I come with you? As you've seen, my quarters have been closed."

"I know," he said without turning to her. "But I'm not the best host. I'm sure you'll find someplace to crash."

"Well, I would stay with Justine, but apparently I'm supposed to be with you at all times."

His shoulders slumped. "Like a babysitter?"

"Precisely." She shrugged. "Besides, if you refuse to cooperate, I won't tell you whatever Justine finds out about Archibald. Remember, she's *my* Erudite friend who has access to the Order's most secret records. She'll only relay information to *me*."

He swiveled quickly on his heels, a wide, naughty grin in his lips. It made him look younger somehow. "Well, princess, now that you've asked so nicely ..." He bowed down, showing her the door.

She walked past him and out into the night.

They walked together down the fairly empty streets, weaving in and out of the darkness as they passed yellow lamplights.

"So, I'm to be with you at all times?" He clicked his tongue, and a wide grin sprouted from his lips. "The Gods must really like me."

Was he being ironic, or had he meant he'd actually enjoy spending time with her? She honestly couldn't say.

"The Gods like *all* their children," Ava countered, stopping to face him.

Liam stepped a little too close. She looked up at him, straight into those emerald eyes that pulled her like a magnet. She breathed in his musky scent, mixed with dry sweat from the fight at the pub, and something else ... something primeval Ava couldn't quite pinpoint. It made her legs shake, and she envisioned herself kissing him.

Heavens, she thought. This was not the time to be losing her mind.

Liam smiled, almost as if he knew the effect he had on her. "Well, princess." His tone was low, his breath a warm caress on the curve of her neck as he whispered beside her ear. "That remains to be seen."

6

AVA

*A*s soon as Ava stepped into Liam's apartment, she wished she could return to the Order.

The place was a one-bedroom space that reeked of stuffy bedsheets and stale air. She cringed as she glanced at the open kitchen and the tower of dirty plates that rose from the sink. An old couch was placed in the center of the living room, near the apartment's only window. It was a sickly shade of brown, and its cushion tops resembled shriveled leaves, which meant there was no reason to keep it, if not for sentiment.

A plasma TV hung on the wall, a few inches to the left of the bathroom door. The wooden coffee table below the TV looked like it was rotting inside. *A perfect match to the sofa.*

Ava's lips curled up. "You *live* here?"

"I don't spend much time inside," he said as if that justified the state of the place.

He hung his leather jacket on a coat rack behind the door, then unclicked the belt that sheathed his sun dagger and sword. He dropped his weaponry atop the kitchen counter—

on the scarce free space he managed to find. The shoulder holster that kept the blessed gun followed suit.

Ava already missed her impeccably clean and welcoming quarters that always smelled like lavender.

"If you don't like my 'décor,' you can fix it with your telekinesis," Liam said.

Her nose wrinkled at all the shoes sprawled before his bedroom door. "My telekinesis isn't strong enough for this. I'm not an Erudite, remember?"

Liam crossed his arms. "If you say so. But you did fling a table at that possessed man back at the pub."

Ava shrugged. "I only pull energy from my essence and link it to my thoughts. It's a trick Justine taught me."

He frowned. "If it's so simple, why don't other Guardians do it?"

She opened her mouth to answer, but nothing came out. She had no idea. "Well, it's not *simple*," she finally admitted. "I can only use the skill for a few moments, otherwise it becomes painful."

Liam gave her an absent "Hmm" before dropping on the couch and turning on the TV to a football game. He sprawled across the cushion tops, barely giving Ava any space to sit. She could probably touch the invisible wall rising between them—it was so evident it might as well be material.

"You don't let people in easily, do you?" she said tentatively as she sat on the couch's arm.

His attention didn't flee from the game. "You've got sharp Guardian skills, princess."

She ignored the irony in his tone—and that silly nickname. "There must be a reason why you do it," she pushed.

He kept watching the screen.

Ava wished she could read a mind like a book, but she wasn't an Erudite or a Virtue, so she had to settle with sensing Liam's annoyance like a gray, sloshy mass going down her throat. The perks of being a child of the Goddess of Love and Life.

Well, Ava hadn't become a great Guardian by letting her charges stay in their comfort zone. Reaching out to Liam wouldn't be easy, though. She might've met him only a few hours ago, but she already knew he would be one of her most stubborn charges.

She sighed and rolled her eyes, praying silently to the Gods for patience.

"Why, Liam?" she pushed again.

He made the same gesture she did, as if he too were asking the Gods for patience. Finally, he said, "When you're in my line of work, getting attached will only bring you pain."

"And yet, you were attached to Archibald."

He glared at her from beneath his eyebrows, finally turning his attention away from the screen. "Archie raised me. He made me who I am. He wasn't just my partner, he was my father *and* my best friend."

Ava nodded. Silence was the only appropriate answer to his words, to his pain.

Time passed, but his eyes didn't release hers. Finally, Liam rolled his shoulders and stretched his neck. "You haven't met many Selfless, have you?"

"One," she said. "He saved a charge of mine from a hungry vampire some thirty years ago."

The memory of the bulky blonde man with kind gray eyes jumped to mind.

Her charge, Miss Schmidt, was unconscious but alive, the dead vampire by her side missing his head—decapitation: the only way to make sure an In-Between wouldn't rise again. Angels and demons too.

"No harm done, sweet cheeks," the Selfless had said when Ava arrived.

Sweet cheeks. Princess. Perhaps being condescending to angels was a habit for the Selfless.

"I've never met a Guardian before," Liam said, pulling Ava from her memories. "Just Archangels." He glanced at the sword he had dropped atop the kitchen counter. "They wanted to take the sword from me, but Archie had gotten it through all the proper channels. The look on their faces …" He snorted to himself. "You baby angels are different from second-tiers. Well, *you* are, at least."

She frowned. "Different?"

"Nicer," he countered, turning his attention back to the screen. "I'm not used to nice."

Ava gaped at him, not knowing exactly what to say. Kind words didn't seem to come easily to Liam, and yet, there they were.

"A little too naïve," he added, "but we can change that."

Ava blushed and looked at her feet. How did he intend on changing *that*?

Liam turned off the game and stood. He took off his shirt and threw it on the sofa.

Ava's cheeks burned when she saw his tight biceps and the small squares on his stone-hard stomach. Scars cut across his trunk, raw lines that denoted a lifetime of battle. Some scars were fresh and pinkish, others a shade darker than his olive skin⬚memories that wouldn't fade. Perhaps she should find the marks disturbing, but to Ava, Liam was beautiful. Scarred or not, the Gods had taken extra time to carve him.

"W-what are you doing?" She cleared her throat as he started unzipping his pants, her heart climbing up her throat.

He frowned at her, clearly unaware of how inappropriate he was being. "I'm taking a shower."

Liam took off his shoes, then dropped his pants on the sofa. When he touched the rim of his black boxers and began to lower them, Ava had to use all her strength to stand up and turn away, but not before noticing how his *happy trail*—she learned the expression from Justine—formed a chalice toward his crotch.

"Do you always behave so improperly?" Ava asked, pointlessly closing her eyes since she had her back to him.

"I thought you accompanied your charges at *all times?*"

"Yes, but I could return to my quarters at night unless my charges were in immediate suffering," she snapped, her voice louder than intended. "Also, I respected their privacy."

She heard Liam's laughter from behind her back. "I take it you haven't seen a naked man before?" He chuckled. "Princess, I thought you were pure … but a virgin?"

"I'm not a virgin. I'll remind you I was human once," she spat, forcing herself not to look back at him. "And I've seen naked men." *But none that looked like Liam.* She cleared her throat. "I simply fail to understand the necessity of seeing *you* naked."

"It shouldn't bother you. After all, I'm your charge, right?" There was a sense of victory in his tone, almost as if he'd made a point she'd failed to understand.

She resisted the urge to turn back to him. "I suppose …" She shook her head and crossed her arms. "The human form is the Gods' glorious work, and an underlying temptation at the same time. Angel, demon, or In-Between, we've all been human once; we've all caved to human needs. Angels especially are known for reacting rather passionately about their basic instincts." She rubbed her forehead, suddenly feeling weary. "In any case, seeing one of my charges in that manner is … uncomfortable."

Especially if said charge resembled a Greek sculpture.

"An underlying temptation, am I?" Ava couldn't see him, but somehow she knew he was grinning. "Why princess, here I was thinking you were exclusive to that asshole Messenger. Is he also a temptation to you?"

Yes. A temptation Ava was certain would consume her sooner or later. Not that there was anything wrong with that. She only hoped she and Ezra were ready for it, whatever *it* was. And she *should* believe they were, *wanted* to believe, but deep down, Ava couldn't.

Before she could say a word, she heard steps and then the bathroom door squeaking closed. She was about to turn around, but the door opened and Liam quickly returned.

The warmth of his body grew closer, and her heart pumped blood madly through her veins. She saw herself turning around and slamming into his hard chest, cupping his cheeks, and drowning his lips in deep burning kisses, their hushed breaths the only sound in the night.

Instead, she kept still, pushing such silly urges somewhere far and deep within her.

His stubble brushed the side of her neck, and he moved her hair out of the way. His breath was smoldering as it hit her skin. "You can sleep on the couch. If you want a shower later …" He handed her a scruffy green towel.

"Thank you," she said, thirsty for something she couldn't name, trying to steady her breathing.

Footsteps creaked on the wooden floor, and then the bathroom door clicked shut. The sound of rushing water came from inside.

Ava exhaled loudly, calming her beating heart. She took the towel and pressed it against her chest. For a moment, she wished she was pressing Liam's body close to hers.

She looked at the dirty broken couch and at the dirty broken apartment. Ava took a deep breath and closed her eyes, listening to her slowing heartbeat.

She might not know what the Gods' plan was, but this must surely be a test. The Gods were good with this sort of thing.

7

LIAM

When Liam was seven, he found his mother dead on the living room floor, her mouth hanging open and dripping vomit, her body twisted in a way that made her resemble a broken twig.

He called—*cried, bellowed*—for help, and then came the neighbors, followed by the police and the state people. Soon enough, Liam found himself part of an adoptive family in which the woman was always angry, and the man looked at him in a funny and far from fatherly way.

He stayed there for a week. Then he ran and ran, and even when the air burned his lungs, and his body begged to stop, he kept running.

One day, a stranger with sandy blond hair and kind gray eyes picked him up from the streets, saying Liam was actually an angel reborn as a human. The stranger claimed he'd been looking for Liam for a long time.

Liam had laughed—and nervously looked around for either an escape route or someone to help. But the man offered food and shelter, and it was raining, and Liam was so hungry he was sure his stomach chewed on itself.

The man was good on his word, though. He gave Liam a roof and food as promised, and he didn't look at him funny. The latter was the only reason why Liam had the deepest sleep of his life during his first night at Archie's.

When Liam told him about his adoptive family, Archie said nothing. His eyes merely grew a shade darker, and then he left.

A day later, Liam saw the man who looked at him funny dead on the TV. Apparently, he'd been *funny* to a whole lot of foster kids.

When Archie came home later that night with take-out Liam *knew*. He just knew. As he stared at his own plate, he muttered, "Aren't angels supposed to be good?"

"No, kid," Archie spoke through a mouthful of food. "We're supposed to slay monsters."

And that was that.

As Liam grew up, he knew he wasn't exactly holy. His entire life—and charming personality—were proof. If anything, he might actually belong to the other side.

He was good at killing evil creatures, though. Archie had told him this gift was holy in a way. So maybe Liam was an angel after all.

He grinned at the demon standing ahead of him, a dark silhouette surrounded by a swarm of angry flies. Liam knew the "flies" were remnants of darkness, buzzing around the source. He had read it in the Selfless schoolbooks *and* experienced it in practice—even if he didn't fight demons all that often.

Lower demons could be a box of surprises. They were much harder to assess than werewolves or vampires. For werewolves, Liam could check the size of their canines, their muscular build, and then he'd know whether to run or fight. Usually he fought. Strong blood-suckers were also easy to assess, since they reeked of old leather. But demons? Not so easy to read. Bigger risk.

Fire swirled in a sphere where the demon's heart should've been. The creature looked faintly human: it had black thorny limbs, and a human face shaped by smoke. It had also come looking for a fight. And maybe the demon would be more than Liam and Archie could handle; maybe it wouldn't. There was only one way to find out.

"Gods, I hate those things," Archie grumbled beside him.

"Well, we *are* paid to kill them." Liam licked his lips and removed his sun dagger from the inside pocket of his black leather jacket.

Archie was quicker, though, and already jolted at the demon.

Liam knew the series his partner was about to try: attack, dodge, swivel. But the mess of shadows and fire opened its jaw in the way of a python—its chin almost touched the floor. A sphere of darkness burst from its throat, sucker-punching Archie mid-way and flinging the old man back against the alley wall.

The harsh thump made Liam wince. His heart tightened, but he knew Archie had withstood worse than this.

"Demons in the Hells," he grunted under his breath, and the thing's attention locked on him.

The demon clawed the space before it with its shadow hand, ripping the air between them with fiery gashes. *A front shield.*

Liam grinned as he remembered the series Archie had taught him when he was only fifteen.

"Bad thing about front shields, kid," Archie had said, "is that they only protect the front."

Liam lunged, and right before he met the demon's shield, he stepped back, turned left, and cut the thing's left ribs with his dagger. The demon shrieked as sparks of fire bled from the cut.

Liam didn't wait for the demon to turn toward him. He swiveled again, circling the creature, and slashed another cut on its right rib. The thing's shrieks exploded throughout the alley.

The demon might've been human once, like most supernatural creatures, but its black beady eyes and pointy shark-teeth showed exactly what it had become. A thing of nightmares.

The creature charged, trying to strike Liam with its shadow claws that ripped flames from thin air, but Liam was faster and dodged, slashing a deep cut across the demon's back with his sun dagger. Sparks and lava burst from the long cut. The demon let out a piercing scream, its hands desperately trying to reach the wound.

This thing was powerful but way too slow. Liam didn't wait before swiveling again and facing the demon. In a swift move, he cut half of its throat open with his sun dagger. Lava flowed from the cut, and ripped flesh fluttered like a flag as the demon's head bent unnaturally to the side. The demon couldn't shriek anymore.

Life—if one could call it that—left those beady eyes as the creature fell limp on the floor.

The shadows disappeared, and the lava turned into black liquid oozing from the cuts. Without the darkness, the demon looked like a human covered in pitch-black soot. The man's face was the only feature that remained uncharred. His black beady eyes stared at the sky, a question trapped inside them.

Liam made the sign of the sphere and kissed the thin golden pendant hanging from the necklace tucked under his shirt, as he always did when a mission went well. Thanking the Gods didn't hurt, and deep down, Liam knew they watched over him. Or maybe Archie had hammered those ideas into him for so long, he had started to believe them.

His partner limped toward him with a pleased grin. "Well done, kid."

Liam ran toward Archie and draped the old man's arm on his shoulders. "You scared me back there." He felt Archie's ribs with the tips of his fingers. They shouldn't be pointing inward toward Archie's organs. "Let's go. We need to get these wounds fixed."

Archie chuckled as they walked. "No biggie. Been through worse."

Liam shook his head. "You've got a broken rib, and you're probably bleeding internally."

"As I said, no biggie." Archie knitted his bushy eyebrows. "Who am I kidding? Guess it's time to retire."

Liam's jaw clenched with disapproval, but he managed to keep his voice dry and polite. "You don't get to retire unless Cap says so."

Archie winced, and Liam slowed down, following his pace. "The Captain said so yesterday, kid."

Liam halted, his mouth hanging open. "Fuck, no. You're my partner. I'll watch over you, all right?"

Archie shook his head. "Trust me, I don't like this either. But I'm not as fast or strong as I used to be. At some point, I'll become a liability to you." He winked and attempted a smile. "Besides, a condo in Florida stops being a bad idea once you cross the big six-o."

A condo in fucking Florida?

In the Selfless precinct, Liam had found a purpose and a family. He wasn't keen on losing the most important part of it. No fucking way.

Archie stopped and cupped Liam's cheeks with his hands. "Son." He only called Liam that when he meant business. "The time has come. They'll assign you a good partner, you'll see. But first, you need to let me go." He chortled. "Come on. It's not like you won't be able to visit me. I'm still your father, you know."

Liam leaned his cheek against the palm of the man who had raised him, the man he'd looked up to all his life. "We'll cross that bridge when we get to it, all right?"

Archie smiled and nodded.

LIAM HAD PLANNED to blend in quietly as they walked into the precinct. He would sit Archie somewhere and fetch Kevin to heal him, and with any luck, the Captain would never know.

Cap was maybe around sixty, but no one knew for sure. Her dark silver hair was cut razor short, and she dressed a blue suit filled with pins that spoke of honorable mentions. And she'd got them for a reason. The woman was fucking relentless.

She was also the first person to spot them. Liam grunted a curse.

Epic shitstorm on the way.

The Captain yelled for Kevin, their healer, as Liam sat Archie down on a chair near a desk towered with papers. The Captain pushed him aside and kneeled so she could look Archie straight in his light-gray eyes.

"You old fool," she grumbled.

Archie winked at her. "Missed you too, sweetheart."

The Captain shook her head and turned around. "Where's Kevin?" she bellowed to no one in particular, a certain desperation in her tone.

The Captain and Archie had history, this much was obvious to the entire precinct. But what it exactly was, no one could tell. Liam had tried prodding Archie about it, but he'd never gotten an answer other than "Mind your own business, kid."

Kevin, a red-haired boy in his early twenties, rushed toward them. "Bloody hells, can't a bloke go to the loo anymore?" Kevin was part of an interchange program with the precinct's counterpart in England, which was clear by his thick Yorkshire accent. "I mean, when nature calls you—" He stopped when he spotted Archie and assessed the damage. "Old Man, do you ever listen?"

Kevin quickly placed his hands over Archie's ribs. Golden light shone beneath his palms, and Archie let out a relieved breath. Kevin, on the other hand, grunted and squeezed his face as if being repeatedly shot.

Certain Selfless could inherit remnants of their angelic powers. With Kevin, it had been healing, since he'd been a powerful second-tier. This was more rumor than fact, but considering Kevin's abilities, the rumor had to be true.

Having a human body hindered him, though—all Selfless for that matter—and healing could cause Kevin a great deal of pain, especially if he crossed the line.

"You ought to watch out, Archie," Kevin said in between grunts of pain. "You can't miss your own retirement party, yeah?"

Liam scowled. "Did everybody know except me?"

"Yes," the Captain said, standing up in that stiff military manner of hers.

Liam watched the scar that cut her face in a diagonal, then quickly diverted his attention to his own feet. "Cap, I'd like to oppose Archie's retirement. You know he can't quit the game. I mean, a condo in Florida?" He snorted. "You know he'll be miserable there. I can take care of him."

He felt like adding that the Captain herself should've retired some five years ago, but her furious glare told him to shut up.

"Can you? Really?" She nodded toward his injured partner and a sweating Kevin. "The evidence says otherwise."

"Go easy on him, Shelly," Archie said. He tried to move but winced in pain instead.

Only Archie was allowed to call the Captain by her name. Liam had tried it once, and he'd gotten two weeks of desk work for it.

"Your boy is as careless as you are," she told the old man, a certain grief in her tone.

It was the Captain who handed them their missions, and it was the Captain who bore the weight of sending someone to their death; the kids she often trained herself, the people she loved like family. Her dark brown eyes and wrinkled skin spoke of a lifetime of trials.

Archie used to call her "a mountain against an unending storm." It fit her all too well.

Kevin fell with his back on the floor and took deep breaths, his chest heaving up and down, his forehead shining with sweat. "I did my best, heh?"

Archie carefully bent down from his chair and tapped Kevin's ankles. "You did good enough, Kev."

The Captain didn't wait another second before handing Liam a paper. "I need you to investigate this claim. No funny business, just detective work. Do *not* engage in a fight, or I will have your ass handed to you on a platter. Understand?" This she said looking specifically at Archie, because she *knew* he wasn't letting Liam go on this mission alone.

"Oy," Kevin yelled from the ground, sensing the same thing the Captain did. "You need to rest, old man."

"I'm fine." Archie smiled in that warm way that assured Liam he had everything under control. "Don't worry about me. I'll tag alone merely as a consultant, all right? Besides, you said it yourself, Shelly. It's easy detective work."

Kevin sat up and shook his head. "Your funeral, you stubborn old sag." He stood up and patted his clothes. "If you all excuse me, I have some paperwork to finish." And off he went, wobbly and weak, doing his best to stand up straight.

Archie turned to the Captain. "I think Kevin would be a good partner for Liam."

The Captain raised a thin gray eyebrow. "Do you realize how hard it was to get a healer like him across the pond?"

"Yes."

"And you want me to assign the best healer in miles to your little guard dog? Denied," she said, then turned to Liam. "I'll hand out a list of potential partners to you later, and you better pick one."

"Yes, ma'am," Liam said, knowing better than to argue.

Archie tapped his own legs and stood. He stretched his arms and exhaled loudly, like he was releasing the weight of the entire world off his back. "Ah, good as new." But Liam knew by the shaking of Archie's knees that he was still in a small degree of pain.

"Old man, are you sure—"

Archie nodded to the exit of the precinct. "Let's roll, kid."

THEIR FOOTSTEPS CLICKED against the concrete sidewalk. The street was deserted, quiet. In Liam's experience, silence was never a good sign. It always preceded trouble.

"Can't I work solo?" he blurted, his hands shoved in the pockets of his leather jacket. "I'm not exactly good at people skills."

Archie frowned. "Your 'people skills' are pretty decent when you're picking up girls at the bar. I believe you took two ladies home last night?"

An easy grin spread on Liam's lips. "Different kind of people skills." He studied his own shuffling feet. "I was thinking we could establish a private practice. You'd do all the boring stuff like research and paperwork, while I'd be out on the streets."

"You'd still need a partner to watch your back," Archie countered.

Hells, this wasn't going as Liam expected. Archie had been his partner since his first day as a Selfless. He had made Liam the detective *and* the man he was today. *Fury Boys*, that's how they were known on the streets. Fierce Selfless who got the job done, but most importantly, a team.

Liam wasn't sure how he was supposed to go on without him.

"Whatever," he said, remembering all the times he had shot that word at Archie when he was a teenager.

Deep down, Liam knew his father had to retire. Archie wasn't as fast or as strong as he used to be, and poor Kevin was having to patch him up more frequently.

It saddened him in a way. When Archie was younger he had been a force of nature, Liam's one and only hero. But his hero was only human.

They found the vampire looming near a dark alley. Drake was his name, and he was Archie's contact with the In-Betweens.

He stared at Liam and Archie with nearly white irises, his pupils tiny black dots. From up close, it felt like staring into a tiger's eyes before it lunged at prey.

"Why have you called me?" the vampire asked, his hands shaking.

Drake's skin was marble white, and sickening blue veins had started growing under it, rising from the bottom of his neck. This vampire was starving. Drake was so thin, it seemed his flesh had been glued to his bones.

"How long since you last fed?" There was pity in Archie's tone.

The old man would fall upon a demon with the fury of the Gods, but he'd always avoid conflict with the In-Betweens, even though they were technically as damned as demons.

"Do you care? Do any of you *holy* ones care?" The vampire gritted his teeth, showing his protuberant fangs. "I ask again, what do you want?"

"We want to know why the attacks on humans have increased in sector thirteen." Liam stepped forward, trying to stand between Archie and the bloodsucker. "A lot of vampires are being generated without going through the natural death process."

"Well, complain to the ones who cursed us for not choosing a side," the vampire hissed. "That was your Gods, wasn't it?"

"And the Devils too," Liam added, watching him, waiting for the moment Drake would lose control. "Don't blame us if you couldn't pick a side when you died." Liam's muscles clenched, and he stepped forward. "But by turning humans, you're stripping them of the choice *you* had."

Archie put a hand on Liam's shoulder and stepped forward. "Drake, the hunger is clouding your judgement." His tone was calm, soothing. "Tell us how we can help."

The vampire gurgled a laugh. "Angels helping an In-Between? We're stuck in the middle of a war we want no part in." He showcased his fangs. "*This* is the price we pay for neutrality, and oh, how *fair* it is."

"There are no neutral sides in the battle against darkness," Liam said. "Which makes you all as good as demons."

"And yet we hate them as much as we hate you," Drake spat. "Your Gods might have given us immortality on Earth and sensitivity to light, but it was the Devils who gave us our hunger for blood." He paced back and forth. "Of course we generate vampires. It's the nature of our curse. But we never pass the annual quota the Order imposed."

Finally, he was opening up.

"What changed?" Liam pushed, his arms crossed.

"Someone's starving us, cutting our legally obtained blood supplies. At some point, the hunger takes over and we attack humans." He looked at the street, as if making sure no one overheard them. "The numbers of starving vampires are increasing, and the main covens can't control them anymore. Then you Selfless or Warriors and Archangels, you're all the same, we're just targets to you all, aren't we?" He chortled. "You come and smite us without asking questions, and the demons just smile and watch because they want the world to burn. I lost three of my coven this week." He shook his head. "We're not alone. Too many werewolves have been hunting on forbidden grounds lately."

"Why?" Liam asked.

"Wolfsugar," Archie deduced quietly.

The powder could be converted into a drug like Xanax. A good deal of werewolves took it as an aid to control the inner wolf, but if wrongly dosed, it could have the opposite effect and force the change, wiping out their control over the beast.

"So, someone's withholding blood supplies from vampires and tampering with a drug werewolves use to control their change. All of this to force In-Betweens to kill humans?" Liam chortled. "My bet's on you guys losing your shit like you always do."

Drake glared at Liam with his predatory pupils. "The dark is on our doorstep. Soon it will be in yours too, Selfless."

Liam had lost count of the times a vampire, demon, or werewolf had told him "the dark was coming." The dark was *always* coming, and it was *always* losing because it was chaos and fury against the light's order and logic.

Archie crossed his arms. "These are serious accusations, Drake."

"It's the truth," he said. "Lilith will not stand by this for long, neither will the werewolf lord."

"Who's Lilith?" Liam asked.

Archie rested a hand on his shoulder. "Let's call it a night, kid. He isn't making sense."

"She's the mother of all vampires," Drake said. "The first human who refused to choose between the Gods and the Devils when given the final choice."

"The first vampire?" Liam frowned. "If she exists, she's damn old."

"Extremely, and also incredibly powerful." Drake added with a sly grin. "She will bring reckoning to the Order *and* to the Devils, to all the creatures on this Earth that threaten us, that force us to make a choice we don't want to make. She will resist, we all will, until there's nothing left of us."

Archie rolled up the long sleeve of his checkered shirt, showing the vampire his bulky arm. Drake licked his lips, his eyes focused solely on Archie's veins.

"What are you doing?" Liam asked, a chill running down his spine.

"We need to be sure if he's serious or if he's lost it. If Lilith is real ... well, the only way to know is by feeding him."

Liam pushed Archie's arm down. "Are you insane?"

"Kid, I've been doing this for over forty years," Archie said with a sharp tone, his face a marbled mask. Liam knew this expression well, and he knew it meant a very serious 'back off.'

So Liam swallowed his fears, his fists helplessly clenched, because that was all he could do, really. Going against his father wasn't exactly an option; the old man was more stubborn than the Cap herself.

Archie stepped forward and gave Drake his arm. The vampire hesitated, almost as if wondering if this was a trick. Then his hunger took over, and he sank his fangs into Archie's wrist.

Archie winced in pain, but allowed Drake to feed.

The vampire didn't stop, swallowing long gulps. *Naturally.* Vampires weren't known for their self-control.

Liam tapped Drake's hunched back. "That's enough, buddy."

The vampire didn't free Archie, so Liam took out his sun dagger. In one swift move, he slashed the bloodsucker's back. Drake immediately let the old man go, arching his spine as he uttered a loud curse.

The vampire recomposed, straightening his stance and cleaning the blood from the sides of his mouth. Selfless blood was stronger than normal human blood—something to do with an angel's holy essence dripping into their human body. It would keep Drake fed for at least a week. Already, the sickly veins had started to retreat.

"Thank you, Archie." Drake bowed to him, then stuck his tongue out and pressed his thumb against it. He touched Archie's wrist, and his fang marks were soon gone. *Vampire saliva, the world's best Band-Aid.* "If angels find out you fed me ..."

"They won't." Archie folded his shirt back toward his wrists and buttoned his cuffs.

Drake peered at him with eyes that had turned to an unnatural silver. "What I told you is the truth. Someone is forcing us to attack humans, causing the Order to fall upon us without mercy. In doing so, whoever is behind this is annihilating the In-Betweens without getting their hands dirty. They're using the Order to do their dirty work."

"And Lilith?" Archie prodded.

Drake gave him a brief grin. "Now *that* was the hunger speaking." Without another word, he turned and left.

"It's not our problem," Liam said as they watched Drake go. "If someone is out for the In-Betweens, then good riddance, right?"

Archie shook his head. "The In-Betweens aren't demons, kid, even though we treat them like it. They don't deserve our wrath."

"They're a fucking threat to humans, Archie. Demons, In-Betweens, they're all the same shit," Liam said, frowning at his mentor. "Your compassion for them makes no sense."

"You could use some of it," he said, then tapped Liam's back. "See you tomorrow?"

Before Liam could answer, Archie turned and walked away.

Liam couldn't help but feel that his mentor, his partner, his *father*, was disappointed in him. He should've followed Archie, should've cleared the air, like he always did when they had a disagreement. Instead, he watched Archie go, the lamplights drenching the old man in a fake halo as he walked under them.

The next day, the Archangel's sword waited for Liam on his desk with all the proper paperwork. Archie's handwriting on a ripped piece of paper said *"Use it wisely."*

Not long after, the old man lay in a hospital bed, his wounds beyond anything Kevin could heal. The boy had volunteered though, knowing he'd probably die before saving Archie. *Then they both would be dead.* Liam could still remember the pain in the Captain's eyes as she forced two Selfless to hold Kevin down and stop him from committing suicide.

To save Archie, they needed a full second-tier, an

ascended angel. But the Order sent a helpless Guardian instead.

The strangest part of it all was that, when the time for his choice came, Archie didn't become the angel he had once been, or one of the In-Betweens he seemed to pity and respect. No, Archie *chose* to become the thing he hated the most.

And Liam would find out why.

8

AVA

*A*va woke with sunlight caressing her skin. A shy gust ventured through the half-open window, bringing in fresh air.

She stretched, rejoicing in her pleasant awakening right before inhaling the musky scent of oak and earth from her large shirt, the one Liam had given her before he'd gone to bed.

It was so big that it worked as a dress.

Since Liam's shirts fitted perfectly against his muscular form, she guessed he must wear this to sleep. *Or perhaps he lent it to his lovers.* But then the shirt would smell like them, and not so wonderfully like him.

She discreetly dipped her chin and sniffed the fabric, but a sting of pain swam down her stiff neck. The old sofa—her new *bed*—was as comfortable as an iron mattress.

"Morning," Liam called out from the kitchen, his mouth half-full with food, most of him hidden behind a mess of hanging pans and piled cutlery on the kitchen counter.

Her heart drummed in her chest. *Had he seen her sniff his shirt?*

By his cocky grin, yes. Yes, he had.

As she approached the kitchen, the scent of burnt pancakes battled with the fresh air that ventured through the window. The burnt stench won, and Ava sighed deeply, muttering a prayer before sitting at the counter.

She looked down at the plate before her. It was filled with two burnt pancakes and scrambled eggs that smelled old.

"I thought I should fix you breakfast," Liam said from across the counter. "As a peace offering."

She turned to him, and her jaw hung open. Now that there was no kitchen clutter between them, she could see all of him. "You're, hmm ... shirtless."

There he sat, bands of muscle perfectly woven together underneath tanned, smooth skin. A soft stubble peppered his jaw, venturing down his Adam's apple. Heavens, Liam was a finely tuned symphony. She barely noticed the scars on his torso because they belonged to the symphony too. And those piercing eyes, smart and clear green, eyes that seemed to know exactly what she was thinking, they were peering at her.

"I'm being a nice host, *princess*," he said. "Usually I walk around naked." He forked a piece of pancake and shoved it in his mouth.

"I suppose I should thank you, then." She cleared her throat and grabbed her fork, stabbing a portion of eggs with it. "Thank you. For the food, I mean. And for not walking around naked."

He wiggled his eyebrows. "I used to be an angel before the Selfless Reincarnation Department turned me into a human, right? I guess I should honor my roots and play nice for a change." He frowned. "By the way, how does the SRD turn angels into human babies?"

"No one has access to that department, not even the Messenger, the Throne, and the Sword. They sign off on reincarnation requests, but after that ..." She shrugged. "You were born like every other human on Earth, but how that came to be? I don't think anyone in the entire Order knows. Other than the SRD, that is."

"Hmm." He observed her through narrowed eyes. "Anyway, I might not remember my time as an angel, but I try to be good." He scratched his forehead. "Mostly because of Archie. If it wasn't for him, I don't know where I'd be right now. Probably in a really fucked up place."

A fog of longing and sadness brushed against Ava's essence, and she wished to blow it away. But only Liam could do that, at least on the long-term.

Short-term, however ...

"Don't even think about it," he said, pointing a finger at her. "No Guardian feel-good bullshit. I'm fine."

He wasn't, but Ava always respected her charge's will.

She looked down at her food, which to Liam's credit, looked worse than it tasted. Heavens, she missed the buffet at the Order, where she could fetch anything her stomach desired: eggs, sausages, pancakes, even tapioca or pho-bo. All the world's cuisines were mankind's gift to the Gods.

Ava ate her breakfast faster than she'd expected. She must've been starving.

"Are you sure you're in this with me, princess?" Liam said without paying her any attention, his focus solely on finishing the last bite of his pancake. "There's still time to back out."

"You're my partner. My first duty is to you, always." She reached for his hand and grabbed it. "Besides, I'm a Guardian. I don't back away from my charges."

No matter how hard getting through to them may be.

She nodded to his empty plate. "You're finished?"

"Yeah." He smiled at her, his eyes soft.

She swung her fingers in the air, and their plates floated

toward the sink. Her jaw hung open as she watched the uncluttered area. "You cleaned the dishes?"

"Thought I should before you complained again." He narrowed his eyes at her. "Don't get used to it."

She raised her hands in mocking surrender. "I won't."

Ava set the two plates down in the sink and spun the handle, all with her mind. Water poured from the faucet as soap floated toward the plates, and soon, a brush started cleaning them.

She felt a pang at the back of her head, but it wasn't unbearable. *Not yet.* Lifting the plates didn't demand the same effort as the table back at the pub, but if Ava did this longer than a few seconds, the dreaded after-effects of using a power that didn't belong to a Guardian would take over.

"I still can't figure out how you do this," Liam muttered to himself.

Truth be told, neither could she. *If not the Gods, than who'd given her telekinesis?*

The thought made her head hurt even more, so she changed the subject. "What's the plan?"

Liam stood and went to his bedroom. "We go to the precinct," he said as he disappeared beyond his door.

After a moment, he walked back into the living room wearing a black shirt that clung to his chiseled form. He took the black leather jacket from the coat rack and put it on.

He had fixed his sun dagger on the left side of his belt and the silver Archangel sword on the right. Liam had taken his weapons with him before going to bed—either he was very protective of them, or he didn't trust Ava. She guessed the second.

In time, she told herself. The Selfless were known for being suspicious. Tricks of the trade, she supposed.

"Have you ever been to a precinct?" he asked as he patted

the gun hidden underneath his jacket, almost as if making sure he hadn't forgotten it.

She cleared her throat. "This would be my first time."

"You'll like it." His lips hooked on the left side of his face as he eyed Ava up and down, his attention entirely hers.

Heat flushed to her cheeks, and she became extremely aware of her bare legs. A part of her wished to pull down the shirt to cover more skin, but another part *wanted*, *needed* him to see her. *All* of her.

Before she could move or speak, Liam shook his head the way one dismisses a thought. A frown creased his forehead as he said, "You should get dressed."

THE SELFLESS PRECINCT—WHICH Liam called the Nine Five—resembled the human police stations Ava had seen while working as a Guardian. Desks towered with paperwork lined the vast space, and people hurried everywhere as the ringing of phones created background noise.

A pair of tough-looking Selfless wearing brown leather jackets brought in a vampire woman. Red lines tracked down the edges of her mouth, and the typical stench of rotting blood wafted from her body. *Definitely a newly turned.* New vampires reeked of coagulated blood, while ancient ones stank of termite excrement. Ava knew this because she had crossed plenty of In-Betweens while working as a Guardian —luckily, they rarely attacked when unprovoked.

The fang marks on the woman's neck proved she hadn't died before being bitten; that she hadn't made *the* choice. This woman had been turned by another vampire.

She trembled, her eyes dazed. Her entire body looked sunken, as if her bones were about to collapse in on themselves. The newly turned couldn't control the hunger, especially if their makers didn't stay to help the transition. And this particular vampire must've been starving before attacking some poor soul—hence her nearly skeleton-like figure and the blood in her mouth.

The Selfless duo showed the vampire no mercy, pushing her toward a row of cells near a big window. Ava frowned at that. Sunlight didn't hurt older vampires, but it could be extremely unpleasant to their newborn, especially one this weak.

Much to her relief, the Selfless put the woman in a cell with no direct sunlight. They were angels after all, and angels abhorred cruelty.

The dress code in the Nine Five seemed to be a leather jacket, jeans, and sneakers—sometimes black military boots. She saw it on the Selfless who engaged in chitchat around the water cooler, in the ones who made phone calls or typed into their computers, and the ones who paced around the precinct dressed the same way too.

As she and Liam moved forward, Ava looked down at her white bodysuit, the belt and linen kilt, knowing she'd draw attention. Sure enough, the voices dimmed and all eyes fell on her.

Men and women nodded at Liam as they passed the rows of desks, but when the Selfless looked at Ava, their mouths twisted in a bitter way.

"Sorry, princess," he whispered, "but the guys are upset with high command for leaving a fellow angel out to dry."

"I understand," she said. "I have no issue with being the focus of their anger. Having a face to blame can help with their healing process."

"Even though you didn't do anything wrong?" He stopped and frowned. It was the most glorious sight, that puzzled look on his flawless face.

She shrugged. "That's unimportant."

"Hmm, curious ..." He observed her a little longer, a hint of amusement hidden in the corner of his lips. Then he kept heading toward the office at the end of the room.

The glass door and glass windows were closed by shutters so no one could see what happened inside. Just as they were about to reach the door, a voice came from behind, "Oy, Liam!"

A red-haired boy in his early twenties—skinny like a stick and with freckles spread all over the bridge of his nose—caught up to them. His eyes were glistening, and his skin flushed. "We have to bring Archie back," he demanded more than said, completely ignoring Ava.

Liam patted the boy on the shoulder. "Kev, I promise you I'll get to the bottom of this."

"And *bring Archie back*, yeah?"

Liam gave him a broken glance that shifted quickly to his own boots. "I'll try."

The boy nodded, his lips pressed into a confident grin. "If anyone can bring him back, it's you, mate."

Grief and guilt oozed from Liam in cold clouds that brushed against Ava's essence. He knew no one could bring Archie back, and the boy must know this too; he simply couldn't handle the fact right now.

"The Messenger assigned me a new partner for the time being." Liam cleared his throat and turned to Ava. "This is Ava, hmm, what's your last name again?"

"Lightway."

The boy frowned. "*Archie* is Liam's partner." He observed her with curled lips. "A fuckin' Guardian? The Messenger lost his fuckin' mind, heh? I mean, her name's *Lightweight* for the Gods' sake!"

"*Light*way," she corrected, using her best Guardian voice, the smooth monotone that always appeased her charges.

"And I'm not here to replace Archibald. I'm only here to help."

The boy kept squinting at her but addressed Liam. "Mate, if they were gonna pair you with a lower angel, the least they could do was give you a Warrior instead of a fuckin' Guardian."

"Kev, go easy on her," Liam said, even though he had told Ava the exact same when they'd first met. "You used to be a Dominion before being reborn, so that means you guys are on the same team, right?"

The boy shrugged. "Dominions are ascended angels, mate. We're *way* more useful than a clueless third-tier."

Something burning swirled in Ava's chest. She was tired of being underestimated just because she was a Guardian, the most harmless of all lower angels. If she was so useless, Ezra wouldn't have assigned her this mission. She trusted his judgement above all else, and she would make him proud whether this boy believed in her or not.

"Thank you for the vote of *confidence*," she said, immediately chiding herself for the bitterness in her tone.

The boy, however, seemed pleasantly surprised. "Not like most Guardians, are we?" He grinned at her in an all-knowing manner. "No offense, love, but you lot only make people *happy*. Wait, not even that; you simply *soothe* them with your weak light. Also, your shields are pitiful. Guardians are only useful when they ascend to Dominions, like myself."

"I'll remind you that you're a Selfless right now, not the Dominion you used to be," Ava countered through gritted teeth.

"True." The boy waved his hand up and down, showcasing her to Liam. "That doesn't change the fact that they gave you a fuckin' kitty, mate."

Heavens, the boy was blunt. Ava couldn't decide if this annoyed her or amused her. Maybe both.

Liam cleared his throat and a flock of black hair fell over his forehead. "She can move stuff with her mind, Kev," he said quietly.

The boy raised his brow at her. "Call me intrigued, love."

"It's not much," Ava said shyly. "My Erudite friend taught me how to do it."

"Odd." The boy tapped his chin with his fingers. "You shouldn't be able to use telekinesis or telepathy, even if only a bit. It's not a part of your Guardian essence."

Ava shrugged, which was the only explanation she had. Justine had never found this odd, but then again, Justine knew less about angelic matters than Ava did.

The boy observed her a little longer, then took her hand and shook it. "Name's Kevin, by the way."

She bowed her head to him. "Nice to meet you, Kevin."

"Didn't know Guardians could lie so well, love."

She winked at him. "We're a box of surprises, aren't we?"

A smile bloomed on Kevin's face, and he slapped Liam's chest with the back of his hand. "Oooh, I like her, mate."

Ava's partner rolled his eyes and then nodded to the closed room. "Captain's busy?"

"Give her time. You know how much Archie meant to her." Kevin turned to an empty desk at the far right, and sadness grew thick in the air around him. "To all of us," he muttered.

"Speaking of which," Liam said, "can you run Archie's call logs from the last five days? Last I saw him, we'd encountered a vampire who claimed someone was tampering with wolfsugar and stealing the vamps' blood supplies."

Kevin's brow crinkled. "Why would someone do that?"

"To increase In-Between attacks on humans."

"Hmm, and then the Order would strike them without mercy," Kevin added with a nod. "It's a lead, I guess. I'm working on the logs already, but they're blocked and encrypted."

"You think Archie did this?"

"Very likely, but I can't tell for sure." Kevin shook his head. "If he did, though, it means he didn't want anyone following his footsteps."

A flash of sorrow swam across Liam's features. "There's only one way to find out."

"Quite right." Kevin bowed slightly to Ava before returning to his desk at the corner of the large common room.

Liam tapped Ava on her shoulder and motioned her to follow him. They took an elevator near the exit that led them underground.

"Do you think the surge of In-Between attacks is being caused by *someone*?" she asked, still getting used to Liam's theory. She'd heard faintly that the number of attacks on humans had grown, hushed whispers within the Order's halls.

Liam leaned against the gray elevator's wall. "All I know is that it's a smart way to annihilate the In-Betweens without getting hands dirty. But why someone would want to do that ... no idea."

The elevator opened to a long cement corridor lined with enormous training rooms that resembled those used in the Order. Big windows showcased ceilings at least three stories high.

Ava knocked on a window, and a surge of power reverberated through her bones. The glass had been blessed, which meant it could withstand strong impacts such as the blast of a holy gun or an Archangel's punch.

Back in the Order, the training rooms were all white, and the ambiance could be programmed to any desired setting:

rain, desert, bursting volcano, or freezing Antarctica; the options were endless. She had never fought in one, only accompanied Justine as an audience because her friend was always flirting with a Warrior—the "cute fight-club types," as Justine used to call them.

Here, however, the walls and floors were padded and dark blue. Ava doubted the Selfless could choose any ambiance. Ropes hung from the ceiling, and parallel bars stood stacked on the left end of the room along with balance beams and pommel horses, which Ava assumed worked as obstacles during training.

It didn't seem fair that the Selfless precincts had less resources than the Order. After all, the Selfless were protecting humans, more so than any other angel. Even worse, their bodies were weaker—stronger than the average human, certainly, but weaker than an angel's.

Perhaps Selfless was a more appropriate name than she had assumed.

Liam entered the last training room and withdrew his silver and blue sword. "Now, princess, I did promise your boyfriend I'd show you how to use one of these."

Ava froze, then glanced down at Ezra's golden and white sword sheathed on the belt around her waist.

Gods, give me strength.

9

AVA

*H*er new partner showed Ava how to steady her base, then proceeded to the basics of sword fighting. *Block, charge, turn. Slash.*

It was hard at first, but the few lessons she'd had during initiation soon bloomed to memory. After one hour, Ava managed to keep a decent base and a good defensive stance, which she counted as a small victory.

Next, Liam told her to run thirty laps around the room. Having the endurance of angels helped, but Ava barely managed to complete the last lap. Her legs hurt, and so did her lungs.

Liam tapped the back of her calf with his foot. "Sixty more."

"Demons in the hells," she blurted, immediately making a note to pray for forgiveness later. Blasphemy wasn't a terrible sin, but it was a sin nonetheless.

Liam showed her no empathy. He simply nodded ahead in a clear command for her to go on. And so she did.

When Ava finished the last lap, her legs caved and she fell

on the floor, panting, her chest heaving up and down. Sweat coated her entire body.

Liam gave her a ridiculously short moment to recover before bending over and offering her his hand. "Resting time's over, princess."

"I'm not a harmless princess." Never breaking eye contact, she got up by herself. Her legs shook with a fury, but they didn't let her down.

He gave her a mocking grin. "I never said harmless."

She smacked a loud slap on his shoulder. Ava didn't approve of unnecessary violence, but this had been extremely necessary. And it'd felt good.

Liam faked an "ouch" with that unnervingly perfect grin still stamped on his face. "You might be a Guardian, but there's something wild and untamed burning in there." He pointed at her forehead, squinting as if he were searching for something.

She straightened her stance. "You barely know me."

"I'm good at reading people." He rubbed the spot she had hit. "Also, you just harmed your charge and that makes my point."

"Well, my charge deserved it," she said, crossing her arms.

A laugh burst from his throat, a genuine, earthy sound that made Ava want to smile too. "Touché, princess."

Liam steadied his base in a clear cue for her to do the same. He then unsheathed his sword and acquired an attacking stance. So did Ava.

"What's the story behind this sword?" She nodded to the weapon.

Liam glanced at his silver blade, which even under the training room's burning LED lights emitted a dim glow. "It's Archangel Michael's sword. It was a gift from Archie."

Ava's weapon dropped to the padded floor, and her jaw almost followed. "You can't be serious."

He nodded at her fallen sword, one eyebrow raised. "Do this during a battle and you're dead."

She blinked and quickly picked up her weapon, steadying her stance. "How?"

"I guess Archie had contacts in high places." He shrugged. "The transfer of ownership went through the legal requirements, by the way. Archie didn't steal the sword, which is what most of you think when you see me with it."

"No wonder Archangels hate you," Ava murmured to herself. "Michael was incredibly powerful, and one of the Sword's most trusted angels. Some say he began his eternal sleep, others say a demon killed him."

"You've met him?"

"No," she said shyly. "Third-tiers don't interact with second-tiers, asides from our direct supervisors, that is."

"So most of you report to ascended angels." He frowned. "But you work with the Messenger, and he's way above a second-tier."

"The only exception to the rule, yes. It's Ezra's way of defying a directive he's not particularly fond of," she said with a soft smile. "In any case, Michael's tales of greatness have been shared through *all* of the Order's halls. Information has a way of slipping through marble and concrete, I suppose."

"Well, it's my sword, and that's all there is to it."

A thought burst in her mind, words of pure sacrilege, words that made her stomach churn and bile surge at the back of her throat. Perhaps, it wasn't the problem with the In-Betweens that had caused Archie's death. Perhaps, obtaining Michael's sword, aligned with an angry Archangel ...

She chided herself. An angel would never harm a brother. Or a human.

Liam pointed his sword at her. "Attack."

Conversation time was over.

She rushed toward him, a scream ripping through her throat. Liam blocked her as effortlessly as blocking a child. Then he charged.

Ava knew her stance was filled with breaches, so he would easily break through. Liam had already turned his sword in his grip so the hilt and not the blade pointed at her —a tactic to cause minimal damage.

His victory was imminent. As if on instinct, Ava's essence flooded through her, hardening on her skin, and when Liam slammed the hilt against her ribs with a hollow thump, it felt like a tickle and nothing more.

"No shields," Liam grumbled as he stepped back.

"But—"

"From what I heard, Guardians can't keep shields for long. Which means you can't rely on them, not with your life."

As much as she hated admitting it, he was right.

Ava forced her shield back into her core, then quickly charged at him, hoping the surprise would grant her a victory.

It didn't.

He fought with *one hand*, the other behind his back in a very gentleman-like manner. Every time Ava spotted an opening in his stance, Liam closed it at the last minute. *He was teasing her.*

Ava's blade met his again and again. The shrieking sound of metal hitting metal screamed through the room.

"You can do better than that," he said, a provocation hidden in his words.

He was using one.damned.hand. An offense, really, which only fueled her rage.

Soon the *clang, clang, clang* of their blades was all Ava could hear, and although her arms hurt and her sword felt as heavy as iron and stone, Liam hadn't shed a drop of sweat.

One. Blasted. Hand.

She attacked again, but Liam turned at the last minute and elbowed her spine, thus smacking her belly on the floor.

Air flushed out of Ava's lungs and she coughed, bile pushing to come out.

"Again," Liam ordered, showing her no mercy.

Ava took a deep breath, centering her mind—and her stomach. She forced herself up and charged, again and again.

Liam must've been holding back before. Now his attacks penetrated all her defenses. Ava lost count of the times she ended up breathless on the ground, but she never took his hand or asked him to go easy on her—either out of principle or pride. Perhaps both.

Her entire body hurt, even her bones. The hilt of his sword had hit her nonstop like a wrecking ball. Her skin felt sore in certain spots, which meant she'd be peppered by purple blotches later. *Mementos of their first lesson.*

"Don't worry; I'll get Kev to help with those," he said, reading the winces of pain in her face.

"I'm fine," she countered before charging again.

For the umpteenth time, Liam swiveled right before Ava attacked, but she found an opening in his moves, a glorious gods-sent opening.

She lowered her sword and hit a punch on his left ribcage, which sent him a step back. She followed up with a kick in the stomach, and then punched him beautifully in his face.

Liam spiraled on his axis, but he didn't lose his balance.

"Good," he grumbled once he steadied, a hand brushing his jaw. "But you need to use your sword, woman."

Woman this time. Not princess.

Ava blinked, only now realizing she hadn't used Ezra's

weapon. She strengthened her grip on the sword, and the weapon pulsed in the way of a beating heart, spreading warmth into her body.

She must be getting tired, and they should probably stop, but Ava had tasted victory and needed more. So she acquired an attack stance and grinned, an invitation for Liam to come and play.

He licked his lips and charged, but much to her own surprise, Ava blocked him beautifully. He kept going at her, but she blocked every single strike, *clang, clang, clang*.

Heavens, it was as if a door inside her had unlocked; Ava couldn't explain how or why. But all too soon, it was over. She felt the opening in her stance, knowing she wouldn't recover in time. That unmerciful hilt stabbed at her stomach, and the impact drew all her breath out, making her bend over. Liam elbowed her back, slamming her belly to the ground. *Again.*

She grunted in frustration as she rolled over and lied on her back, her chest heaving up and down.

Sweat coated her body, but it also coated his. The roots of Liam's hair were peppered with sweat, his black shirt glued against his skin.

He pointed his sword at her, his breathing ragged. "That was pretty good, princess."

"Stop calling me that," she groaned, then flung her sword against his in an arch, sending both weapons clanging against the ground to her left.

Liam glared at the weapons, but Ava wasn't done. She opened and closed her legs in a scissor shape, tripping him on the floor. She then rolled atop him and pinned both his hands to his sides. "Aha!"

Those clear emerald eyes widened, and his tantalizing lips opened in a surprised smile.

Only now did Ava realize that she sat astride Liam, his

entire body hard and sweaty against hers. His scent, that marvelous oaky fragrance so natural to him, burst from his every pore.

His Adam's apple went up and down as he stared at her. "You're full of surprises, aren't you?"

Liam's gaze burned and trapped Ava at the same time. She couldn't break free; his attention was a physical thing that kept her there just as she was. The urge to do things she hadn't done in a hundred years surged inside, but she forced it back down.

Heavens, what's happening?

Liam must've sensed her distraction, because he pushed Ava up with his waist and rolled over her, pinning her on the ground and trapping her arms above her head with one strong hand.

He grinned at her victoriously. Normally this would annoy Ava, but all she felt was his strong body perfectly fitted against hers, as if they were two pieces of a puzzle. Desire swam up and down inside her, an electric current that charged all the parts Ava tried to ignore.

Liam looked down at her chest and swallowed, then focused on her lips. "This position suits you," he croaked.

Her throat dried. "I preferred being on top." She flushed at the double meaning of her words. "I-I didn't mean—"

She did, but he didn't need to know.

His nose was inches from hers now, his dark hair falling over his forehead. "You did well today. Needs to be better, but good for a first time."

"Why, thank you," she said with pride, but halted at the strong musky scent that now drowned her.

Ava's reasoning slipped away as she sniffed the curve of his neck.

He growled inwardly. "You like?" His voice was a sensual murmur that set Ava ablaze.

"Hmm." She stared at him intently, taken by a delirious trance, her lips half open, inviting, *begging*.

She had felt this urge before with Ezra, the unyielding pull, but it had never been so strong, and Ava had always managed to control it.

This ... this was different. Liam's green eyes devoured her, made her forget who she was. Her hard nipples grazed the fabric of her bodysuit, a reaction of her body to his. When her nether parts ached for Liam's touch, Ava knew she'd lost the battle.

He lowered his mouth to hers as his free hand slid atop her left rib, stopping right under her breast, his thumb brushing the fabric ever so slightly.

"Ava," he muttered, her name a prayer.

When he nibbled her lips, her mind spun. She arched her back, killing any space between them. Call it adrenaline, but something primeval had taken hold of her, and she brushed her crotch against the hardness of his.

He grumbled low in his chest before deepening their kiss, his tongue venturing into her open mouth, consuming her. She replied with hunger, taking in all of him.

Ava freed her hands from Liam's grip and wrapped her arms around him, trapping him to her, bringing him closer—if that was even possible.

Their breathing grew in unison, fast, shallow, mingling with their feverish moans.

Heavens, Liam was going to take her, and she would let him. The pull between them assured Ava this was meant to be, but a faint voice in the back of her mind told her to stop.

Liam was her charge, and she barely knew him. But Gods help her, Ava couldn't break free. Within those moments, all she wanted, more than the air she breathed, was *him*. So she lowered her hands to his belt, ready to unbuckle it.

The hinges of the training room's door creaked, jolting Ava from whatever spell had taken hold of her.

Liam glared down at her with the same horror she felt, which meant their feverish trance was over for him too.

Heavens, they had almost ...

Liam let her go and rolled to the side, then stood up and gave her his hand.

She didn't take it.

Justine stepped into the room and stared at them, a curious frown creasing her forehead. Then came a mischievous grin. "Was I interrupting?"

Guilt mixed with shame filled Ava as she pushed herself up. She had almost had relations with her charge *and* partner in a training room. *Gods forgive her.*

"No, not at all," Ava said, her tone weak.

Liam turned to Justine, his arms crossed. "You got information for us?"

"For *Ava*, pretty boy." Justine winked at him.

"What did you find?" Ava asked, focusing on Justine and trying to ignore Liam's magnetic presence.

Justine walked closer to them. "Well, the records didn't have any leads, but I talked to a friend of mine." By her naughty grin, this friend was less of a friend and more of a lover. "He said that if you want information, your best bet is a guy named Jal."

Liam ran a hand through his sweat-soaked hair. "Fuck."

Ava turned to her partner. "Do you know him?"

"No, but I've heard the name." He shook his head. "Damn it, we're going to need the Captain's approval for this."

"Why?"

"Because Jal is a second-tier demon."

10

AVA

Once Ava was done showering, Justine handed her a towel and then underwear, followed by a fresh bodysuit and white linen kilt. Thank Heavens for her friend. Ava's old clothes were damp with sweat.

She took the elevator to the precinct with Justine, but Liam stayed behind to finish his shower and lock the training room. Ava suspected he'd done so because he felt equally ashamed—Gods, Ava's lips were still swollen from their exchange.

If they couldn't even be in the same elevator, how could she keep being his Guardian? A chaos of fear and desperation gnawed at her chest. Ava would never forgive herself if her lapse in judgement damaged her relationship with her charge. She had never lost reason in that manner, especially not because of a male—granted, an incredibly handsome one. But Ava wasn't an animal in heat.

She tapped the empty sheath attached to her belt as the elevator went up. "Oh. I forgot my sword."

"I'm sure your *partner* will grab it for you," Justine said with a naughty grin. "Speaking of which, what happened

89

down there? I mean, don't get me wrong, thank the Gods you're not some asexual creature." She looked up and raised her palms as if in prayer. "But you and Mr. Hunky were really going at it from what I could see."

Angels could be quite promiscuous—something to do with the raw power coursing their veins—but Ava had never given in to these urges. Her head had always been in the right place, her priorities in check. *Until a few moments ago.*

She closed her eyes, her fingers brushing her lips. They still tasted like Liam. "I couldn't pull away from him. His scent was so overpowering. Something in my mind just snapped."

Justine blew air through her lips. "Sweetie, it's normal. It's not like he's your soulmate; it's just sex. Also, you haven't gotten laid in a hundred years. You were bound to explode sometime." She grabbed Ava's hand and lowered it. "I just assumed it would be with Ezraphael. Then again, your new partner is a *fine* specimen."

Justine's words didn't make Ava feel any better, but she appreciated the effort.

As soon as the elevator doors opened to the precinct, Justine's attention fell on the tall red-haired young man pounding at the keyboard on his desk, his attention fixed on his computer screen.

"Who's that?" she asked, biting one of her wine-colored nails.

"That's the precinct's healer," Ava said, then dropped her voice to a whisper. "Please don't get involved with him. Kevin seems to be very important to Liam."

"You're one to talk." She nudged Ava with her elbow before walking to Kevin and giving him her hand.

Kevin immediately scrambled to his feet and kissed the back of Justine's hand, a goofy grin on his face.

Ava sighed helplessly at the effect her friend had on males

—and some females too. She couldn't recall the last time someone had resisted Justine's charms.

"Isn't she a little old for him?" The firm tone of Liam's voice came from behind Ava's ear, his breath brushing on her skin.

A shockwave ran down her spine as she turned around to face him. He stood absurdly close, so much that her nose almost bumped against his chest.

The sharp scent of a freshly bathed man invaded her nostrils, waking something in her that was best kept asleep.

He stared down at Ava, his presence, his flesh, all too close to hers. The same force from before pulled her toward him. She cleared her throat and stepped back, fighting as hard as she could.

Liam frowned at her, as if she were a puzzle he couldn't decipher. Then he handed her Ezra's sword. She thanked him and sheathed it.

"I'd like to apologize," she started, but he gently stamped a thumb on her lips. His soft touch vaporized the words on her tongue.

"I'm the one who should be sorry," he said. "I don't know what came over me. You're my partner, Ava, and the only angel who's willing to help. I ..." He shoved his hands in the pockets of his leather jacket. "I should've never jeopardized that."

"I can say the same." She smiled, but something inside her deflated. "I'm happy we cleared the air."

"Yeah. This type of thing can happen when adrenaline is high," he said with a confident shrug. "It's normal."

Normal? Had this happened before with another woman?

"I suppose it is."

Just the thought of him being so close to another female sent flames down Ava's chest. She took a deep breath to steady her nerves. Perhaps she should visit the Order's medical department when she had the chance. There must be something wrong with her brain.

She turned back to Justine and Kevin, who talked eagerly with each other. Justine looked to be in her early thirties, whereas Kevin was at least eight years younger. However, time and age were unimportant for immortals, so why was Liam worried?

Ava observed his concerned frown and finally understood what truly bothered her partner.

"Justine treats her lovers kindly. You have nothing to worry about." She thought twice. "Well, mostly."

Liam raised an eyebrow. "Mostly?"

Ava blushed. "Once, I passed by her room in an inopportune occasion and heard sounds of both pain *and* enjoyment." She raised her hands. "As long as both parties are happy and safe, I will not judge."

Liam observed her. "Anyone else would. Angels can be very judgmental. Humans too."

"Well, I try not to be."

His attention locked on her lips for a moment, but then he cleared his throat and nodded to the Captain's office. "Come on."

Liam knocked on the glass of the closed door. The word "Captain" was engraved in it, but no name came after. Just Captain.

"Enter." A woman's voice rang from inside, her tone dry and raging like a sandstorm.

The Captain sat behind a dark wooden table with her feet propped up on her desk, her attention fixed on the open window. The sound of car horns and voices ventured inside, but the Captain didn't seem to listen as she held a glass filled with amber liquid.

She must've been around sixty, and she had short gray

hair cut in a military fashion which matched well with the silver embellishments—medals—pinned to her navy suit.

On the wall opposite to the window was a brown leather couch that sat two people, but Ava doubted they'd be using it. Something about Liam's twitchy manner told her he planned to get in and out quickly.

He walked toward the Captain's desk. Ava closed the door behind her and followed.

The Captain's drink stank of whiskey. Ava knew the scent well. Her mother had given her a glass to help cure a cold when she was only fourteen. The whiskey didn't help—Ava threw up most of it—but back then, the medical sciences weren't as evolved as today.

The Captain kept looking outside and ignored them completely.

Liam straightened his stance. "Little early for that, isn't it, Cap?"

"Had a rough night, kid," she said before taking a sip.

"Yeah, I can relate." His tone was weak and mournful.

A warm pulse beat from Ava's sword, pushing against the sheath. Ava frowned at it, then at Liam and the Captain. *Had they also felt it?* They paid her no attention, so they couldn't have.

The sword beat again then stopped, almost as if it had been caught doing something mischievous. Ava glared at it. The weapon pulsed again, hard and at once, connecting to something deep inside her.

The Captain's office turned into blurred smudges that reshaped into a living room bathed by late afternoon sunlight.

What was this place? Ava had never been here before.

A bulky man sat on a couch. The afternoon light turned his hair a fiery blonde, but Ava could see little of his face since the light came from the window behind him, drenching his features in a penumbra.

A boy sat next to the man, his skin too attached to his bones, and his face smudged by so much dirt it had turned into a dark shade of ash. The boy resembled an abandoned puppy, but it was the eyes, clear green and fierce, that told her who he was.

Liam.

They sat on the same brown couch from Liam's apartment, only this time the cushions were fluffy and looked comfortable.

"You've been through a lot, kid," the man said.

That man must be Archibald, and this … this must be a memory. But how Ava stood here, she couldn't explain.

Liam shook so hard she wondered if he was freezing, but he didn't utter a word.

Archibald gave him a soft smile. "What you've been through is called a test of faith." He laid a hand on Liam's shoulder, and the boy flinched. Archibald immediately pulled back, giving Liam the space he needed.

The boy's gaze locked on the floor's wooden boards, and after a long silence, Liam mumbled, "What's faith?"

"It's something that lives right here." Archibald pointed to Liam's heart. "It's how the Gods speak to you. Keep listening to your faith, and you'll be just fine."

Ava frowned at Archibald's definition of faith. It was certainly unorthodox, but at the same time, beautiful.

In the blink of an eye, the room vanished, and she was back in the Captain's office.

She glared at Liam, then at her sword, which now behaved like any other inanimate object. She waited for it to pulse, but nothing happened.

What in all the Heavens?

Liam and the Captain kept speaking, completely oblivious to what had just happened to her.

"Cap, you saw what they did to Archie," Liam said, his lips tight and fury in his tone.

A gray cloud pricked inside him, pushing against Ava's Guardian instincts, an agony at things long gone.

Ava wasn't an Erudite, so she shouldn't have been able to enter someone's mind. Then again, she wasn't supposed to lift objects with her thoughts either.

Nothing made sense.

She cast a suspicious glance at the sword, wondering if the weapon had played a part in what happened, but that sounded insane.

The lines in the Captain's expression hardened, and she took another sip of her whiskey. Her attention went to the window, or perhaps way beyond it. "The Messenger told me to give you a mission involving damage control on vampire attacks from sectors fourteen and thirteen."

Liam turned to Ava with a frown that begged for an explanation, but all she could do was shrug.

He turned to the Captain. "What did you tell him?"

"That I'd assign you the mission." The Captain glanced at them, her brown eyes slightly inebriated. "You and your new *partner*." The last word came out with a chuckle.

"I'm not taking a new mission," Liam said. "Look, someone might be tampering with wolfsugar and stealing legal supplies of blood from the vampires. It's why the number of attacks have multiplied, and I think it might have something to do with Archie's death. I have a lead, Cap."

The Captain spun her glass in small circles and watched the liquid swirl. "Of course you do."

"But if Ezra ordered us—" Ava silenced at the pleading look Liam sent her, a look that told her he needed Ava on his side now more than ever.

A Guardian's first duty was to their charge, but this was

different. She would be going directly against Ezra's orders, and defying him in such manner felt like sticking a blade in her heart.

The Messenger trusted her. He wasn't only her boss and mentor, he was her friend. Perhaps more than that, considering he had kissed her. But now Ava had also kissed Liam, and nearly done things with him she shouldn't have. Guilt hung heavy on her shoulders, sticky and pitch black.

This was wrong, so very wrong. But when she watched the glistening desperation in Liam's eyes, Ava knew she had no choice.

Gods help her.

She straightened her stance and wrapped both hands behind her back. "Yes, we have a lead."

The Captain observed her through narrowed eyes. "Guardians aren't known for rule breaking. But I guess that if you stick with this one," she nodded to Liam, "common sense leaves you pretty quickly." She turned to him. "I take it that if you're here, it's because this *lead* will force a contact with a second-tier demon?"

Even drunk, the Captain was quite perceptive.

"I need answers, Cap." He nodded to her drink. "We all do."

The Captain inhaled a long breath, then leaned back against the chair. "I can delay the paperwork. And you have permission, of course, though unofficial."

"Don't we need an official permission, though?" Ava asked.

"I can't give an official okay for this, not when the Messenger requested a new mission for Liam. But I can stall." She pointed her glass toward Ava. "Are you fine with following him, angel girl? If Liam dies while facing a second-tier demon, he can always come back as a human or an angel, whereas if *you* die …" Her hands mimicked a small explosion. "Poof."

"I was assigned to help my charge in any way I can." Liam winced at that, as if the word "charge" bothered him. *Good.* Now he knew how Ava felt when he called her 'princess.' "If my life is endangered, so be it. My charge always comes first."

The Captain raised an eyebrow at Liam. "She has good intentions, but she's too green, kid."

He scratched the back of his neck. "I know."

Ava shot him a glare of pure death that seemed to amuse him.

"She learns fast, though," he added. "We made progress with sword fighting today. And she can create shields."

"On myself, yes," Ava said quietly. "I'm not certain if I can protect us both."

Liam snorted. "You don't have to protect me." He nodded to the Captain. "We'll also try to find Archie, Cap."

"If you do, you'll have to kill him."

The words seemed to punch Liam, and he took a step back. "You can't possibly—"

"I know what you're going to ask," the Captain said as sunlight peered through the window, highlighting all the wrinkles on her skin and the darker shades of gray in her silver hair. "The answer is I tried. I really did."

"Cap, we need to bring Archie in. We have to help him." Liam stepped forward. "He's family; not just to me, but to the entire precinct. Come on!"

"He isn't one of us anymore." There was pain in the Captain's eyes, and she took a long gulp of her drink. "There's no salvation for him."

"There's always salvation." Ava stepped forward and immediately regretted it after the furious glare the Captain sent her.

"There's no hope for the damned," the Captain countered

through gritted teeth. "An angel, of all creatures, should know."

"That's not fair," Liam grumbled.

The old woman laughed loudly. "And since when is the Gods' will fair? Go do what you have to do kid, but at the end of the day, we'll still be on this side and Archie on the other."

Liam shook his head and turned to leave. Ava followed, but right before they reached the door, the Captain said, "There are wheels spinning in the background, Liam. Something big is happening, but I can't guess what. Be careful." She looked at Ava, and she could swear the Captain's expression softened. "I assume you can mask your power?"

"I can."

"Good." She turned to Liam. "Give her some normal clothes, will you? Otherwise your new partner will stick out like a sore thumb." The Captain poured herself some more whiskey. "You don't want that where you're going."

11

AVA

*A*va would never get used to wearing jeans, black boots, and a leather jacket. At least her tank top was white, a small remnant of her Guardian attire.

"Why do you Selfless dress this way?" she grumbled, still adjusting to the rough fabric of her jeans. What a remarkably itchy material ...

"It makes blending in a lot easier, princess," Liam said as they entered the Chinese restaurant. "Remember to mask your essence so they think you're a Selfless like me."

Ava nodded and gathered her essence in her core, wrapping a thin layer of her light around itself. Masking essences was easy when it came to humans, but the supernaturals had sharper senses. And Ava was about to step into a den *full* of them.

Ignoring her uncomfortable jeans was easy after that.

Liam led her past the nearly empty tables, then through a fume-filled kitchen, finally taking dimly lit stairs that led down to an iron door in the basement. Liam knocked on it twice and a sliding peephole opened, showing unnaturally crisp purple eyes.

Vampire.

Loud music boomed from inside, and beams of green and purple light moved haphazardly throughout the space behind the vampire.

"Name your business," the creature ordered.

"We're here to see Jal," Liam said, holding his chin high in a proud, if not defiant, manner.

The vampire lifted his nose and sniffed both of them. "Jal wants no business with the Order."

"We all know the Selfless and the Order aren't exactly the same thing."

"You're all angels, no matter your wrapping."

Liam leaned forward and whispered, as if admitting to a wrongdoing, "We want to make a deal."

The vampire's eyes lit up. "A deal from a Selfless? Oh, Jal will like this very much."

The door unlocked and opened to a vast club that boomed with loud music. Neon lights flooded the packed dance floor which was walled by two rows of lounges. The place reeked of cigars, sweat, and alcohol.

"Heavens, it's only four in the afternoon," Ava muttered to herself. "How can they be partying at this time?"

Liam grinned down at her as if she had said something amusing. "There's no right time to party, princess," he yelled over the music. "Especially when you have forever ahead of you."

They snaked through the crowd, and Ava caught scents of wet fur and coagulated blood, typical for werewolves and vampires. But there were also other scents: sweet, citrus, musky … so many, so different. That could only mean one thing.

Humans!

With her heart pounding against her chest, Ava narrowed her eyes to see men and women being bitten and scratched on the dance floor. She gripped her sword's hilt, and just as she was about to unsheathe it, the vampire who'd let them enter stopped her.

He shook his head in a silent warning. "They're here of their own will."

Liam crossed his arms. "And I assume you have the turning requests approved by the Order?"

"Of course." The vampire's smile didn't meet his eyes. "Then again, some of them simply enjoy feeding us. Becoming a creature of the night isn't for everyone." He turned and moved forward, a clear sign for them to follow.

"What's the assessment, princess?" Liam muttered as they followed the vampire.

Ava peered through the humans' emotions and sensed nothing but elation and eagerness coated by sexual arousal, a red, candy-like cloud that emanated from their bodies.

"They're here because they want to be." She scoffed. "Why would they choose this?"

Liam shrugged. "When you don't know if you'll go to the Heavens or the Hells, living forever seems like a pretty good idea. Not to mention that some people don't feel like reincarnating. Growing up is a pain in the ass. I'd give anything to avoid going to school again."

Ava repeated the words she'd learned during initiation. "Giving yourself to the In-Betweens is the choice of the weak."

"Is it?" He gave her a quizzical frown that said he knew more than Ava ever could.

An icy wave smashed against her at once, a freezing void that reverberated within Ava's bones. It was peppered with delirium and something sad and tortured, something that made Ava want to scream and cry at the same time.

She turned to the lounge on the left, where three demons played cards at a round table.

The source of darkness.

Two demons worked the cards without paying Ava any attention, but the third observed her with piercing dark-brown eyes and a hint of a smile. Darkness oozed from his back like an oil leak in the ocean, thrumming against her essence. The darkness shaped large wings, and when she narrowed her eyes the shadows disappeared, giving way to magnificent draconian wings that were at least the span of a school bus.

Wine colored scales that turned black at the tips coated the demon's wings. They shimmered when light from the dance floor hit them, stealing the color—green, purple, sometimes blue.

Absolutely breathtaking. A demon's wings shouldn't be this majestic, but then again, Ava had never seen demonic wings in real life until now.

The demon spread them wide, a silent warning that in here, *he* was king.

Ava didn't need introductions to know who Jal was.

His long dark hair cascaded down his chest in the way of a silk curtain, his deep bronze skin smooth and flawless. As a second-tier, Jal looked remarkably human, unlike the lower demons who accompanied him.

Swarms of shadows covered all of the first creature; the only visible feature in the darkness was its slit yellow irises. The other demon looked more frog than human with its gray skin and round, jawless face. It grinned at Ava, showing teeth that resembled thousands of needles before returning its attention back to the game.

It was said that the darkness could make weaker demons take monstrous forms, but for some reason, the light didn't have the same effect on angels. Why that was, Ava couldn't say. Ezra had once told her this was the devils' test, something to churn the weak from the strong. Unlike the light, the darkness was unmerciful and cruel. "Survive that, and you can survive anything," he'd said.

This was why Jal looked perfectly human, apart from his draconian wings. As a second-tier demon, he had conquered the darkness in the same way that Archangels, Virtues, and Dominions had conquered the light.

The stench of sulfur invaded Ava's nostrils as she and Liam climbed the stairs to the lounge. *Demonic scent.*

Jal's wings transformed into shadows again, disappearing behind him, but he kept watching Ava.

A predator about to attack.

"You okay?" Liam asked her as they stopped before the table, his broad shoulders shielding her.

Ava nodded, but she was actually far from okay. She had never faced a second-tier demon before. Heavens, she had barely managed those third-tiers back in the pub. Imagine one like Jal, whose darkness slipped through every pore.

Her hands started shaking, so she gripped the hilt of Ezra's sword to steady them.

The weapon pulsed once. Strings of warmth connected with her core, and a calming sensation invaded Ava, almost as if Ezra himself had whispered the words of the Gods in her ears.

"Demons and angels only reveal their wings when they want to fly, fuck, fight, or show off," Jal said nonchalantly, throwing cards at the table. "Why do you think I showed you mine, pretty angel?" His tone was hard and playful at the same time.

To show off, naturally. It was why many ascended angels often walked with their wings on display.

A realization hit Ava like a car crashing against a wall: Ezra rarely hid his wings within his light when she was around. Did that mean he was showing off ... or that he wanted to become *intimate* with her?

She cleared her throat, steadying her voice. "You wanted to scare me, but you failed, demon."

"Did I?" A laugh rumbled in Jal's chest as he leaned back in his chair. Then he turned his attention to Liam, who still stood between them. "I can't remember the last time an angel was crazy enough to step into one of my properties. Surely my fame has preceded me, but perhaps you're foolish enough to ignore it."

"The Selfless are no angels," Liam countered, his tone steel and stone.

"You say tomato, I say tomahto. Besides, I'm not a fool. *You* are a Selfless. Your companion?" He clicked his tongue. "She's as pure and angelic as they come, Liam Striker."

Liam masked his surprise beautifully, but Ava could still sense it stabbing his core. "How do you know my name?"

"I had many dealings with your former partner," Jal explained. "He never cared to introduce us, though. My guess is you weren't ready."

Liam's throat bobbed, but he never lost focus. "We have a proposal for you."

Jal's eyes flashed yellow, and a grin spread across his squared jaw. "If you'll excuse me, gentlemen," he said to the demons as he stood.

Jal walked down the rows of the lounge, and Liam and Ava followed.

Below, on the dance floor, a sea of creatures ground against each other, dancing, fornicating, *biting*. A shudder coursed through Ava's body, and she focused on the path ahead.

Once Jal reached the end of the club, he stopped before an iron door.

The room inside was a small square with no windows that reeked of cigars. One round wooden table stood in the middle, accompanied by one chair. A wooden box rested atop the table.

Jal closed the door behind him and opened the box. He picked a cigar from inside, then dropped on the chair, propping his black leather boots on the table.

Here, with cold light shining over his features, he looked remarkably handsome, almost angelic. His black shirt clung to his muscled frame, much like Liam's, and his ebony hair curtained the left side of his face in a graceful wave. Ava felt envious of such silky hair, wishing her tresses had the same shine.

Was it a sin to envy a demon?

Music still thumped outside, but at least now they could talk in relative quiet.

Jal raised his index finger. It caught fire briefly, enough for him to light his cigar. He inhaled and then puffed a circle in the air, his attention never leaving Ava.

"I love it when angels need a favor. It's not often that you do, of course. Angels aren't as stupid as the humans I make deals with." He smiled mischievously. "Perhaps you'll prove me wrong, pretty angel."

"Your deal is with me," Liam snapped.

Ava's hands closed into fists, her nails biting into her palms. Higher demons made deals with humans in exchange for their souls. So when the human died, they were stripped of the choice, and their fate could only be determined by the demon who damned them in the first place.

"You should be ashamed." The words sounded stupid as they left her lips. After all, a demon could feel no shame.

Jal inhaled deeply, then exhaled a cloud of smoke. "Unlike most demons, my terms are clear in my contracts. The humans know what they're getting into, and they accept that. Wasn't it your Gods who granted them free will?"

"Why, you can't possibly—"

"We need answers about my partner's murder," Liam cut in, his face a marbled mask.

Jal motioned to Liam's head with a pleased grin on his face. "Oh, I like what's going on in there. You have revenge written all over you, Selfless. It adds flavor to your essence." He inhaled before puffing another ring of smoke in the air.

"What can you tell us about Archie's murderer?" Liam pushed.

Jal angled his head, locking his attention on Ava. "Your boy here wants to kill whoever murdered his partner. Are you okay with that, Guardian?"

Ava knew Liam sought revenge, but she would help her charge make the right decision. They would bring the murderer in for questioning, if they found him. Let the Throne and the Virtues handle their judgement.

"Liam will come around," she said, barely believing her own words.

Jal snorted, then took a lengthy inhale. He puffed it toward Liam in a stream of smoke. Her partner didn't wince or move, simply stared down at the demon as smoke brushed past his face.

A deep laugh rumbled in Jal's chest, and for a moment, Ava wondered if there was a dragon underneath his skin. "I can tell you *something* about his murder," he said, "but nothing in life comes for free."

"Name the price," Liam said.

The demon peered at him, his sinuous eyes assessing Liam thoroughly. "Archibald made many enemies on my side. What was it that we called you? Ah, yes, the *Fury Boys*. Funny that he's one of us now." He shrugged. "Some demons would love to get their hands on the famous Archibald Theodore Brennan, you know."

"Then they have a death wish," Liam countered, his tone

cold, hiding the fury that raged beneath. "Archie can take any demon with his eyes closed."

"Lower demons perhaps," Jal said with an enigmatic grin, almost as if he had won a veiled battle. He raised his hands in surrender. "My point is, information about your partner is valuable. I'm only agreeing to help because Archibald was kind to the children of the night." He nodded toward the club beyond the closed door. "And since he was kind to them, I'll return the favor."

Ava frowned. "You stand with the In-Betweens?"

Jal inhaled and puffed smoke through his nose. "I don't play nice with other demons. Unless we're playing cards, that is. Their money is as good as any, and the suckers love to lose."

She remembered Liam's theory. "Someone is tampering with wolfsugar and stealing blood from vampires. This smells a lot like demon work to me."

Jal glared at her, his nostrils flared. "I'd never—" He stopped and took a deep breath. "If I wanted them dead, I wouldn't be trying to keep as many of them fed and under control, would I?"

So it was true. Someone *was* forcing the In-Betweens to attack humans, bringing the wrath of the Order upon Jal's "children of the night."

"Who's behind this?" Ava asked.

Jal gritted his teeth. "If I knew, they wouldn't still be alive."

"Did it have anything to do with Archie's death?" Liam's tone was hollow, empty. *Hurt.*

"Maybe." The demon considered this for a second or two. "Probably."

Liam grunted in frustration, rubbing his forehead. "Name your price, demon."

Jal tapped his fingers on his chin. "I lost a bet with one of the werewolf lords. Well, *the* werewolf lord."

"No fucking way." Liam crossed his arms, muscles bulging underneath the fabric of his shirt. "Ask for anything else."

Jal gave them an amused grin. "I don't *need* anything else. I need the necklace of Achmelladin." He took a phone out of his pocket, tapped the screen a few times, and then showed it to them. The screen displayed a golden necklace with an emerald the size of a fist. "It amplifies a psychic's powers."

Liam whistled. "That must've been a really bad bet."

Jal inhaled and then puffed another breath of smoke. "Neutrality has its costs." He placed the phone on the table.

"A demon who is neutral?" Ava asked with a snort. "Who cares for the In-Betweens? That's rare."

"Not rarer than an angel doing the same." At this he glared at Liam, as if sending him a hidden message. Jal then returned his attention to Ava, assessing her from top to bottom. "Hmm, beautiful."

Liam stepped in front of her, a growl rumbling deep in his throat, a sound remarkably similar to Jal's draconian grunts.

"Bring me the necklace," Jal said with amusement. "And I'll tell you what I know about Archibald's murder."

"Not yet." Liam raised his index finger. "We're supposed to steal from Lothar, the strongest werewolf to date. Throw in a personal favor in the bundle, and we'll have a deal."

Ava wanted to ask Liam if he believed negotiating was wise, but it seemed he and Jal were trapped in an invisible battle.

"I'm not a fan of bargaining," Jal spoke through tight lips.

"Lothar is a type five In-Between," Liam said. "That's almost like fighting a fucking Archangel. Stealing from him is worth more than one simple answer."

"Oh, your father taught you well." Jal licked his lips. "Fine.

You get information about Archibald's murder, *and* a favor from me."

Ava couldn't be certain if relying on a demon's favor was wise, but Liam looked pleased with the deal.

"Where can we find this Lothar?" she asked.

"Your partner will know." Jal nodded to Liam and stood, stretching his free hand to him. "Lothar isn't keen on security, since no one is stupid enough to try to murder him. Or steal from him, that is."

"We'll get the necklace." Liam shook the demon's hand, and a soft shadow ventured through their veins. The deal was sealed.

Liam and Ava left the club, rushing out of the Chinese restaurant. As soon as they stepped on the cold street outside, Ava stated the obvious. "This was a bad idea."

"Of course it was." Liam took his phone from his pocket and punched in a number. "Kev, I need you to fake an inspection letter. Also, get the guns ready."

AVA

*O*nce they arrived at the precinct, Kevin handed Liam two holy guns strapped to a crossed belt. Her partner fixed the weapons around his own trunk, and when he was done, Ava could barely see the guns underneath Liam's leather jacket. There was also Michael's sword and a sun dagger hanging from the belt around Liam's waist. When Ava thought there was no space left in his body for more weapons, she spotted Liam hiding knives in his boots.

"Got you something too, angel girl," Kevin told Ava before handing her a sun dagger. "It's not much, but Liam would kill me if I gave you a gun." He waved his hand dismissively. "In any case, I doubt holy blasts can inflict much damage on a type five like Lothar."

Ava shuddered as she looked down at her belt where her sun dagger and Ezra's sword were sheathed. The In-Betweens usually kept to themselves, which was why Ava had never faced one. A werewolf lord at that, with claws that could rip her to shreds and teeth so sharp they could bite her arm off ... Even with Liam by her side, she might be walking to her death.

The fact that her partner carried enough weaponry to free a small country didn't help ease her fears.

She followed Liam across busy streets packed with people and cars stuck in traffic jams. A symphony of angry horns erupted non-stop, but soon rush hour would be over, and then the city would be quieter, though never completely silent.

"Werewolves don't like sharing, but hopefully we won't have to use all of these." Liam tapped the guns hidden under his jacket.

"Hopefully," she said, failing to mask the fear in her tone.

"Don't worry." He retorted without glancing back at her, an intense frown creasing his forehead. "I can be compelling if I want to."

She observed him. "You're thinking of all the ways this could go wrong, aren't you?"

"Why princess, how do you already know me so well?" He gave her a charming wink.

Before she shot him a snarky reply, Ava spotted an old man across the street. He had a trimmed beard the color of snow and shoulder length white hair, which made a beautiful contrast against his ebony skin. His piercing, clear blue eyes narrowed at her. Wise eyes, clever eyes, something *ancient* hidden within them. But it was his clothes that rang an alarm in her head.

He wore a gray t-shirt with the Rolling Stones logo—Justine had introduced the group to Ava in the past. The man's worn jeans were fashionably ripped at the knees, and his sneakers were as red as strawberries. Ava expected a young human to dress this way, but an older gentleman?

This is prejudice, she told herself. *He may dress as he so wishes.*

As if he'd heard her thoughts, the man smiled and tilted his head at her in either thanks or a silent greeting.

Ava squinted at him, wondering if they'd met somewhere, but she remembered all her charges and she had never seen this man before. Just as she was about to approach him, a speeding car cut through the space between them. When it passed, the man had vanished.

"Are you okay?" Liam placed a hand on her shoulder. "You look like you've seen a ghost."

"Perhaps I have," she mumbled, then looked up at him to meet those blazing green eyes focused on hers.

The pull from before came stronger than ever, a *need* Ava tried hard to control. Liam clenched his jaw and his nostrils flared, as if he were fighting the same battle.

"We're here." He let her go and stepped back.

They had stopped before the entrance of a fancy apartment building with glass doors. A doorman dressed in a bland beige uniform promptly let them in.

Jal wasn't joking when he said Lothar didn't worry about security.

They walked across the glass-paneled hallway until they reached the elevator. Liam pressed the button to call it down and waited.

"Most supernatural creatures hate bureaucracy, like everyone else, so that's our trump card." He pulled the fake inspection letter Kevin had prepared for them from his pocket. "Still, things might get ugly. Maybe it's best if you wait here."

Ava considered his offer. The path she followed became increasingly dangerous, and she wasn't a Warrior, no matter how hard Liam trained her. In fact, Ava despised violence. But she would not fear, and she would not cower. Her charge needed her, and she never abandoned her charges. Never had and never would.

"Stop treating me like a porcelain doll," she said under her breath.

He blinked at her. "I'm not. It's just—"

"I'm not strong enough?" This might be true, but Ava slammed both hands on her waist, silently daring him to say it. "I can guarantee you that I'm—"

He took her hands and pulled her closer to him. "It's not that, Ava. Look, a type five werewolf isn't a harmless puppy."

Ava's lips parted as she realized his request hadn't been for her. It'd been for *him*. Liam didn't want to see her hurt.

She cupped his right cheek. "Wherever you're going, I'm following. You're my charge."

He winced at that. "Guess you found your own version of 'princess,' haven't you?"

"Yes, I have." She grinned victoriously.

The elevator door opened, and they got in. Liam pressed the button for the thirtieth floor.

"By the way, the name's partner, not charge," he said as they went up.

She looked pointedly at the shifting floor numbers. "And the name's Ava, not princess."

"Of course." He put a hand to his heart. "My apologies, *princess*."

Heat burst inside Ava's head. "Oh, you annoying man!" She quickly stamped her hands over her mouth. "I apologize. I didn't mean to insult you."

Liam let out a busty laugh. "Of course you did." He pulled her hands down, stepping closer to her. "You should let this side of you out more often."

"What side?" she whispered, her attention lost in his stare.

He brushed her jawline with his thumb. "The human one." His tone was low but soft, and it made Ava want to pin him against the wall.

As if on cue, the elevator clicked open to the thirtieth floor, showing a red-carpeted path. They stepped out, walked to number sixty-three, and knocked three times.

Liam took the paper from his pocket and slammed it against the peephole.

A rough voice that could either be a man speaking or a dog growling came from inside. "I can smell you, Liam. You have no business here."

"Haven't you seen the inspection notice?" Liam countered. "It's been approved by a Virtue."

"Which Virtue?"

"Does it matter?"

The werewolf snarled behind the door.

Liam rolled his eyes and read the name on the paper. "Virtue Suphiel Eriksson."

Suphiel was a powerful Virtue, and coincidentally, Justine's immediate superior.

Ava knew then that Kevin must've asked Justine for help with faking the notice—perhaps it hadn't been faked at all. Justine had her way with the Order's males, even her supervisor. Without meaning to, Ava's thoughts went to Ezra.

"Never heard of this Suphiel," the werewolf said from behind the door, and then all was silent for a moment. "But I guess I have little choice in the matter."

The door opened, revealing a bare chested man in jeans. He was much bigger and stronger than Liam, which was to say worlds. Liam towered over Ava, who at five-foot-seven wasn't as petite as most women. Lothar might as well be a small giant.

The werewolf's muscles, bulged and swollen, felt misplaced against the creature's human form. His arms alone were two times thicker than Liam's.

Ava felt like a squirrel facing a lion.

Lothar grabbed the paper. "This is foolish," he said after reading it. "I'm not storing illegal wolfsugar."

Liam shrugged. "Heard you ate one of your pack leaders a few days ago." He let himself in, and Ava followed. "I've seen the remains. They looked like the work of an angry werewolf in a drug haze."

"He challenged me," Lothar said with gritted teeth. "I did it on my own, no wolfsugar needed." This he added with a proud and ferocious grin.

Fear crept up Ava's spine, but Liam kept his nonchalant manner. "Then you won't mind if we look around, right?"

"You disrespect my home and my word." Lothar bared his teeth, and his eyes glowed a sharp red. "Angels are no better than the demons who cursed us into monsters. You all want to see us burn."

Liam gave him a bored look. "Someone's been taking drama lessons."

Ava let Liam and the wolf man argue as she walked around the apartment. When she cast a quick glance inside Lothar's bedroom, there it was—the necklace, hanging before a mirror. The green emerald flashed dimly against sunlight.

Heavens, Lothar really did not care for security.

Ava sent Liam a glance, and he nodded. *Message received.*

Lothar must've caught a part of that message, because he growled at Ava. "Nothing there for you to see, *Selfless.*"

At least she had masked her essence well, not that it made much difference. If Lothar turned into a werewolf, he'd take her as dinner either way.

Liam waved the notice in front of the werewolf's nose. "The inspection encompasses the entire apartment, *my lord.*"

Lothar's bark promised Liam a world of pain. Unfazed, her partner tapped the werewolf's back and turned him toward the kitchen. "Now, why don't you show me your kitchen cabinets?"

Oh, Liam was good, but Ava had to be careful now. Werewolves were known for their sharp hearing.

She increased the wrap around her essence as she walked

into the room, each step nearly mute. Ava had masked her essence so well that Lothar wouldn't be able to see her.

She grabbed the necklace slowly, softly. A single chatter of the golden chains would alert the beast, but Ava kept her hands firm.

She placed the necklace quietly in her jacket pocket and stepped out of the room. When Ava dared a glance forward to the kitchen, she locked eyes with Lothar, who snarled at her.

"Hide your essence all you want, bitch. I can still smell you," he growled.

Before Liam could react, Lothar grabbed the crossed belt around her partner's chest and kicked Liam toward the closed door, ripping the belt in two and separating him from his holy guns. Wood snapped as Liam broke through the door and flew into the corridor.

His groans of pain came out shallow from outside the apartment.

Lothar grinned at Ava as he took one of the guns.

Heavens, she'd face her final death today.

Instead of shooting her, the werewolf lord pressed his hand around the gun, and metal crumpled like paper until the weapon turned into a ball of iron. He dropped it to the ground and laughed an unnatural, graveled sound. He then left the other gun atop the kitchen counter, as if daring Ava to lunge for it.

The bones in Lothar's body cracked underneath his skin, reshaping him entirely. His nose stretched into a snout, and his legs turned hinged. Dark hairs sprouted everywhere as his hands morphed into claws.

Fear froze Ava where she stood. Her first instinct was to run, but she wouldn't have time to pick up Liam in the corridor and take him with her, not when he was likely injured. She had to buy Liam time by keeping Lothar busy.

She pulled out her sword and remembered her first and only lesson with her partner. *Steady base, tight defense. Quick, simple movements.* She spread her essence atop her skin, hardening her protective shield just as Lothar finished his transformation.

The mighty wolf man stood on hinged legs, his dark grey fur long and silky under the sunlight that peered through the windows. He snarled and crouched on all fours before lunging at Ava.

The ground shook beneath his steps, and Ava gripped the sword harder, even if her hands quivered violently. She might drop her only defense against the beast any second now.

Instead of crashing into Ava, Lothar suddenly halted and stood straight, towering over her. He watched the tip of her sword with amusement.

Drool dripped from his snout and fell on the floor. He growled a laugh, then slapped the sword out of her hand the way one would slap a bug. All too quickly, he punched Ava through the open door and into his bedroom.

Her body crashed through the bed posts and then slammed against the wall. Her spine and skull pounded with pain, her vision blinking in and out as she fell on the mattress. When Ava patted the back of her head, her hand came back bloodied. Either her shield was too weak or this creature was too powerful. She had no time to find out, because Lothar prowled toward her, crouched on all fours, his murderous sneer showcasing sharp teeth.

What wafted from his essence was violent and raw, but strangely enough, Ava caught a dose of harmless mischief mingled with it. Like he was *playing* with her. In all honesty, would she still be here if Lothar wanted her dead? He could've also shot Liam when he'd grabbed his holy gun, but he hadn't.

Heavens, was she already losing her mind?

From the living room floor, Ava's sword pulsed, beating in time with her heart. She felt the pulse thrumming under her skin, down to her bones, and then deeper, so much deeper, piercing through her essence. Each beat tore a rift inside her, a warm, golden line that grew with every thump.

Beat. Rip. Beat. Rip.

The gunshot came from the living room and slammed into Lothar's back. The werewolf whined and crumpled on the floor, but he would recover quickly.

Liam leaned on the kitchen counter, the left side of his forehead painted red. He had the smoking holy gun in his hand.

Ava didn't flinch. She jumped from the bed and ran toward him, picking her sword up from the floor on the way. Angry barks erupted from behind her, but she didn't look back. Liam fired again and again, blue blasts that shot past Ava and hit the werewolf chasing her.

A fourth shot was followed by the thump of a bulky body hitting the ground.

Liam grabbed her hand as she reached him. "Let's go before he heals."

They were almost at the door when Liam shouted in pain and let go of her hand. The werewolf had sunk his sharp claws in Liam's left leg. Blood burst from Liam's ripped veins, and arteries too, considering how far the blood sprayed.

Lothar reacted slowly, blinking in and out of consciousness, the human in him fading. Ava could see the beast trying to take over behind his red eyes, but also the man trying to stop it.

Sweat bloomed in Liam's forehead as he held screams. He withdrew his sun dagger and slammed it into Lothar's claw. The wolf growled in pain, sluggishly letting go of his leg.

"Go Ava," Liam ordered through gritted teeth, his calf in shreds. "Now!"

"I'm not leaving you!"

She sheathed her sword and tried to snatch Liam up, but the half-conscious wolf man let out a long snarl, his eyes glinting with fury and something primeval, something that hadn't been there before.

Even in his wolf form, Ava had been able to see a part of Lothar beneath the beast, but now he seemed devoid of logic and reason, the human in him completely gone.

"Fuck," Liam muttered before Lothar grabbed his good leg and swung him out of the open window.

AVA

*A*va's breath caught in her throat as Liam spun midair. He grabbed the edge of the balcony's glass railings just in time, and his body thumped against the surface from the other side. His fingers strained to prevent a deadly fall, but by the pain carved on Liam's face, he wouldn't hold for long.

Ava ran toward the window that led to the balcony, but something snatched her foot—the injured werewolf had grabbed her calf.

Lothar was extremely weak and bordering on unconsciousness, and still, he grabbed her with the strength of an iron chain.

The sword's pulse beat inside Ava, and her chest began to glow. The glimmer swam down her legs, rushing through her veins, until it concentrated on her calf. The pulse beat again, and her tendons shone bright before smoke burst from her skin, the scent of burnt dog hair and flesh invading her nostrils.

Lothar howled in pain and let her go, brandishing his

burnt hand in the air. She turned to Liam just in time to see him mouth a curse and fall.

Lothar's barks boomed behind her as Ava flung herself out of the window and over the balcony, falling fast, cutting through the air.

She reached Liam mid-fall, pressing his muscular frame against her. The befuddled look on Liam's face called her an idiot.

She didn't care.

Ava pulled her shield from within her essence, hoping it would be enough, even though she knew better. The rift inside her beat in unison with the sword on her waist, and a thick layer of molten gold spread across their bodies, coating their skin. She and Liam became golden statues in a deadly fall.

Would they bleed red or yellow?

They hit the ground the way a comet ends life on a planet. The sidewalk caved with the impact, and a wall of debris rose around them, quickly leaving a cloud of pulverized concrete dust hanging in the air.

Even with Ava's strongest shield, bones should've cracked, organs should've been smashed. Instead, Ava felt as if she had landed from a small jump.

The few people on the street screamed and ran away, one or two drivers left their cars to do the same. The clean-up teams would have fun fixing this.

Liam gaped at the layer of shiny gold on his skin, which had started receding back into Ava until they were both as they used to be.

"What the Hells," he muttered, glaring at her.

A wolf's howl came from the building's top floors, and Ava scrambled to her feet, helping Liam up. She swung his arm on her shoulders and off they went.

Liam winced and held grunts of pain. The deep cuts on

his leg poured blood, and Ava could see half of his tibia. Sweat beaded on his forehead, but he kept limping on one leg, his breathing shallow and ragged.

They managed to reach a small park, not far from Lothar's building, before Liam let go of her and fell on the ground. "I can't. You need to run, princess." He unsheathed his sword. "I'll buy you time."

He coughed and a trickle of blood flowed down the edge of his mouth. Damned the Hells, his lungs might've been punctured.

She sat by his side. "I'm not leaving."

The pulsing light inside her shot through her veins again, making her hands glow. Ava stared at them in wonder. This glow was different from the one that had burned Lothar—Ava had no idea how or why she knew that. While the other glow sought to burn and destroy, this light was warm, soothing. Suddenly, she knew exactly what to do.

She spread her hands on Liam's leg, and he recoiled in the way of someone being branded by a hot iron. But the pain couldn't have been that bad, since his leg soon relaxed under her touch.

The rift inside Ava's essence hurled warmth, as if a shining summer day had burst within her. The light in her hands spread across his leg, penetrating skin and bone, mending limbs and tissue as easily as Ava could lift a finger.

"How are you doing this?" Liam wheezed, then coughed more blood. "Have you ascended to Dominion when no one was watching?"

Ava glanced behind her back, fear and hope making a strange mix. If she had become a Dominion, she would have wings by now, but there was nothing there. Ava quickly realized why. "I haven't forced emotions onto someone else. It's the last power required for a Guardian to ascend to Dominion."

Liam glared at her healing hands. "Well, it seems to me you're almost there."

Another howl came from the werewolf's apartment, and a gray dot fell from the top like an arrow ripping through the air. Then a harsh thump followed, similar to the one they made when they landed.

Lothar might've broken some limbs, but he would recover quickly from the fall. Experience had shown her that a werewolf's body could be remarkably resistant.

The deep, bloody gash on Liam's leg still glared at her, but she also had to fix his lungs, or he'd drown in his own blood soon enough. Ava urged the light to flow, but the glow began to wane. She pressed her hands harder on Liam's leg, praying the light would obey. Instead, it blinked out.

The beating pulse of light was gone, the rift in her essence fast asleep. She tried to summon the light again.

"Gods, please," she prayed.

Nothing happened.

Lothar's howls cut closer. She turned around and in the distance saw the werewolf running on its four paws. He'd be here soon.

"Princess." Liam took her hands and kissed them. "You need to go. I'll see you on the other side, yeah?"

Ava could envision Lothar's claws deforming Liam's face in one strike, then tearing his body in two, blood splashing everywhere. The thought made bile thrash in her stomach.

Liam might return as an angel, but Ava had never lost a charge, never given up. And she wouldn't start now.

She gave Liam an assuring smile as she tried to control the shaking of her body. "You're my partner."

She stood and turned toward the incoming beast whose red eyes glinted with raw and primeval madness. Lothar was so big that the impact of his steps coursed through the ground and went up the bones in her legs.

"Ava, run!" Liam screamed.

Instead, she took the necklace from her jacket pocket and held it toward the wolf man. "I'm sorry we stole from you."

The beast stopped a few feet from her. He shook his head, and when he blinked at her, Ava spotted the human underneath the wolf.

Lothar took a shuddering breath and shook his head again, as if he were still fighting the beast. When he stood on his hind legs, Ava knew the human had won the battle.

He growled at her, drool dripping on the ground, but something else brushed against Ava's Guardian essence, something that hadn't been there before. Something sweet and soft like a feather. *Mercy.* Then a bark, and even though Lothar hadn't used words, the command was clear: return the necklace.

"I-I can't," she said. "We need it to find out who murdered Liam's partner."

The wolf man cocked his head to the side, then whined at Liam, a frown full of pity on his forehead. He was sorry about Archibald, that much was clear.

"Yeah, me too," Liam said.

Lothar growled, and his gray hairs stood on edge. Liam seemed to understand what the wolf man had tried to convey, because he chuckled. "Well, I couldn't exactly ask. We both know you'd never give it to me, no matter how much you liked Archie. He might've treated you kindly, but I was always an ass to you and your packs."

Lothar chortled at this, his tongue sticking out, which made him resemble more of a Labrador than a fierce wolf.

Liam nodded at his injured leg as if to make his point. "Besides, I entered your apartment and shot you five times. If that hadn't drawn out the wolf, I don't know what would."

The wolf man huffed something akin to a laughter. "Rules of the game." The words scraped Lothar's throat, each letter labored and heavy, as if forming them had been hard for him.

Liam nodded. "Call it even?"

A gust of wind came from above, and a feeling of peace and safety invaded Ava. She looked up to see a winged shape landing, then magnificent silver wings with golden tipped feathers stood before her.

Ezra unsheathed his sword and faced the werewolf. "I'm quite certain that harming a Selfless is against regulations."

Lothar growled at Ezra, his fur standing straight. Words formed on his snout, but they came out drawled and deformed. "Wicked angels."

"Hey, we did it for a reason," Liam shouted from behind, then coughed blood.

But Lothar hadn't meant to denounce them to the Messenger. He was *calling* Ezra a wicked angel, which was nothing short of blasphemy.

Ezra kept his sword aimed at Lothar. "The necklace is part of an ongoing investigation. You will provide it peacefully."

The werewolf's nostrils flared, his pointy ears up. He swayed back and forth on his hind legs, almost as if trying to decide whether to attack or run. "You watch us suffer." A bark, followed by the snapping of his jaw. "My children, drugged. You murder them. The Gods don't listen." He pointed at Ezra and snarled. "Soon the injustices will be repaid. Pray I don't find you on the battlefield."

With that, he crouched and left on all fours, each paw strike a punch on concrete.

Ezra sighed and sheathed his sword. He turned to Ava and placed both hands on her cheeks. "Are you all right?"

She smiled at him. "I am now."

He glared at Liam, the fury of the Gods crisp in his blue irises. "Your duty was to protect her!"

Liam pressed his lips so tight they became white. He was about to say something, but instead he broke into furious coughs that painted his hand in red.

"Please help him," Ava begged.

"He's better to the Order as an angel." Ezra's tone was a wall.

"He's my charge." Tears piled in the back of her throat. "Please?"

Ezra shook his head and grumbled something under his breath. He then kneeled and placed one hand on Liam's chest, another on his leg.

"Don't blame Liam for this," Ava said. "I *chose* to be here."

Ezra didn't utter a word or even look at her as light shone from his hands.

Heavens, he was furious.

She cleared her throat. "How did you find us?"

"Your name was on the inspection warrant. I put a track in the system for Ava Lightway. I needed to be sure you were safe." He turned to Liam. "Lothar is a type five. He's not the werewolf lord without a reason."

"I know," Liam said, his cough now gone.

Ezra brushed his own hands as if he were a doctor cleaning up after surgery. Liam's skin and flesh looked perfectly fine, not even a scar remained.

"The Virtues will have to work overnight to wipe the minds of the people in this quarter." Ezra stood and turned to Ava, disappointment in his tone. "Why did you steal from that creature?"

"It's a lead into the vampire attacks on sector thirteen," Liam said as he forced himself up, still getting used to pinky new flesh and mended bones.

Ava went to help Liam stand, but the proud glare he shot her stopped her midway.

"Is it?" Ezra narrowed his eyes at Liam, then focused on Ava. "Does your charge speak the truth?"

The Captain's words echoed in her mind. *"Stick with this one, and you might have to go against everything you stand for."*

Ava hated lying. She had done it once or twice when she was alive, but never had she lied as an angel, and especially not to Ezra. The Messenger had shown her nothing but love and understanding since they'd met a hundred years ago. She should tell him the truth; perhaps he could help. But Ezra knew the one rule Guardians lived by: a charge *always* comes first. And her charge *needed* her to lie, lie to an angel Ava admired and cared for.

A bitter taste coursed down her throat as she swallowed. She remembered Archibald telling young Liam about faith, and that it rested inside one's heart.

"Yes," she said, silently praying for forgiveness. "Liam's telling the truth."

Ezra observed her for a moment, then his shoulders relaxed.

He had such unwavering faith in her ...

"Well then." He laid a hand on her cheek and kissed her forehead. "I expect a full report within two weeks. After that, we'll discuss your new mission."

"A new mission?" she asked.

Ezra scratched the back of his neck, glancing quickly at Liam and then back at Ava. "It has been decided that the three high angels are to choose mates, angels to help them manage the Order, kin souls who can act as our right hands."

"So you'll have a harem?" Liam asked, arms crossed. "Because mates also have sex with each other, right?"

"Don't mistake a mate for a soulmate, Selfless. A mate is a friend and advisor, a soul similar to ours, someone we trust. Sometimes mates do become lovers because of this kinship, but not always." Ezra's tone swayed as he glanced at Ava.

"And yes, an angel can have many mates, but I only wish for one."

Ava gulped and stepped back. "Me?"

Ezra leaned forward, his lips an inch from hers. "I would be honored if you'd consider standing by my side. As I've said, we don't need to be romantically involved." He brushed a stray flock of hair from her face. "But I'd be lying if I said I didn't wish we were."

Ezra was the most blessed of all high angels. Some even said he was close to becoming a Seraph. Ava loved him for his light and kindness, and the idea of being with him in *that* way had crossed her mind more than once.

"Your boss wants to fuck you senseless, princess," Liam sneered, then raised his hands in surrender when she glared at him. "Just saying."

"Show respect," Ezra snarled. "High angels have had mates since the beginning of time. Like the Messenger before me and the one before him as well."

Ava knew that, of course. She just never expected to be chosen as a mate, not this quickly at least.

"F-forgive me, Ezra," she stammered, "but this has caught me by surprise."

"I understand." He cupped her cheeks softly. "There's time. Just think about it. You always have a choice. I would never hold a denial against you."

"But why me? There are several who would be more qual-ified, Dominions even—"

"I don't play by those ridiculous rules, Ava. No angel is more worthy or better than another. Besides, no other angel is *you*." He raised her chin gently. "Promise me you'll consider it. Believe me when I say I need you by my side. I always have. *The Gods* need you by my side."

She froze at that. If the Gods required this, then she must follow their will. Ezra would know; he was their messenger.

What *she* wanted, whatever it was, would have to take second place.

"I'll consider it, of course," she said.

Ava had wanted to be with Ezra for so many decades ... she should've said yes to him immediately. Perhaps she was simply in shock. Maybe tomorrow she'd realize how happy she was.

Ezra bowed his head to her, placing a hand over his heart. With a swoosh of his wings, he rose to the sky and disappeared beyond tall skyscrapers.

NIGHT HAD FALLEN QUICKLY while they headed back to Liam's apartment. They walked in silence through dark and empty streets, the air between them heavy as iron.

The tinge of sulfur warned Ava that a demon approached. Jal cut into their path from a dark alley, his hair black as night, much like his shirt and jeans. Moonlight contoured his wings, peppering the wine and black scales with silver.

Ava guessed that people passing by wouldn't see the dragon demon, just the creature that looked like a man.

"You know how to put on a show," Jal said, extending his hand to them.

Ava handed Jal the necklace, and he gave her a mocking bow. He then placed the necklace in his jeans pocket. "A deal is a deal. I'll tell you about Archibald's death."

"His murderer's name," Liam corrected as he stepped closer.

"I said I'd give you *information* about his murder." He winked at Liam. "I don't know who killed Archibald, or if it had anything to do with the attacks on the In-Betweens."

Liam's fists clenched. "You bast—"

"Do you want the info or not?" Jal leaned closer and whispered, "Word on the street is he was killed by a blessed blade."

"That's ridiculous." Liam sneered. "Another Selfless would never—"

"Who said anything about a Selfless? There's not many of you carrying blessed blades around, is there?" Jal's gaze lingered on Ava.

"An angel would *never* murder a human or a Selfless," she spat. "We're not demons."

"The line between good and evil is blurrier than you imagine, pretty angel." Jal looked at his own nails. "I will tell you this: a psychic I know had a vision, and I need the necklace to amplify it."

Liam's eyebrows shot up, and he crossed his arms. "What was this vision about?"

"Maybe once she sees all of it, I'll tell you." He gave Liam a mischievous grin. "Maybe not."

Liam rolled his eyes. "I'll remind you, *demon*, that you owe me a favor."

"Is this how you want to use it, *Selfless*?"

Liam watched Jal, anger slipping through his skin. Finally, he said, "No."

The demon chuckled victoriously, then turned to Ava. "You seem to be more responsible than your partner." He pulled two metal business cards from his pocket and handed them to her. Four thin lines that shaped circles cut the metallic surface. "If you two look in the right places, you'll soon find your way back to me. This is for when that day comes."

Ava took the cards gingerly, as if touching the same object as Jal could infect her essence with darkness. Even now, she could feel the gripping cold oozing from him, dancing around her, threatening to swallow her entirely. But within the demon, beyond the coating of darkness and cold, there was something else that burned like a furnace or a sun. Something kind and pure.

Nonsense. Demons couldn't be good. Jal certainly wasn't the exception.

The demon shot her an enigmatic grin that told Ava she had unveiled something important, but what it was, she had no idea.

Without a word, his draconian wings spread wide and he took off into the night sky.

1 4

AVA

*A*va's spine prickled as she sat up on the couch. She rubbed her stiff neck and stretched her back. Heavens, sleeping here would be the doom of her.

Her attention drifted to the closed door of Liam's room. They hadn't spoken much since the werewolf incident, even though Ava assured him what happened hadn't been his fault. To this, Liam merely nodded absently and said nothing.

Dinner—take-out that tasted like rubber—had been dead quiet. Ava wanted to talk about Jal's accusations, to break the invisible wall between her and Liam, but she was a Guardian, and a good one, which meant she knew her partner needed time. Time to release his guilt, to let the anger and helplessness swirling inside him quell.

She patted the worn, brown sofa, remembering the trembling boy with burning green eyes and a life of pain etched in his frail body. The bulky man who'd adopted Liam flashed in her mind, the man who oozed kindness and patience. Perhaps one day, she would meet Archibald again.

As a demon.

She shivered at the thought and looked up, wondering

why the Gods allowed such pain upon their children. But she knew better than to question the faith.

Someone in the Order couldn't have killed Archibald. Unlike demons, angels would never kill one of their own. Jal was clearly lying; the dark creatures were good at that.

Archibald must have dug in the wrong places and found whoever orchestrated the attack on the In-Betweens. An angel would *never* be behind that. Whatever he found, however, had cost him his life.

As an experienced Selfless, Liam should've seen right through Jal's lies, but he didn't. *Mind games.* The demon was playing with them, and Liam fell for it.

She glanced at Ezra's sword, resting within its sheath on the coffee table. It lay there, quiet, asleep. Her new Selfless clothes—a white shirt, black leather jacket, and jeans—lay tousled on a nearby chair.

"I'll become Ezra's mate," Ava told herself absentmindedly, the words coming out of their own will.

Ezra said he needed her, and that was all he had to say, really. Perhaps this was meant to be. A frown tensed her forehead. If it was, why hadn't she agreed to be his mate when he asked?

No matter. She would say yes now. After Ava finished her mission with Liam, she would become Ezra's mate and that was that.

The door to Liam's room flung open, and he came out fully dressed. He didn't exchange a word with her; he simply went to the kitchen and made himself some coffee.

Ava stood and walked to him. "Why aren't you speaking to me?"

He took a sip of the warm dark liquid. "Why didn't you tell me you could heal and create shields like a Dominion?"

"I can't. I have no idea how." She glanced at her sword. "I swear it wasn't *me* doing it."

He followed her gaze to the weapon and chortled. "Your *sword* did it?"

She crossed her arms. "I told you I can't explain it."

"It doesn't matter. We need to go to the precinct." He nodded toward her big t-shirt. "You should get dressed …" He was going to call her princess, Ava could feel it on the tip of his tongue. Instead he went with "Ava."

Something in her chest cracked. Damned the Hells, why hadn't he called her by that stupid nickname? And more importantly, why did she *want* him to?

Well, standing here wouldn't give her an answer. In silence, she grabbed her clothes and went to the bathroom to change.

AVA SPOTTED Justine as soon as they set foot in the precinct. Her friend didn't wear her light-gray Erudite's bodysuit. Instead, she had on a yellow dress with a low neckline. Her hair was up in a high ponytail that made her look like a teenager. Justine's red shoes matched perfectly with her lipstick and the red belt around her waist.

She leaned on Kevin's desk, talking to him with a sweet smile that spoke not of lust, but of … respect? Kinship? No, Ava had to be mistaken. Justine never looked at her lovers in that manner.

Kevin had a goofy grin as he listened to her. Then again, it wasn't just him; half of the men in the precinct seemed entranced with Justine's beauty.

"Justine?" Ava asked as she approached her friend. "What are you doing here?"

Justine turned to her and smiled before pulling Ava to a remote part of the precinct, toward the cell blocks. Ava glanced back quickly, but Liam and Kevin had already engaged in conversation, barely noticing they had left.

"Top of the morning to you," Justine said as they passed by a cell that contained a bald vampire with white eyes. He bared his fangs at them, and they increased their pace until he was out of view.

Justine settled for a spot near a window. Ava leaned on the right side of the sill and her friend on the left.

"Kevin and I went on a date yesterday," she whispered, her eyes shining. "Oh, it was glorious!"

Ava couldn't recall the last time she had seen Justine so ecstatic, both when she was a human *and* an angel.

"I'm glad for you." Ava glanced down the corridor and into the main room where Kevin showed Liam something in his computer screen. "Just be careful. My relationship with my partner is rather delicate at the moment."

"Oh, so your charge is your *partner* now?"

"He's both." Ava cleared her throat. "Look, Kevin seems to be like a brother to Liam, so—"

"I know what you'll say. Look, I couldn't possibly hurt him." Justine's gaze shone with glee. "He's a perfect gentleman. We went for dinner yesterday and we watched a movie, and at the end of the night," she wiggled her eyebrows, "we went our separate ways."

Ava frowned. "Since when do *you* go home separate ways?"

"Kevin is different." She shrugged. "I want to get to know him better."

Ava narrowed her eyes at Justine. "Could it be that you actually like him?"

Justine waved a hand in the air. "I like all of them, sweetie."

Ava had watched over Justine for many years when she

was human, and after Justine died and became an Erudite, they quickly became friends. Ten years had passed since, which meant that Ava knew Justine like the palm of her hand.

"You really like him," Ava insisted, a mocking grin on her lips.

Justine furrowed her brows, then glanced back at Kevin's desk. "Perhaps, but try not to tell anyone. I have a reputation to keep. Now, what's the problem with Mr. Hunky?" She nodded toward Liam, who glared at Kevin's screen.

"I don't know yet." Ava blew air through her lips. "Ezra asked me to become his mate, by the way."

Justine gasped and slammed a hand over her own chest. "Gods be damned!"

"That's blasphemy," Ava hissed.

Justine rolled her eyes. "I'll pray for forgiveness tonight." She looked back at Kevin's desk, then leaned toward Ava and whispered, "This is insane. Sure, you spend a lot of time together, as friends and work colleagues, but that's all it's ever been. I mean, you've always had a major crush on him, but you guys haven't even kissed."

Not really. Ezra did kiss Ava when she brought Liam to see him, but she kept that to herself. If she told Justine, her friend would demand explanations she didn't have.

"Becoming his mate makes sense." Ava shrugged. "So does giving myself to him as a friend *and* a woman."

Justine raised her palm. "Fine, but how do you know Ezra's your soulmate?"

"I don't." Ava crossed her arms. "A mate is different from a soulmate. Technically, I could simply be a companion to him, not a lover. Plus, soulmates aren't real."

"Of course they are. In fact, mates are a derivation of soulmates," Justine said. "It's in the books, you know. The mating bond is weaker than a soulmate bond, but it's a bond nonetheless. Call it what you will, but you would be kind of marrying Ezra."

Ava had always wondered if Justine's fixation with soulmates was the reason why she had so many partners. Like she was trying to find her soulmate the way one finds a needle in a haystack.

Ava snickered in disbelief. "Justine, soulmates live in the pages of ancient books and in there only. In any case, I won't become Ezra's soulmate. I'll simply help him rule the Order with the Throne and the Sword."

She would also bed the Messenger. Ezra had made his intentions clear, and the thought of giving herself to him wasn't at all unpleasant.

Justine rolled her eyes. "The angels in the books might be long gone, either to their final deaths or the Heavens, but you can't be sure that the whole soulmate thing ended with them." Her friend tapped her fingers on her own chin, the Erudite in her taking over. "If Ezra asked you to be his mate, your connection might go deeper than you both assume. I mean, just the way you two look at each other ..." She gave Ava a naughty grin. "Some books say the bond between soulmates snaps like thunder, and that it shakes the world below the two lovers' feet. Do you feel something like this with Ezra?"

Ava shook her head.

"Maybe the bond will snap once you're mated." Justine shrugged. "What did you tell him?"

Ava leaned on the wall and stared out the window. "I said that I'd consider it."

Justine raised her brow in surprise. "I assumed you'd say yes without thinking twice."

"So did I."

Justine looked back at Liam, who was still talking to Kevin. "Is that why Mr. Hunky is Mr. Cranky today? Maybe *he's* your soulmate." She narrowed her eyes at him, as she always did when she tried to read someone's mind. "Yup, he wants to get in your panties."

Ava glared at her, heat shooting up her cheeks. "You read this in his mind?"

"No, but you don't need to be a mind reader to know that."

"Justine," she said with reproach, but her friend's playful manner vanished as she focused on Liam.

"He's a torment of many different things. He blames himself for almost getting you killed." She slapped Ava's shoulder. "Thanks for letting me know that a werewolf almost ripped you to pieces, by the way."

"It wasn't Liam's fault," Ava said before heading toward him. "He has to know I don't blame him for anything. Will I have to tell him this a thousand times?"

Justine held Ava's arm, stopping her. "It's not only that. He doesn't know how to feel about you. There's this undeniable connection between you two, which we all witnessed yesterday." Justine winked at Ava. "But he's conflicted. You're his partner, and he doesn't know how to protect you." Her eyes widened. "Since when do you heal and create shields like a Dominion?"

Ava gasped at how far Justine's mind-reading abilities had gone. Heavens, she was only dead for ten human years. If her telekinesis could go beyond basic, Justine would ascend to Virtue in an eye-blink.

"I can't create shields and heal," Ava said. "I have no idea what—" Well, she did, but saying it aloud might make it even crazier.

The sword.

Her friend continued, "There's also that hot demon's absurd accusation." She slapped Ava's arm again. "Seriously, you wouldn't tell me that someone in the Order might've killed one of their own?"

"It's a lie, Justine," Ava said quietly. "The demon is trying to turn us against each other, deviate our investigation. Also, this needs to stay here. No one can know."

Justine tapped the side of her forehead. "No one gets in here, dear." She squeezed her eyes at Liam. "Ezra's proposal irritated Mr. Hunky, by the way, and he can't figure out why." Justine gave her a wolfish grin. "I can think of a reason."

Ava leaned her forehead on the window's cool glass. "I feel like I failed him."

"Liam or Ezra?"

She closed her eyes. "Both."

Justine laid a hand on her shoulder. "Maybe you did, maybe you didn't. What you can't do is fail yourself."

"What's that supposed to mean?"

"You've always been in love with Ezra." Justine bit her lower lip. "But maybe that changed. Do you still want to be with him?"

"It's what's right." Ava shrugged. "And I've wanted it for so long. Besides, I'm a servant of the Gods, and this is their will."

Justine frowned. "It's *Ezra's* will."

"He's the Messenger, Justine. His words are their words."

Justine winced as if she had just stepped barefoot onto cold ice. "Look, no one knows for sure who he talks to when he speaks to the Gods. For all we know, he might be channeling a guy named Bob who likes to mess with us." Before Ava could protest the absurdity of her statement, Justine continued, "Also, arranged marriages might've been a thing in your time, but that has changed."

"Justine, it's fine, really," Ava said. "*I'm fine.*"

She narrowed her eyes at her. "Are you?"

"Don't even think about going into my mind," Ava

warned. "You taught me how to raise mental barriers, remember?"

"I could break your feeble wall in an instant." Justine let out a curse under her breath and crossed her arms. "Fine. If being with Ezra is what you really want, I won't stop you."

"Thank you."

Ava peered through the window, and her gaze fell upon the old man from yesterday. Across the street, he watched her beneath a newsboy's cap that clashed with his youngish attire—a black Nirvana shirt this time, but the same ripped jeans and red sneakers.

"Friend of yours?" Justine asked, then shrugged. "He's got good taste in music. Also, for an old guy, he's kind of hot."

"I don't know him, I think." Ava muttered. "I'm not entirely sure."

"Well, whoever he is, he's blocking me," Justine said. "Can't get a peep into his thoughts."

The man tipped his hat to Justine, and then went on his way.

15

LIAM

*L*iam had taught a fair share of Selfless how to fight, but Ava topped them all. Only two days of training made her faster and more daring. Yesterday, she smacked three punches on his face, and with her sword, she drew a graze on his stomach that ruined his shirt.

He'd expected her to fight back, since he attacked her with no mercy. It was for her own good. Ava had almost died because of the path Liam took, the one that would likely lead to his damnation. All because she wouldn't abandon him like the good Guardian she was. And perhaps, that would doom her as well.

If Ava died because of him, Gods, he'd never forgive himself. So Liam furiously charged and slashed, but Ava was never able to heal herself or create that golden shield again. Which meant that Kevin became a guaranteed presence during their trainings, especially after Liam cut through Ava's shoulder blade by accident.

The scream had erupted from the bottom of her throat, but Ava pressed her lips tight and kept it in, a hand clutched on her bleeding shoulder blade. He'd watched her then, that furious glare on her face, refusing to show weakness. Her blue eyes glinted with suppressed tears as Kevin worked to heal her, and when he was done, Ava didn't ask for a break. She simply fixed her defensive stance and told Liam, "Attack."

He did, of course. Again and again, day in and day out.

Something wild and untamed lurked underneath his Guardian, and the detective in him wanted to find out more. But they had barely spoken since the werewolf incident.

He knew this frustrated her. Princess was a Guardian, so talking to her charge was a big part of her job. But what was there to say, really?

Ava would become the Messenger's mate, even though she hadn't confirmed it yet. It was one of those nearly inevitable things people could sense, like the scent of rain when it's about to fall.

Hells, Ava should've rejected Ezraphael on the spot. He wasn't even her boyfriend; Princess had said so herself. How could she be considering this?

Maybe because she was like the rest of them, always obeying, never questioning. *Mindless cattle.*

When they did speak, Liam would insist they should at least consider the fact that there's someone evil in the Order, while Ava, stunning, stubborn, overly-devoted Ava, persisted in calling it blasphemy.

Liam was so different from her. He knew when to chase the facts, regardless of his devotion to the Gods—if he had any, which in all honesty, he probably didn't.

Also, he could catch lies the way a dog catches the scent of meat. Jal might be a lying demon, but he hadn't been lying when he said an angel might've killed Archie.

Liam pressed the golden symbol of the Gods hanging around his neck, the gift his father, his partner, had given him when he'd first joined the precinct.

Someone in the Order had murdered Archie, and Liam would find out who.

Ava worried about him, that much was clear. She had prayed yesterday at night, when she thought the door to his room was closed—Liam had left it slightly open. He'd watched her from behind the slit, her intertwined hands, her soft whispered words as moonlight sneaked through the window and graced her with a quiet, cleansed beauty. He remembered the training room, and trailing his thumb across her skin, the taste of her lips...

It was just an adrenaline rush, he told himself. But adrenaline didn't make him almost fuck his Guardian in public space.

Ava was sleeping this morning when he woke, her breathing slow, peaceful.

Was she truly closer to the Gods than he was? Could that asshole Messenger be worthier of her?

Obviously, yes. Liam was far from angelic material.

As she slept, a strand of strawberry-blond hair brushed her face. He walked quietly to her, his steps mute. Liam had experience on how to approach someone in silence, a skill that saved his life many times before. He gently swept the strand off her face, and Ava smiled softly. He couldn't help but smile too.

Liam didn't like Ezraphael. He seemed like a pompous bastard, but in the end, it was Ava's decision. It might be a stupid decision, but it was hers to make.

Liam looked down to his heart and poked it, like Archie used to do.

How I wish you were here, old man.

In all this mess, one thing was certain: Liam would avenge Archie. Whether Ava, her Messenger, or the Gods approved it or not, he didn't care.

Ava moved and grumbled, and he quickly stepped away, standing where the sofa began.

She blinked and stretched, inhaling a deep breath. She arched her back, which pushed her breasts against the shirt he'd given her, the mark of her nipples clear beneath the cloth.

Liam looked away. Whatever connection he had to her, sexual desire, kinship; it would have to be ignored.

Princess frowned when she spotted him. "Were you watching me?"

He nodded.

"Why?"

He ran a hand through his hair and looked out the window. "I don't know."

She seemed to consider that. "I'm here to help you, Liam."

"Are you?" he countered.

Guilt immediately slashed through him. He *knew* she was. Ava had proven her devotion to him nonstop since the day they'd met. He might have called her princess to irritate her at first, but as he got to know Ava, he realized he called her princess not because she was frail, or pretty—but Gods help him, she *was* the most beautiful thing he'd ever seen. No, now he called her princess because Ava had become precious to him. Also, her new partner looked remarkably cute when she was annoyed, which was a damn good reason to tease her.

"I'm here for *you*," she stated from below her earth-colored eyebrows. "Always." This without an eye-blink.

Liam's throat bobbed at the upcoming words. "I'm sorry I couldn't protect you."

Ava's lips parted slightly, her brow scrunching with annoyance. "How many times do I have to tell you? I chose my path. I knew the risks. And I will keep helping you, regardless of my commitment to the Messenger."

He winced. "So it's that serious, huh?"

Ava looked at the ground. "It's my duty to the Gods. Perhaps a duty to myself and also to Ezra."

"Yeah. Sure." He nodded toward the kitchen. "There's milk and cereal. I'm heading off to the precinct. You know the way."

~

INSIDE THE BLUE padded training room, Liam ordered Ava to run a hundred laps and after that, they practiced her attacks. Princess was better with defense but being good at only one thing had never won a fight, not when it was a werewolf, a bloodsucker, or a freaking demon against her.

They began basic battling, and their swords clanged as they charged against one another. She did her series well— *attack, push, step back, charge*—but if she were to fight demons or In-Betweens, Ava needed to be much faster.

Kevin watched them from a bench on the left side of the room, his darting gaze following their moves.

Liam wished Ava could tap into the power he'd witnessed. She would need it for where they were going after they were done here. He suspected that adrenaline had brought her abilities to surface, the feeling she had no way out. So Liam attacked her as if she was his worst enemy, any trace of mercy gone from him.

Today, Ava's life would depend on her fear of losing it.

Two swift moves, two moments where Ava failed in her defenses. Two deep cuts, one on her thigh, another on her back.

She fell to her knees, blood flowing from the cuts, but again, she didn't scream. She held the cries inside her throat, her mouth clasped, her entire body shaking. Like a fucking Valkyrie.

"By the Gods, Liam!" Kevin shouted as he ran to her.

He rested one hand on her back and another on her thigh. Ava's blood ran down the gaps between his fingers.

A soft shine glowed from Kevin's palms as he worked tirelessly on her cuts until finally, Ava was healed. The only clue she had been injured was the dried blood on her ripped clothes.

Dark circles contoured Kevin's eyes, and his cheeks were slightly sunken in, the cost of too much healing. If he'd been a Dominion, the side effects wouldn't have been this extensive, but a human body could only withstand so much angelic power.

"Ava, I'm not trying to hurt you," Liam said, his tone soft. "It's just that I already lost one partner, and I can't lose another. You *have* to be ready."

"I understand." Her tone was hoarse. She tried to smile but failed, and it broke something in him.

Gods, Liam wanted to hold her, to beg for her forgiveness, and he also wanted to kiss her senseless. He shook his head, sending the thoughts away.

Wobbly, Ava stood up. Kevin took the cue to hurry back to his bench.

She pointed her sword at Liam and said, "I'm ready."

He admired her, this harmless Guardian and fierce warrior all in one. Then he attacked.

Just before their sword clanged, Ava charged at him with all her might. Like something had snapped behind those sky-blue irises.

Ava attacked hard and at once, pushing him back, and almost slashing a deep gash on his leg. She didn't give him time to breathe, *clang, clang, clang*. There it was, that fire he'd seen rumbling beneath her meek surface.

They ran, jumped, and furiously clashed. Sweat coated his face, and it coated Ava's too. His muscles ached, his breathing was ragged, but oh, this was fun!

"Oy!" Kevin shouted from his bench. "You do know I can't heal anymore, right? For at least two days! I'm fucking drained!"

They didn't care.

She charged, and Liam slammed his blade against Ava's so hard that sparks splintered from the hit.

"Bloody hell!" Kevin yelled, hands slammed on his head. "You two stop! Now!"

They kept pressing their swords together, the screech of metal against metal piercing Liam's ears.

Ava could've won if he hadn't been stronger or more experienced. Soon enough, her muscles began to shake. She fell with one knee to the floor but kept the strength in her block. She smiled through gritted teeth, that wilderness burning beyond the peace and devotion to the Gods.

"Well done, *princess*," he said through hushed breaths, leaning his weight onto his sword, onto her. "You could kill an In-Between this way."

Ava gaped at him as she held her block, her blade criss-crossed with his. "You called me princess."

Liam rolled his eyes, but a soft smile creased his lips. "Only because you hate it."

The adoring way in which she looked at him said thank you. So she *liked* to be called princess? Women could be a fucking puzzle.

He stepped back and lowered his sword. From the bench, Kevin exhaled in relief.

Ava stood and watched Liam intently as they moved in a circle, the tips of their swords nearly brushing on the floor. Two predators waiting to attack.

"What do you think, Kev?" Liam asked, his attention fully on Ava. "Is she ready?"

Kevin shrugged. "Well, it's not like you have a lot of time on your hands."

Ava frowned. "What do you mean?"

"Kev found a blip in the radar two days ago," he said. "It's a small blip, but it could lead to something."

"A blip?"

He and Ava still moved in circles, like perfect clockwork. "There's somewhere you and I need to go."

"And where's that?"

He stopped and sheathed his sword, wiping sweat off his forehead with the back of his arm. "Go shower, then meet me upstairs."

She sheathed her sword and crossed her arms. "Liam, where are we going?"

He gave her a weak smile. "Where your boyfriend told us to go."

16

AVA

"Why are we following Ezra's orders?" Ava asked as they walked through wide streets towered by abandoned warehouses. Dusk had started to settle, drenching the half-decayed constructions in an eerie blue-grey.

"Maybe I've decided to obey the Gods," Liam said mockingly, his tone low.

She stopped and raised an eyebrow at him. "I'm not *that* naïve."

"Well, we *are* investigating illegal vampire action in sector thirteen, aren't we?" He nodded forward and kept walking. "That makes it official business."

He unsheathed his sword and scanned the surroundings as they went, his muscles clenched. She followed him, grasping the hilt of her sword a little too tightly.

"And unofficially?" she asked.

"Archie had an informant named Drake," he whispered. "I tried looking for him, but his coven has moved. Two days ago, one of his own was killed here by another Selfless."

"The blip in the radar."

He nodded.

A clanking sound sprouted from the left, and Ava's muscles tensed. Liam closed his stance and pointed his sword at the origin of the noise, his movements graceful and quick.

A tin can rolled from behind a dumpster, followed by a black cat that jumped atop it.

"Keep your guard up," he said as they moved on.

The carcasses of buildings and rusting cars sprawled on the empty sidewalks made the industrial quarters feel like a cemetery. A soft wind spread the tang of saltwater and rust through the streets.

The harbor mustn't be far.

"If we find Drake's coven, we find Drake," Liam said. "And then we interrogate him."

"You mean you'll ask for the name of Archibald's murderer."

He nodded without glancing at her. "Knowing Drake, I bet he'll know who in the Order tried to silence Archie."

"Those were a demon's lies, Liam." Ava blew an exasperated sigh. "An angel would never harm a human. We are devoted to the Gods' creations. It's why we exist."

"Why Guardians exist," he corrected. "What about the others?"

She shook her head. "That's sacrilege."

"Everything is sacrilege to you." He nodded behind them, showing her the way they'd come. "You're free to go, princess."

She looked back at the abandoned street and pictured herself in her room, at the Order, where she didn't need to learn sword fighting or defy the will of the Gods on a daily basis. Then she glanced at Liam, who had stopped to watch her.

An inch of fear glinted in his clear green eyes, and a

longing sensation wafted from him, brushing against her skin in a soft caress. He didn't realize it, but he was asking her to stay. He *needed* her to stay.

A voice in the back of her mind, *her* voice, whispered words she couldn't understand. Ava concentrated, but all she could discern was the question, *"Why do you think you're here?"*

She shook her head and inhaled deeply. "You're right. If there's an absurd possibility that someone in the Order has betrayed the Gods, we should investigate." Heavens, spending so much time with Liam had begun clouding her judgement. "But don't be surprised when we discover Archibald's murderer was a demon or an In-Between."

He smiled at her, and Ava saw that little boy in Archibald's living room. "Sure thing, princess."

Warmth filled her chest. Ava never imagined she'd come to like that silly nickname, yet here she was.

They walked on, their careful steps nearly silent, until Liam raised his arm and Ava halted.

"Listen," he whispered.

At first, she couldn't hear a thing apart from the wind coursing through the empty streets. Then grunts in the distance. The clanking of a blade on concrete.

They hurried through abandoned factories that echoed their steps, immense man-made caves with hollow halls, until they reached a red-bricked compound with broken windows and a missing roof.

Voices came from inside.

Two piles of rusting machinery stood by the entrance, and Ava and Liam hid behind them before peeking into the warehouse.

A Warrior, clad in an obsidian bodysuit and kilt, faced a vampire female. The guns and daggers he should have been carrying laid strewn on the floor. All he had was his sword, which he pointed at her with a shaking grip.

Ava's instincts urged her to run the other way. Warriors were skilled fighters. They rarely feared anything, but this one was *terrified*.

Ava angled her head left and understood why. A headless body clad in black was splayed behind the vampire woman, twisted in all the wrong angles. Ava followed a track of blood on the ground that began on the severed neck and went past the Warrior. There, not far behind him, was his fallen partner's head, staring at Ava with milky eyes and an open mouth.

Before she could cry in horror, Liam held her gaze. His stare oozed assurance, and Ava knew that as long as he was here, she would be fine. So she swallowed back the scream and nodded.

The remaining Warrior kept pointing his shaking sword at the vampire female. "You'll pay for your sins, creature."

The woman laughed ice daggers. She wore a dark green Victorian dress decorated with black ruffles on the hem of her skirt and on the edges of her corset. Her orange-red hair was tied in a loose bun atop her head. The woman's clothing belonged to the 1800s, but she might be much older than that. Her skin was a flawless porcelain, and it reminded Ava of a doll her mother had once given her.

This vampire might be strikingly beautiful, but when she snarled through red lips, her neon-blue eyes fixed on the Warrior, Ava saw her true nature: a bloodthirsty beast. The headless body behind her proved that.

"And who will make me pay?" the vampire asked, her tone cold. "You? Your partner?" She nodded to the headless corpse behind her.

"You monster," the Warrior growled.

She stamped a hand on her chest and forced an innocent

look on her face. "I'm no monster. You murdered one of my own, so I murdered one of yours. Quid pro quo." She smiled and licked her lips. "Now you, I'll kill for fun. Slowly, piece by piece, until you beg me to finish." She bared her fangs at him. "Remember this day, Warrior. Vampires will *not* go down silently."

"He needs help," Liam muttered to Ava. "Stay here."

"Wait," Ava whispered, trying to grab his arm, but he'd already slipped through her fingers.

Liam pointed his silver and blue sword at the vampire as he walked toward the Warrior. "You know the punishment for killing a member of the Order is death, right?"

The woman watched him with interest, her attention bouncing from Liam to the sword he wielded, back and forth, as if she couldn't decide on which she should focus. Finally, she said, "And what punishment is given to angels who murder an In-Between without cause?"

The vampire pointed to a dark spot at the end of the vast space, and Ava narrowed her eyes. Another body laid sprawled on the floor, a man dressed in black, almost blending in with the darkness. His skin was milky white, and his gaping stare lifeless. His head had been severed from his body, like the dead angel behind the vampire.

"Drake," Liam grumbled under his breath. He turned to the Warrior, red anger pulsing from him. "Why the fuck did you kill that vampire?"

"He attacked us," he said, his attention going from Liam to the woman.

Liam's lips curled. "Drake would never do that. He knew better than to mess with angels, even when he was starving."

The Warrior knitted his brows and looked down at Liam as if he were a cockroach. "Know your place, *Selfless*."

Her partner spun on his feet the way water flows, and

then he was behind the Warrior, his blade on the angel's neck.

The Warrior snorted. "You won't kill me."

"I'll ask again." Liam pressed the blade on the thin skin of the Warrior's throat, drawing a line of blood. "Why did you murder that vampire?"

"It was the bloodlust." The warrior gulped. "It made him kill humans."

"Lies!" the female yelled, her voice broken gravel and glass. "They promised him blood supplies. It was a trap!"

"We didn't," the Warrior's voice quavered.

Foggy gray tendrils danced around him in a wayward manner. *Untethered, unreliable.*

He was lying. An *angel* was lying.

"You will die today," the vampire assured matter-of-factly.

Ava couldn't say what urged her to move. Maybe it was shock. Maybe it was an instinct to protect her charge since this situation could only end in a disaster.

She tried to ignore the infuriated glare Liam sent her as she ran toward him, but it burned right through her.

As soon as she stopped by his side, he whispered, "What in the Hells are you doing?"

"Being your partner, I suppose." She turned to the woman and pointed Ezra's golden sword at her. "Let us go. We'll interrogate this angel and find the truth."

"You're here." The female growled in anger, showcasing her protuberant fangs. "Damned the Hells, not now."

Ava exchanged a confused look with Liam.

"Do I know you, vampire?"

"No, angel girl." The woman's fists clenched. "But if you're here, it means that your partner is ..." She shouted something akin to a bark.

"I think the vamp's going crazy," Liam muttered, his

sword still fixed against the Warrior's throat, preventing the angel from moving.

"I'm perfectly rational, you fool!" The vampire pointed at Liam, showing a red, manicured fingernail. "How did *he* know I'd run into you? He made me promise I'd help you remember if our paths crossed. That bastard!" She bared her fangs and shouted again, a vein popping on her forehead.

"Who's this *he* you speak of?" Ava asked, never lowering her sword. "And remember what?"

"It's for your godsdamned *partner* to know." The vampire turned around and let out one last guttural roar. She then fixed her hair and straightened her posture, taking a deep, calming breath.

Her blue eyes turned into red-emeralds, and she snapped her attention to the Warrior. "You scum!"

"How dare you offend—" The minute his eyes locked with hers, he dropped his sword, his expression blank.

"Walk out of this warehouse and never stop. Even when your feet bleed and your bones ache, you will continue. Walk, Warrior, walk until you draw your last breath," she ordered, her tone a deep, low drone.

The Warrior nodded, his mouth hanging half-open. He turned around, nearly slashing his own neck—thank the Gods Liam was quick and removed his blade just in time.

"Hey!" Liam shouted after him. "Warrior, what are you doing?"

The angel didn't reply. He simply walked back and stepped on his fallen friend's head. Ava looked away, but she couldn't block her ears. A jolt of electricity swam up her spine at the squishy sound of meat and bones crushing.

The Warrior continued to walk out of the warehouse, moving like a robot, until they couldn't see him anymore.

"Vampires can't glamour angels," Liam said, his tone weary and uncertain.

"I just did, darling." The vampire shrugged, turning her red eyes toward him. "And now it's your turn."

Liam grunted and shook his head, as if he had gotten dizzy for a moment, but he didn't back down. Ava took his free hand, making sure to keep her sword aimed at the vampire woman.

"What are you doing to him?" she demanded.

"Isn't it obvious?" The vampire licked her lips eagerly. "Not many can resist my glamour like he's doing right now. He's a strong one. Always has been."

"I-I don't know you," Liam grumbled lazily, as if he was falling half-asleep.

"You don't, but your tales of bravery precede you," she said, a certain sorrow in her tone. "It doesn't matter anymore. The past is gone."

Liam swayed and almost dropped his sword, but Ava held his hand tight, her fingers biting into his skin. He quickly recomposed himself and pressed her hand back.

"I'm here," she whispered to him.

"I know," he croaked with a weak smile, then looked at the vampire woman and raised his sword.

The vampire frowned at Liam. "Why isn't it working?" She glanced at Ava and her eyes widened, as if she had just unveiled a big secret. "Of course! *You* are the path to him!"

The vampire approached them with careful steps, her gaze locked on Liam's. "Interesting," she muttered, but what was interesting, Ava couldn't tell.

"Stop right there!" The tip of Ava's ivory and golden sword drew a drop of blood from the woman's chest.

The vampire's shining red eyes turned to Ava, and a heavy weight fell upon her body, as if she had been frozen inside a block of ice. Ava couldn't move her feet, her hands, or even her neck. The glamour might've taken hold of her lungs too, but a sharp inhale proved her wrong, bless the Gods.

Ava had heard of a vampire's glamour, but this was much stronger. An angel like her should've been able to free herself from it. Heavens, even a Selfless could. And yet, that Warrior hadn't, despite being arduously trained to combat In-Betweens.

The woman took Ava's sword from her stone-hard hand and laid it carefully on the ground. Then she walked away and called Liam with her finger. "Come to Lilith, love."

Lilith. Queen of the damned, more legend than truth, and yet here she stood, the most powerful vampire in history.

Ava scoffed. That vampire might be Lilith, but Liam would never take orders from ... The clang of metal hitting the ground clanked from Ava's side. Out of the corner of her eye, she saw Liam had dropped his sword, his gaze locked on the vampire's.

"No!" Ava yelled, but this didn't stop Liam from going to Lilith.

The vampire turned to him and draped her arms over his shoulders. Liam rested his hands on her waist casually, easily, the way a lover would. Her lips were stupidly close to his.

"Don't touch him!" Ava yelled, tears piling in the corners of her eyes. "Liam!"

But her words couldn't reach him.

She pushed the glamour that held her in place with all her essence's power, but it didn't work. Ava glared at her sword on the floor, begging it to beat again.

Nothing.

"Don't hurt him," Ava croaked, angry tears sliding down her face. "By the mercy of the Gods, don't hurt him."

"Mercy?" Lilith frowned at Ava. "Your Gods know no mercy, angel girl." She turned back to Liam and cupped his cheeks. "Such a fine specimen ..."

The vampire pressed her red lips against Liam's. He opened his mouth to her, deepening their kiss as he wrapped his arms around her lower back, bringing her closer to him.

Something red and irrational birthed inside Ava, and a furious scream ripped through her throat. "Let him go!"

Instead, Lilith kissed him deeper.

Ava's fury vibrated from her core, pierced her own skin, and then slammed against the invisible bonds that kept her in place. A chaotic power with a thirst for blood bloomed inside her. That hungry, raw thing would destroy Lilith's shackles soon enough, and once it did, Ava would bring the fires of the hells upon the vampire.

17

LIAM

*L*iam's mind felt fuzzy. Something wasn't right, but he couldn't tell what. He looked at the empty white space around him. *Wasn't he in a warehouse just a moment ago?*

Someone stood before him, a blurry form that grew into focus as it approached.

"Ava?" he muttered.

She smiled at him, that beautiful grin that calmed every inch of his soul. Instinctively, he smiled back. She was so perfect and so ... naked.

He stepped back and looked away, clearing his throat. "Hmm, princess, you forgot your clothes."

"I did." She walked to him and only stopped a few inches away. Ava straightened her spine, showcasing her full breasts, her pink nipples hard.

An invitation.

He swallowed dryly and took another step back. "No, there's ..." His head hurt and spun. "There's something wrong."

She stepped closer and wrapped her arms on his shoulders. Her flesh rubbed against the fabric of his shirt, and his hands found their way to her lean waist.

Her skin was so smooth ...

That familiar pull took over him, the same one from the training room, the one that told him to make Ava his right here, right now.

"You want this," Ava whispered in his ear, then moved her waist, rubbing her crotch against his. "Your body betrays you."

"I ..." he swallowed, sand walling his throat. He looked into her blue eyes, like the sky on a bright summer day, then cupped her cheek with his left hand. "What's happening?"

She poked his chest, the way Archie used to do. "Why do you think you're so drawn to me?"

His thumb brushed her smooth, rosy lips, and a delirious pain grew under his pants. "You're so beautiful."

"Try again." She bit his lips softly, and it took all his strength not to fuck her right then.

"You're strong, Ava, so much more than you know." He nibbled at her lower lip. "It burns inside you."

"Like it burns inside of *you*," she whispered in his ear, her breath soft tingles on his skin.

"You're light," he realized, his breaths heavy. "*My* light."

"And you're darkness." She smiled, showing protuberant fangs that suddenly became normal teeth. "*My* darkness."

"I ..." An alarm wailed in his mind, warning him this was wrong.

Ava leaned her head left, freeing the path to the curve of her neck. He kissed her smooth skin and drowned in the soothing lavender scent of her hair.

The alarm silenced.

Ava's body moved sensuously, grinding against him. He couldn't take it anymore. He parted his lips and drowned her in them.

Gods help him, he'd never let go of her.

His tongue danced with Ava's, venturing, discovering, and he pressed her harder against him, his fingers digging into her full bottom.

All too soon she interrupted their kisses, her breathing ragged. She grinned and looked to her left. "Don't you find that interesting, angel girl? That of all the creatures in this universe, you were paired with the one that seems to be yours?" She caressed Liam's forehead with the back of her hand. "How lucky you must be." She placed a finger on his lips, and he opened his mouth. She pushed her finger forward, and he bit it gently. "So *very* lucky."

Liam couldn't make sense of her words; all he wanted was to kiss Ava again. He heard a dim voice in the distance, a familiar sound ... *Ava's voice*. It screamed his name, but he must be mistaken. Ava was standing right in front of him.

"Michael." Ava nudged her nose with his. "You've always looked for her, haven't you? Your light. Your darkness."

Michael? Was that his name? He didn't know, couldn't remember. Ava's words felt like a foreign language sometimes.

Again those screams came from a distance, pain etched in them, desperation ... but he didn't want that; he had enough of it every day, throughout his entire life. He wanted the light and peace Ava brought him, something he had never known before.

How could he have lived this long without her, his partner, his *princess*?

"Tell me," Ava said, "why do you wield this sword?"

The Archangel's sword magically appeared in his left hand. Michael's. *His.*

Ava's fingers danced sensuously across the hilt.

"Archie gave it to me," Liam said before stamping a soft kiss on her lips, bringing her closer to him with his free hand. It felt as if they had a world between them, and he couldn't bear that, not when Ava was so close.

She licked his lips in return, and he forced his tongue inside her mouth. Ava moaned with pleasure, her muscles softening beneath his embrace.

She pushed him back softly with her hands, her breathing ragged. "A wonderful gift," she said. "That can only be wielded by an Archangel."

"Not true." Liam shrugged. "I'm human."

She raised an eyebrow. "And why do you think that is?"

The fuzziness in his mind grew, and Liam thought he would faint. He held Ava closer to him, like she was his lifeboat.

"I *chose* to come back as a human," he said mostly to himself, a hint of doubt behind his own words.

She kissed him and he closed his eyes, reveling in her smooth lips and the feeling of her breasts against his skin.

His chest was naked now. *Where had his shirt gone?*

"Think again," she whispered in his ear.

"It was dark and cold …" He stared at her, knowing he should think harder, try to remember. "I was *forced* to become human."

Ava disappeared, and an angel with curly hair the color of ripe lemons now stood before Liam. His wings were the color of the sea.

Gabriel.

Liam had seen Gabriel in the Order. The Archangel had spared him from getting on a fight with an angry Archangel.

Gabriel stretched his hand toward Liam. A bleeding gash cut across his forehead, his sweat mingling with red. "Follow me, brother."

Swords clanged in the background, the dry smell of sand, fire, and blood invading Liam's nostrils. Then Gabriel and the battle were gone, leaving Liam alone in the whiteness with Ava standing so perfectly close to him.

All he could focus on were her lips, and then he was drowning in them again. He couldn't pull away; he didn't want to.

The words burst in his mind, *"To the hells with Gabriel and his wars."*

"Take me," Ava said with a wicked grin. "Take me right in front of her."

She pushed her tongue into his mouth, and he forgot about everything, forgot who he was.

The sword disappeared from his hand and he repaid her needy kisses, then trailed a blazing path with his mouth toward her collarbone. When she stepped back a little, he pulled her back to him, hungry, needing.

"Ava," he whispered, cupping her cheek. "I'm not letting you go."

But Ava's neck was strained like an invisible rope pulled it back. The peace and comfort, the love he had felt before, it all crashed into him as if Liam was made of glass and he was breaking. He tried to hold on to that immense happiness, he tried so hard, but it was already gone.

He swayed back and almost fell to the ground. With a hand slammed on his forehead, he blinked, trying to focus.

They were in a dark warehouse. The cold of the night pierced through the fabric of his shirt where his jacket was zipped open. He patted it because he was sure he'd been chest naked only a second ago.

Liam spotted a woman a few steps ahead, but she wasn't Ava. It was the vampire with red hair.

Liam withdrew a sun dagger from his belt and pointed at her. "What the Hells is going on?"

The woman didn't move. Her neck was strained because there was a blade held tightly close to it, almost cutting her flesh. And behind that woman, holding the sun dagger, stood Ava, her face strewn with tears, teeth clenched.

His Valkyrie.

The fury in Ava's blue eyes almost didn't suit her—or perhaps it suited her all too well.

Liam swallowed and stepped forward, sheathing his dagger because Ava seemed to have a pretty good hold on the vampire.

"She's a jealous one, your soulmate." The vampire grinned, her red lipstick smudged on the sides of her mouth.

Hells, he hadn't been kissing Ava; he had kissed that *thing.* She had glamoured him!

Liam spat on the floor as if it could take the bitter taste from his mouth.

"There's no such thing as soulmates," Ava said quietly from behind the vampire.

The woman rolled her eyes. "Believe what you will, angel girl. Your faith does not change simple facts."

"Who are you?" Liam demanded, wiping spit from his mouth with the back of his jacket.

"Her name is Lilith," Ava said.

The vampire chuckled. "Thank you for the introduction, *princess.*"

Ava pressed her blade deeper into Lilith's neck, drawing thin droplets of blood. "Don't call me that."

"I apologize." The vampire raised her hands. "Truce?"

Ava didn't move.

"This position is highly uncomfortable for me, dear." The vampire swiveled quickly, opening a gash on her own throat as she faced Ava.

Liam spotted his sword on the ground behind him and quickly snatched it. He had the tip of the blade at the back of the vampire's neck in no time. "Touch her and I swear—"

"If I wanted your love dead, she already would be, Selfless," Lilith said, her attention solely on Ava.

His partner glared at Lilith, her head held high, silently defying the vampire. Ava's hardened expression went beyond simple rebellion. It lacked the mercy and compassion so inherent to her.

"Princess." He stretched his free hand toward her, hoping it would catch her attention.

Ava blinked, as if drawn from a trance. She nodded, the Valkyrie gone and replaced by the meek Guardian. She walked to Liam and took his hand.

Lilith turned to them. The gash on her neck had already begun to heal. Flesh mended, weaving over itself, and then Lilith's cut disappeared without leaving a scar, though her full cleavage remained drenched in her own blood.

Ava gripped her blood-tainted dagger so hard that her knuckles became milky white. "I-I shouldn't have ..." Her hands began to tremble, shock finally hitting her.

"Why not?" Lilith asked, rubbing her neck. "You're remarkably good at slashing flesh. A poor little Guardian. Who would've thought?"

"I didn't mean, I ..." Ava bit her lip. She closed her eyes and inhaled deeply. "No, I *did* mean it. I wanted you dead." Her voice faltered. "How could I?"

"It's okay," Liam muttered softly, wishing his words would appease her. "You'll get used to it. You did good, Ava."

"Hardly a sin to wish a vampire dead, isn't it?" Lilith fisted both hands on her waist and nodded to him. "You and your partner still have a long way to go. *He* must teach you."

"Who's *he*?" Ava asked through trembling lips.

A giggle twittered in Lilith's throat. "In time."

"Enough of this nonsense." Liam pressed the tip of his sword on her collarbone, drawing droplets of blood. "If I was Michael, then I was *forced* to become human. Why?"

"Your frail human shell can't withstand the rest of your memories. I can't see them either." She watched the blade that drew her blood and scoffed. "I'm bored now."

Her eyes glimmered ruby red before everything darkened, and a freezing cold pierced through him.

"My children are suffering, and we're impatient." Lilith's words were a faint whisper echoing around them. "Stay away from the Order. You're both precious to him."

The fading light of sunset blinked back, filling the warehouse in twilight. And Lilith was gone.

18

AVA

*A*va watched steam rise from her coffee cup. The events from the warehouse replayed in her mind nonstop, keeping her awake through the night.

She cringed at the memory of Liam and the vampire kissing, at Lilith's body snaking around his, and then his mouth taking hers with the thirst of a man lost in the desert. Just the recollection of their passionate exchange made bile swirl in Ava's stomach, and her throat tightened.

She had watched. All of it, and she couldn't lift a finger. Literally, thanks to Lilith's glamour.

Ava had cried Liam's name until her throat felt like shredded paper, but he didn't listen. Just when she had given up, her eyes stinging with tears, she felt the pulse of her sword. That familiar warmth spread through her, and the rift of light and heat opened inside her essence. Molten gold burst from her core, covering her entirely. *The shield.* It could break the glamour. Ava didn't know this, but the rift inside her somehow did.

Lilith's glamour shattered, but the vampire was so busy

making out with Liam that she didn't notice Ava approaching until it was too late.

At first, Ava had wanted, *needed,* to kill Lilith. Something primeval inside her said Liam was hers and no one else's. Instead of ending the bloodsucker, though, Ava swallowed her fury, and a rush of guilt swam across her. She had never wished to end someone's life before.

Once they returned to Liam's apartment, she prayed tirelessly during the night, begging the Gods for forgiveness. Hate was something new to her, something alien and *wrong.* She hoped praying would redeem her.

Ava took a sip of her lukewarm coffee, feeling like she was at a crossroads: one path leading to her salvation, the other to her doom.

Liam sat across from her, and by his frown and the dark circles under his eyes, he had barely slept during the night. Like her, he also stared at his coffee.

"We should tell the Captain," Ava said quietly, breaking the silence, "and then report to Ezra."

Liam snorted. "You trust your boyfriend blindly." He sipped his coffee, then shook his head. "We tell the Cap and Kev. Not a word to Ezraphael or any other angel."

"Not even Justine?"

Liam shrugged. "I guess Kev would tell her either way."

Ava narrowed her eyes at him. "Ezra could help us, Liam."

"How can you be certain of that, *princess?*"

This time, he'd used her nickname to spite her. Ava knew the difference in his tone by now, but starting another argument wasn't smart. So she brushed it off. "I've known Ezra since I became an angel. I trust him as much as I trust Justine."

"Really?" Liam took another sip. "You don't tell him half of what you tell her."

Ava crossed her arms. "It's a hierarchy issue. If he knew I

was disobeying his orders, he'd have to assign me to another charge. And punish me, of course."

"He paired us together, Ava." Liam's words hung dry in the air like the single beat of a drum.

If Ava and Liam were indeed of the same fabric, as Lilith had said, then it was a remarkable coincidence that they had been paired together.

Could Ezra have done this on purpose?

Ava snorted to herself. *Impossible.* Ezra wanted Ava to be *his* mate, not Liam's. It made no sense to pair her with a supposed soulmate. And what were soulmates, after all?

Folklore, nothing more.

Eternity was a long time, which was why most angels had several mates. Only a handful spent their lives with one partner, and even so, they didn't share the soulmate bond.

Because it wasn't real.

Some Virtues said that the ancient scriptures had been mistranslated; that the Erudites who wrote them meant *mates* as in kin souls instead of *soulmates*—one soul.

It made sense. In all the branches of the Order, in the entire world, there was no record of soulmate bonds backdating to thousands of years. Not to mention that the concept of half-souls existing and completing each other seemed ludicrous. Each essence had its own worth, its own purpose.

She cleared her throat. "We both know better than to believe the words of a vampire."

"Yeah." He gave her a weak smile. "But that Warrior killed Drake to silence him. So no word to the Messenger, not until we know who's behind this. Agreed?"

She let out an exasperated sigh but knew there wasn't much she could do to convince him. "Fine."

This wasn't wise, but it wasn't imprudent. If they wanted Ezra's help, they would need a strong case. Right now, they juggled smoke and mirrors. They needed concrete evidence.

Liam watched her from across the kitchen counter, his expression revealing nothing. Finally, he said, "I saw a memory of the Archangel who helped us. Gabriel. I can't explain why, but I think it might have something to do with Archie's death." He glanced at his own arms like they were a piece of clothing. "And with me."

Ava nodded. "Then we go to Gabriel for answers."

"We will." He smiled sadly at her. "But first, I want to train some more with you."

She shifted on her seat. "You think Gabriel would attack us?"

"No, but if shit goes down—and it always does when you least expect it—I want you ready, or at least as ready as you can be."

Nothing in the world could prepare Ava to face off with an Archangel. If he hurt her charge, though, she would pierce her sword's blade into Gabriel's gut and slash his flesh until his blood rained upon her, and ... Ava cringed at her own thoughts, skipping a breath.

Heavens, she'd have to pray tonight, something she'd been doing all too often since becoming Liam's partner.

The Selfless bit his lips and shook his head, as if he were dismissing something that had come to mind.

"What is it?" She reached out and laid a hand over his.

He stared at her fingers, his thumb brushing her skin. "You shouldn't become Ezraphael's mate."

"It's my duty," she said, a knot clogging her throat. "We're not soulmates just because a vampire told us we are. Soulmates aren't real."

"I know, but it *felt* ..." He frowned, then turned her hand softly, laying his palm over hers. His skin was wonderfully warm, and she couldn't help but relax under his touch.

"It doesn't matter." He pulled away and crossed his arms. "Besides, we're partners, and we shouldn't jeopardize that. Right?"

She nodded. "Right."

That inviting pull between them told Ava to crawl on the counter and drown Liam in violent kisses, to vouch her eternal devotion to him.

Instead, she closed her eyes and inhaled, assuring herself that this wasn't because of some ridiculous connection.

Soulmates? No, this was simple attraction.

A familiar voice at the back of her head, her *own* voice, whispered, *"Fool."*

As soon as they entered the Order's hall, Ava found Justine, who had just come out of the elevator. Her friend's eyes widened in surprise when they met Ava's.

Justine's dark brown hair was fixed in a bun, and she wore Ava's golden dress—the one she had used during last year's ball. Her earrings were made of tiny rubies hanging down like a curtain, and a grim feeling pierced Ava's gut. Images of dripping blood, red as those shiny stones, flashed before her eyes.

She shook her head, and the images were gone. If Ava believed in silly things such as bad omens, she'd be worried.

"What a lovely coincidence!" Justine said, hugging Ava with strength. She turned to Liam and slammed both hands on her waist. "Give me back my friend. You *train* her way too hard, Mr. Hunky."

Liam lifted one charming eyebrow. "First, it's just training, nothing *else*. Second," he turned to Ava and frowned, "is that what you two call me behind my back?"

Ava gulped. "Sometimes."

171

Liam rolled his eyes, but his half-manly, half-boyish grin made Ava smile too. He nodded to Justine. "Going out with Kev?"

"We're going to the opera." She beamed with excitement. "How fancy is that?"

Liam cocked his head to the left. "Tell Kev he better be on time tomorrow."

"Sweetie, if tonight goes as well as I hope it will, he'll have to be a little late." She tapped the bridge of her nose knowingly.

Ava wished she could tell Justine all that had happened to them, all the things that had kept her awake at night.

"You okay?" Justine asked as she laid a hand atop Ava's shoulder.

She observed her friend, who had been shining with happiness before noticing Ava's torment. "I didn't sleep well, that's all."

Justine gave Liam a naughty grin. "Oh, *really?*"

He bit his lip and looked away, his mouth twitching bitterly.

Justine cringed and turned to Ava, a breath hissing through her teeth. "Oh, did I hit a nerve?"

"It's fine." Ava smiled. "Go enjoy your date. We'll talk tomorrow."

Justine narrowed her eyes. "I could force your mental barriers and see all that's going on in there." She pointed to Ava's forehead. "But lucky for you my date is waiting. Tomorrow, then. Promise?"

"Yes. We'll tell you and Kevin everything. Go enjoy yourselves."

Justine kissed Ava goodbye, then tapped Liam's shoulder. "You play nice, Mr. Cranky."

"I thought it was Mr. Hunky?"

She winked at him. "It depends on your mood."

With that, Justine waved goodbye and left.

Ava and Liam went up to Gabriel's office, the air in the elevator heavy with silence, a brick wall between them. Ava wished to break it, but she didn't know how.

The elevator opened to a beige carpeted corridor. They stopped before a door with a golden plate that read 42—according to the help desk, this was Gabriel's office, the one he occupied on the lower floors of the Order, the floors third-tier angels like Ava could access.

Since Gabriel supervised quite a few Warriors, his presence in the lower levels was often a requirement. They had been lucky, really. If Gabriel had been in his usual office, in the upper levels of the Order, he'd be close to unreachable.

Before Liam could knock on the door, a kind voice came from inside. "Come in."

Gabriel's office was different from Ezra's. The walls were a soft silver, and the golden floor showed their reflection. A wide array of swords and weapons hung on the walls, and for a moment, Ava felt as if inside a shiny gunroom.

Gabriel was lying on a white padded sofa near an open archway which showed the city beyond. Curtains fluttered gently with the soft wind that came through.

He had a book in his hands, his blue-green wings hidden within his light. *There and not really there.* Ava remembered Jal's words: Demons and angels only reveal their wings when they want to fly, fuck, fight, or show off.

Apparently, Gabriel wanted none of those.

He closed the book and smiled at them in a dreamlike manner. "To what do I owe the pleasure?"

Liam took one step forward. "You *knew* me."

Gabriel frowned, as if he thought Liam had lost his mind. "Of course. We met in the hall a few days ago, didn't we?" He snorted to himself. "I believe I saved you from a terrible beating."

"No, I meant you knew me before *this*." He pinched his own skin.

Gabriel froze, his lips half open. He cleared his throat and stood, leaving the closed book on the sofa. He paced in circles, his hands behind his back.

Liam walked to him. "What happened to me?"

Gabriel stopped, sadness coating his expression. "You don't want the truth, Michael."

So the vampire was right. Before Liam was a Selfless, he'd been the legendary Archangel Michael. And if Lilith was right about this, could she be right about them being soulmates?

No, absolute nonsense.

"I need to know what happened," Liam said. "It's part of an investigation."

"An investigation?" Gabriel knitted his brows. "Of what?"

Liam looked back at Ava, silently asking for help.

"We can't disclose the case." She stepped in. "By orders of the Messenger."

"Hmm." Gabriel turned to him. "I assume it has nothing to do with your partner's death?"

"It doesn't," Liam said without hesitation.

He could be a remarkable liar when needed.

Gabriel narrowed his eyes at Liam, assessing him. Then he ran a hand through his curly hair and sighed. "I'm not certain if this is wise."

"I don't care," Liam replied through gritted teeth, fists clenched. "Why was I turned into a human, *brother*?"

Gabriel recoiled slightly, as if Liam had hit him with a punch. It was a strange thing to witness, a mighty Archangel recoiling before a Selfless.

"You don't understand. I can't—" His tone came out strangled, as if he were fighting a battle within himself.

"Why?" Liam demanded.

"You don't want to know."

"Why!" he bellowed, his face turning red.

"To forget!" The words burst from Gabriel's throat, and he inhaled deeply. "You *had* to forget."

"Forget what?"

Gabriel crossed his arms and looked out of his open window. "Betrayal. Pain. Oh, the things we've done, Michael ..."

Liam opened his mouth to say something, but an alarm wailed throughout the Order, piercing Ava's ears.

Gabriel's eyes widened, and his jaw dropped. "It can't be."

"What happened?" she asked, her voice muffled by the alarm, the shrieking sound reverberating through the golden floor of Gabriel's office.

"The Order." Gabriel swallowed. "It has been breached."

Air vaporized from Ava's lungs, leaving a vacuum in its place.

The Archangel hurried to the wall and picked up a holy gun and a sword. He tossed another holy gun at Liam, and her partner caught it midair. Liam strapped the weapon in the holster underneath his jacket, then unsheathed his sword.

Gabriel glanced at the silver blade and grief oozed from his irises, but then he shot out of the room. Liam followed and so did Ava.

Her heart beat inside her ears as she unsheathed her sword, blood pumping through her veins. Heavens, who could've breached the mighty headquarters of the Order, the trunk that held all other branches together?

Who would be insane enough?

Her hands shook and she gripped her sword tighter, trying to hide the fear that swirled inside her.

They hurried to the open elevator and pressed the button to the hallway. Her skin was cold and clammy with sweat.

As they descended, Liam cupped Ava's cheek with his free hand. "Are you okay?"

She stared at him. Gods knew what awaited for them in the hall, but of one thing Ava was certain: she'd protect Liam with her life.

For him, she would be ready.

"Yes," she said quietly, laying a hand over his. "I'm fine."

"Judgement day is falling upon us, brother," Gabriel said, his tone grave and mournful.

"You should visit the Nine-Five." Liam turned away from Ava and took his gun from its holster, unlocking the safety with a loud click as the elevator slowed and stopped. "Judgement day is child's play for us."

19

AVA

The elevator's door slid open to reveal a wild river of beasts pouring through the broken entrance and windows of the hall. Warriors pushed back, attacking the incoming streams to contain the flow, but there were too many creatures and they slipped through easily.

In the middle of the hall, the disciples of the God of War formed circles around Erudites and Guardians, their brothers and sisters who knew nothing of bloodshed and violence.

They had been the first to die. Bodies in white and light-gray bodysuits were strewn across the marble, joining beheaded werewolves and vampires.

Blood from both sides painted the floor red.

Gabriel's wings flashed on his back, then boosted him toward one of the windows, across the hall, where a pair of vampires fed on a screaming Guardian.

Ava thanked the Gods that Justine wasn't here. Her friend was an Erudite, like many of the bodies piling across the hall, their silver bodysuits drenched in red. But none had perished more than Guardians. Red made a stark contrast against the white of their suits.

It was easy seeing herself in those bloodied piles; a corpse with a milky and unblinking stare, lost amidst all the others.

Without thinking, Ava stepped back and into the elevator, her heart thrashing within her chest, every breath a slash in her lungs.

"The Gods are with me, and I'm with the Gods," she muttered to herself, her entire body trembling, including her sword. "Even if I walk through the wastelands of the Hells, I will fear no evil, for the Gods are with me and I'm with the Gods."

"Ava, I won't let you get hurt," Liam said.

His voice snapped her out of her desperation.

He was out there, where werewolves and vampires dashed across the hall, drawing rivers of blood, and he was *smiling* at her, a silent assurance that he'd protect Ava with his life. Liam was *her* charge, and he was out there where the rivers of blood flowed freely, and Ava was here, scared witless inside the elevator.

She forced herself to step out and back into the hall. She swallowed and strengthened the grip on her sword.

Liam turned toward the cruel madness ahead, the muscles on his back clenching. "Remember the dual battle instances we practiced?"

Fighting back-to-back against unseen enemies had been easy, something between battling and ballroom dancing. The shifting muscles on Liam's back had told her what their next move was, so after a while she could easily follow him. But they had only practiced twice and against thin air. Her entire experience was based on imaginary attacks.

Ava took a deep breath, trying to steady her nerves. Then she slammed her back against Liam's.

"Ready?" he asked.

"Does it matter?"

His chuckle reverberated through his ribcage. "Not really."

Liam led the way, a holy gun in one hand and his sword in the other. He shot four blasts ahead but kept moving. Ava followed, his every step also hers.

A werewolf charged at her from the left, and she turned in a half-circle. So did Liam, their bodies moving in unison. He faced the beast, and Ava heard the blast of his gun followed by a splash of blood. From the corner of her eye, she saw the werewolf slump on the floor. The gaping hole in his left eye still oozed blue smoke.

This wolf wasn't as strong as Lothar, and that's why it easily perished.

Her stomach clenched and her legs weakened, but she kept going. One flaw in their stance could cost them their lives.

Liam dropped his empty gun on the floor. "Damned the Hells. That was my last shot."

"Why are the In-Betweens doing this?" Ava mumbled as they pierced their way into the bloodbath.

"You know why."

She did, and at the same time, she didn't. Lothar and Lilith could have requested a meeting with the Order, voiced their concern. This act of desperation was … exactly that.

It struck her then, that the In-Betweens might have asked for help already, but their pleas probably remained unanswered. After all, depositions by In-Betweens held no value in the Order's courts.

A vampire yanked Liam away, trapping him in a strong hold. Before Liam or Ava could fight back, the creature's fangs sank into his neck.

Ava saw red; she *felt* red, pulsing, beating, *burning* inside her. Red. Gold.

The rift. It bled the same energy that created her shield. Warmth swam across her body, sharpening her senses. Every movement felt faster, more fluid. Before Ava knew it, she had circled the vampire and slashed her blade across his midsection with surgical precision, missing Liam by a few inches.

The vampire's waist fell on the floor, guts and organs pulled by gravity. Liam shoved the upper half of the vampire away and glared at her.

"T-the Gods are with me," Ava muttered, her teeth clattering as she glared at the vampire's bleeding half. "And I'm with the Gods."

Liam stepped around the fallen body and cupped her cheek with his free hand. "Princess, you can use Erudite skills, and maybe that applies to Warriors too." He looked around. "Right now, you need to be a Warrior. Can you do that for me?"

"You're hurt." She nodded to the blood on his neck which had stopped flowing.

"This little thing?" He smirked. "Come on. It's not enough to tickle, let alone turn me."

She gave him a weak smile, holding back her tears.

He kissed her forehead. "You're doing great." With that, he slammed his back against hers.

They pierced through the crowd of moving bodies, slashing and dodging in perfect synchrony. Ava didn't know how, but she felt faster than before. Suddenly, she was perfectly aware of every tendon and bone under her skin.

She quickly spotted Lilith amidst the clashing bodies. The vampire queen fought back to back with Lothar the same way Ava did with Liam.

Lothar, a giant wolf man two times Lilith's size, slashed and ripped everything in his path. With one strike, he shredded a Warrior's face into bands of flesh and bone splinters.

The werewolf lord chuckled to himself, something between a growl and a bark. "You show us no mercy, servants of the Gods!" His barks were clear amongst the sounds of battle, even though forming words strained his thick throat. "Now no mercy falls on you!"

Lilith scoffed. "Such a taste for the dramatic, dear."

Her eyes shone red as she glamoured an incoming Warrior, stopping the woman in her tracks. Lilith jumped over her and bit half of her neck off.

"There you have it, princess," Liam muttered to Ava. "The werewolf lord and the vampire queen got tired of taking shit and decided to come out and play."

Ava didn't say anything, just remembered Lilith's words. *"Stay away from the Order."*

She'd tried to warn them.

Amidst the blood bath, Lilith caught sight of her and stopped. Her neon-blue eyes shone red, and a sudden urge to run and never stop took over Ava. She shook the urge away, the rift inside her beating in unison with her sword, flooding her with light and blocking Lilith's glamour.

Why was Lilith trying to save her?

A Dominion with peach-colored wings zinged past the arched windows, landing amidst the crowd of bodies to Ava's right. A vampire jolted toward the Dominion, but the woman glared back at the creature and he stopped in his tracks. The vampire began shaking, then stepped back, muttering something Ava couldn't understand. The Dominion kept her focus on the creature, and the vampire kneeled on the ground.

"Please, no more," he whimpered, veins bulging under his neck.

The Dominion handed him her holy gun. Tears streamed down the vampire's cheeks.

"Thank you," he whispered before shooting himself in the head.

C.S. WILDE

Ava turned to Lilith, who'd witnessed the same scene. The vampire queen's glistening red eyes tried to tell her something, but she couldn't figure out what.

Reality wavered around Ava. Dominions, the evolution of Guardians, didn't force harmful emotions onto others. But then again, this was battle, and battles were not won with mercy.

The thought left a bitter taste in her mouth.

She looked around and noticed that apart from the Dominion and Gabriel, there were no second-tiers here. And the three high angels were nowhere to be seen.

Where was the cavalry?

As if on cue, the domed ceiling rumbled and three angels broke through, falling upon the hallway like ripe apples: the Messenger, the Throne, and the Sword.

They stood amidst hills of bodies, grand like the Gods themselves. Ezraphael, with his silver and golden wings. The Throne, Agathe, a woman with raven hair and raven-feathered wings. And the Sword, Talahel, with his long red hair tied in a braid, the sides of his temples shaved, and his wings of a fiery orange.

Agathe and Talahel charged forward, slashing bodies as if they were made of butter, their movements too fast to follow. *A blur of light and death.*

So quickly the balances had tipped. This was not a battle anymore; it was a slaughter.

Ava should've rejoiced, but the In-Betweens were being drugged and starved, and no one listened, no one cared. In a way, she understood why they revolted against those who killed them without second thought.

The Order had failed them.

"You watch us suffer," Lothar's words echoed in her mind. *"My children, drugged. You murder them. The Gods don't listen."*

The Sword vaporized many In-Betweens with his red

182

light-blasts, and the Throne vanished into a cloud of smoke just as a werewolf charged at her, only to reappear behind her enemy and slash his throat.

Each high-angel had a unique power particular to their essence. Powers not shared by anyone in the Order.

While the Throne and the Sword worked the hall, Ezra stood still, his attention locked on Lothar and Lilith.

The werewolf lord rested his forehead against Lilith's as if saying a silent goodbye. He pushed her away when Ezra ran toward him.

Blue thunder cracked around the Messenger's force field, forming a sphere around him. Lothar dodged at the last minute, and Ezra tore a round hole on the marbled wall, raising a cloud of debris on the spot.

The clean-up teams, whatever remained of them, would need weeks to fix all this.

Ava looked for Lilith but couldn't find her anywhere. The vampire queen was gone.

"Fight me!" Lothar bellowed, his barking words an effort for him. "With honor!"

The round, invisible shield around Ezra was coated with dust.

"Gladly," he said through gritted teeth, his loose light hair draping over his face. His force field blinked out, and the dust fell on Ezra's silver bodysuit.

The Messenger ran toward Lothar, a golden layer wrapping his hand—a shield—and with one mighty strike, Ezra sucker-punched him. Lothar slammed against the opposite wall of the hall. Marble cracked, and Ava thought the hall would crumble upon everyone in it.

Perhaps it already had.

This was not the Order. Not *her* Order. This was something else.

Lothar shook his head, centering himself. He then rushed toward the Messenger, and Ezra withdrew his sword.

Their strikes were thunder and storm, booming loudly across the now-quiet hall. Most screams and cries had ceased. Agathe and Talahel had cleaned up the place, and the surviving angels helped their fallen comrades. All vampires and werewolves were either dead or had fled.

A howl of pain sucked Ava's attention back to the fight.

Blood trickled down the edges of Ezra's lips, and the left side of his face was a dark shade of purple. Lothar was in worse shape. He wheezed and almost tripped twice, a hand slammed on his ribs. He had a black eye, and his snout bent on an unnatural angle. And then there were all the deep gashes across his body. Ava counted at least one or two fatal wounds.

Everything happened so fast …

Ezra fixed his silver hair behind his ear. "Repent for your sins, creature."

Lothar growled, "After you."

"We only hurt those of you who have broken the law, and yet you come to our house and murder innocents."

"You murder our innocents too. We are desperate." Instead of focusing on Ezra, Lothar found Ava, and his eyes, sad and resigned, rested on hers. "Evil triumphs when good does nothing."

"Say what you will," Ezra spat. "Your treason must be punished."

Ava wanted to intervene, to beg Ezra for Lothar's imprisonment instead of his execution. But Ezra was faster, and in a moment, he was upon Lothar.

"Wait!" she yelled, but Ezra didn't hear, or perhaps he simply ignored her.

The werewolf lord didn't fight, he just stared at Ava as Ezra slashed his throat open. Blood sprayed from the wound, but Ezra wasn't done. He couldn't be, because Lothar could heal. He pulled Lothar's head back while pushing his body down with his foot, stressing the tension upon Lothar's neck until it ripped free of his body. His spine dangled under his neck.

Ava dropped to her knees and hurled.

"Ava!" Ezra said, truly seeing her for the first time, blinking away the bloodlust that had taken hold of him.

He threw Lothar's head away like garbage before running to her.

Ava stumbled back, bottom to the floor as she pushed herself away. Her shifting feet slid on the bloodied marble. Her breathing was frantic, ragged, and she couldn't focus, couldn't think. She had to get out of here. *Away from him. From everything.*

Warm liquid made her hands slip, and she glanced down. Her palms were soaked in red.

"The Gods are with me," she breathed.

"Ava, please." Ezra reached for her, but a pair of black army boots stepped between them.

"Don't touch her," Liam said. "Lothar didn't deserve to die that way. He was desperate; they all were."

Ezra's glare was anger and contempt, his lips white because he pressed them too hard. His clothing was splattered with Lothar's blood.

Red on silver.

"They killed our brothers and sisters," Ezra countered. "What did you want me to do, *Selfless?*"

Ava inhaled deeply, centering her thoughts as she glanced at the bodies strewn across the hall. Both sides wrong, both sides right. It made her head hurt.

She wiped bile from her lips with the back of her arm, staining her leather jacket. It didn't matter. By now she was half covered in blood anyway.

She forced herself up, trying to ignore Lothar's fallen body in the back of the hall and how it sucked all the hope and faith and kindness out of her.

She grabbed her sword from the ground, and the blood on her palm tainted the handle. The beating of the sword reverberated faintly from the blade into her bones.

"Why did you give me this sword, Ezra?" Her voice came out weak and broken.

"Ava ..." Ezra tried to step toward her, but Liam blocked his way again.

The Messenger sighed as if he were searching for the right words. "The sword is a facilitator," he finally said. "It helps you unveil the power of your essence. It's supposed to push a third-tier angel into becoming a second-tier." He rubbed the bridge of his nose, staining it wine red. "It's because of the sword you hold that I ascended many centuries ago. I figured it could do the same to you."

Ava frowned, slightly confused and yet relieved that she hadn't lost her mind. The sword *was* doing something to her after all. "Why would you want to speed my ascension?"

He tried to step closer, but Liam pushed him back.

Ezra blew out an exasperated breath. "Because you need power to walk with a Selfless. It was dangerous, Ava, and just the thought of you getting hurt—"

Liam snickered and crossed his arms. "See, I have a different theory. I think you wanted her to ascend so you'd have a powerful mate by your side. I've seen what she can do, and I'm betting you know exactly how powerful she is."

Ezra's blue eyes beamed with fury, but he didn't move an inch toward Liam. Instead, he turned to Ava. "I'd never use you in this manner. Ava, you *know* me. I gave you this sword because I trust your abilities, and I trust *you*. What I said remains true. I need you by my side; the Gods need you by my side, with or without the sword. We must help the Order shed light into mankind's path."

Ava looked at the fallen corpses and at the red blotches splattering the hall's marbled floor. An irking sensation prickled beneath her skin. "Is this how we'll do it, Ezra?"

He followed her gaze and blinked, as if only now he could see the rotting death around them. "We had to." He frowned at a small mountain of werewolf bodies. "Gods, we …" He swallowed. "Revenge is not the way of the Gods."

From a distance, the Sword and the Throne watched him intently.

"But we had to do it." Ezra turned to Ava, nodding to himself, his eyes glistening. "We had to, Ava, they attacked us. Please …"

She didn't know what to think. Almost as if in auto-pilot, she asked, "Why did you pair me with Liam?"

Ezra's eyebrows scrunched in confusion. "He needed the guidance of a Guardian." He seemed to sense this wasn't enough for her, so he puffed out a breath. "Liam is fire, Ava, burning without thinking twice. You're water, soothing and calm. He's impulse; you're common sense. It might've been unconventional, but I truly believed you could help him."

She stepped closer and peered into Ezra's eyes. As far as she could see, they spoke the truth; they always did. The bloodlust she'd seen as he ripped away Lothar's head had given way to something frail and breakable, like a thin layer of ice.

"Ava, please," he mumbled, his voice falling. "I meant you no harm. I truly believed the sword would help you."

"I know." Ava sheathed her sword and turned toward the exit.

She didn't look back, even when Ezra called her name, begging her to return.

AVA

*W*ater cascaded down Ava's body, cleansing her from the dirt and blood—souvenirs of battle—that clung to her skin. Her tears mingled with the flowing water. It felt as if more than blood and dirt were being taken from her.

Her lips quivered as she prayed for the dead, but there was no point. Angels and In-Betweens weren't like humans. Their bodies *were* their souls, and once they died, there was no Heavens for them, no Hells, just … nothing.

The thought of someone disappearing into nonexistence made Ava sob harder. She stifled her cries with her hand.

A soft knock came from the bathroom door. "Ava, you all right?"

"Yes." She gulped and took a deep breath. "I'll be out in a minute."

"Take as long as you need." She could feel Liam's forehead stamped against the door outside, or maybe it was just her imagination. "I'm off to bed."

Liam had heard her cries, of this Ava was certain, and yet he did not push, did not intervene. Instead, he gave her the time and space she needed. And right then, she loved him for it.

"You need anything?" he asked quietly, trying to hide the worry in his tone. It felt like a gray mass as cold as ice, prickling against Ava's Guardian senses.

"No, I'm fine," she said. "Thank you."

For a Guardian, she was becoming awfully good at lying.

AVA STEPPED into a dimly lit room. The scent of pine wafted from the wooden walls and floor. Persian carpets extended under her feet, and old tapestry paintings hung on the walls. The paintings showed the three Gods and the three Devils, fighting in heavenly battlefields crowded with Seraphs and Wraths. *The armies of the Heavens and Hells.*

Other scents suddenly overcame the pine, stenches of decay and blood so strong that Ava gagged. She might've lost her mind, but she could feel an invisible force trying to kick her out of that room.

She spotted an open door that led to the outside. The wooden floor creaked below her hurried steps. When she burst out of the place, she inhaled the cool night air, once then twice, soaking in all of it.

The moon hung high in the night sky, drenching the garden in silver light. All the plants were brown, dry and cracked, the tree trunks bare and black. Their curling branches were leafless, and yet, the dead garden had a stark sort of beauty that made Ava smile.

In the middle of the garden stood a metal gazebo filled with rococo swirls and a table fashioned in the same way. A thick layer of white paint coated both the gazebo and the table, capturing the faint moonlight.

The old man with the newsboy's cap, the elder who

followed her, sat at the table, his concentration on a chess game he played. He moved one piece forward, and his opponent, a young woman whose skin shone green and gold, smiled. Her dark green hair floated around her like waves crashing against the shore.

A sense of safety and love cascaded through Ava, flooding her with awe so grand that her knees buckled. She fell over them in a trembling heap. Without meaning to, she started to cry because the Goddess of Life and Love, *her* Goddess, the mother of all Guardians, stood before her.

The elder turned his attention to her, and so did the goddess. She smiled at Ava but didn't say a word. Then she shook her head, her mane of hair dancing around her in slow motion. Every piece of her started dismantling, as if the Goddess was a tree shedding leaves in autumn.

She quickly gave place to an old bald man with a knowing grin and infinite kindness behind his eyes. The God of Knowledge and Logic stood up from his chair. He drifted toward Ava, his robe fading at his feet like a floating ghost. As he did, he shed his form once again to reveal a tall broad man with a flowing mane of red hair and strong muscles, a mighty sword attached to a belt around his waist.

The God of War should've been threatening, intimidating, and yet, all Ava felt was love and acceptance. He, *they*, loved her like she loved all her charges: unconditionally. And they were so proud of her, they didn't need to say it. The sensation bloomed and spread inside her heart.

"My Gods," she croaked, crouching on the ground until the tip of her nose touched the ashen earth. She shook and cried as she whispered, "Holy Gods in the Heavens, I am your servant. So long as I exist in your infinite Glory, the Gods are with me and I'm with the Gods."

A warm finger touched her chin, lifting it up. This time, it was the Goddess of Love and Life, smiling down at her.

"What is your purpose, child?" she asked with all their voices, a mix of tunes. But there were more than three voices there. Ava counted at least six.

She parted her lips to answer, but couldn't; she was shaking so much. She swallowed and tried to compose herself. "To help mankind, my Goddess."

"You are special, Ava, so much more than you think." The Goddess smiled before shadows wrapped around her, changing her features. Her kind eyes shifted into a predatory yellow, her teeth sharpened, and her nose fell on the ground in the way of a rotten fruit.

A freezing cold stabbed through Ava. The sensation she was alone in an empty room took over completely; a place where her screams would remain forever unheard. She cried but not with joy or fulfillment.

This time, she cried in fear.

She knew this devil from the depictions in the books. Belzebub, devil of Death and Desperation, his nose two reptilian slits, his skin a slimy gray. His oily dark hair dripped down his features. A face grew from his neck, a woman with purple shining irises, skin dark as the night, and hair silver like the moon. Berith, devil of Chaos and Violence. She smiled upon Ava, and Ava tried to recoil, but Belzebub never released her chin. His fingers were colder than ice and burned her skin.

A third head grew beside Belzebub's, a man with a face of marble, his skin white as snow, his hair blue flames catching fire. Mammon, devil of Ignorance and Envy. His clear blue eyes sparkled, and his sharp toothed grin told Ava he'd feast upon her soul.

"Do not fear the dark, Ava." They spoke at the same time, their shrill, cold voices mingling with the warm, assertive tones of the Gods as if they were part of the same thing, the same universe. *Balances shifting.* "Show your light to him. Let him show his darkness to you."

Ava's head hurt and she cried, forcing herself to move, but she couldn't. "P-please," she mumbled. "Let me go ..."

"Tell us, Ava," the voices rumbled. "Why do you think you're here?"

She woke with a scream stuck in her throat.

AVA

*T*he next day, when they arrived at the precinct, Ava found Justine sitting on a chair. Kevin handed her a glass of water and most of the liquid spilled from her trembling hands. She still wore Ava's golden dress.

"T-the halls were painted red this morning," she stammered as Ava approached. "No bodies but so much blood, I couldn't stay there. All my fallen brothers and sisters ..." Justine's breath hitched, and Ava rested a hand on her shoulder. "I was enjoying a fun date while they suffered."

"If it helps, most of the blood was from the In-Betweens," Liam said from behind Ava. "Now, *that* was a massacre."

Ava glared at him, and he raised his hands in surrender as if her eyes had held him at gunpoint.

"It doesn't help," Justine said quietly. "Two of my research group are *dead*. I wasn't there. I couldn't—" She looked at her own hands. "I couldn't help them."

"It wasn't your fault," Ava said, her tone soothing.

She whispered the words of the Gods to Justine, assuring her that they were with her and she was with them. Golden sparkles floated from Ava's lips and dove into her friend's skin. This normally worked when appeasing her charges, but Justine hadn't been one in a while now. Besides, an Erudite's telepathy could often block a Guardian's empathy.

Justine sniffed. "Thanks for trying, dear." Her expression shifted, quickly turning into something dark and bitter. "What they did is unforgivable. We must show them the wrath of the Gods, show them why *no one* has dared to attack the Order until now, and why no one ever will again."

Ava frowned. "That is not the way of the Gods."

Her friend snorted and took a gulp of water, steadying the glass with both hands. "It's the only way now."

Ava couldn't believe her words. "The path of the Gods is the path of forgiveness, of love and understanding. Now more than ever, we cannot forget that. Otherwise we won't be any better than the darkness we're trying to fight."

"The servants of the Gods are *not* pushovers," Justine snapped at her, glaring at Ava with disgust. "At least, most of us aren't."

Ava gaped at her friend, ignoring the sting in her chest. "Fighting for revenge will only feed the darkness until it swallows everything and all of us."

This seemed to stop her friend's rage. Justine's shoulders slumped. "I-I'm sorry," she croaked, setting the glass on the table. "I'm so sorry."

"It's okay." Ava kneeled on the ground, facing Justine. "A lot of Erudites and Guardians died yesterday. They deserved better." She took Justine's hands. "But someone is forcing the In-Betweens to attack humans, and the Order is annihilating them because of it." She spoke as if this justified the attack. She knew it didn't.

Both sides wrong, both sides right.

Justine's lips curled. "Why should we help the In-Betweens when they chose to stay neutral? They certainly never helped us."

"That isn't a reason."

Justine snorted, then caressed Ava's cheek with her thumb. She sniffed back her tears. "You should ascend straight to Seraph, you know. You'd make an amazing queen in the Heavens."

"How's the debugging on Archie's phone?" Liam asked Kevin from a few steps back.

Ava's partner might act nonchalant, but pink, blurred tendrils of sympathy wafted from him and brushed against Justine. Her friend couldn't feel it, of course, but Ava could.

"Done five minutes ago." Kevin nodded to a desk in the back so they could give Justine and Ava some privacy.

"Took them long enough," Justine chortled. "You should go." She grabbed a tissue from a box on the table, then wiped her nose with it. "He's your charge."

Ava stood and laid a hand on Justine's head. "Once upon a time, so were you."

Justine smiled at Ava and patted her hand. "I'll be fine." She nodded to Liam. "Go to him."

"I'll return soon." She squeezed Justine's hand before walking toward the two men.

Kevin handed Liam a piece of paper as Ava approached. She inspected what was scribbled on the surface.

844-483-2293.

"It's Archie's last call," Kevin said, pointing at the number. "I tried tracing it, but it's blocked as Hells. No one took my calls."

Liam peered at the number. "Hmm." He picked his own phone and dialed, leaving it on loud speaker.

A click and then a voice.

"Liam," Jal said from the other side, his tone low and tired. "Your timing isn't perfect, but we have no choice. Does Ava still have the cards I gave her?"

2 2

LIAM

*L*iam pulled Ava to a corner of the precinct near a window, where they could have some privacy. He peered at her tired and yet fierce blue irises, hoping they could show him her thoughts.

Ava had cried last night. He'd heard the muffled sobs while she was in the shower. Gods, he'd wanted to break through that door and hold her, wrap his arms around his Guardian and only let go once all her tears dried. But Princess didn't need that. She needed space, and he gave it to her, all through the night and also during breakfast.

A mournful silence had filled the air around them this morning, a heavy grief over things lost. The streets and his job made Liam tough, prepared him for shit like that, but Ava was different. She had never faced sudden and ugly deaths, the kind that stuck to someone for years, especially in their nightmares.

He feared yesterday's bloodshed would change her, darken her soul, if only a bit. Hells, years as a Selfless had certainly darkened his, but Ava remained true to her nature.

Justine might've lost sight of what mattered, but Ava

196

never did, not for one second. Even after seeing her brothers and sisters bleed, after discovering her future mate was manipulating her, even after witnessing Lothar's unfair death, Ava didn't lose sight of what was important—of who she was or the principles she stood for.

She was clearly hurting, but she was still standing. The strongest woman Liam had ever met.

"Are you sure you want to do this?" he asked her in a whisper, hoping she would say no, that she would agree to stay in the precinct with Justine and Kevin, where she couldn't be hurt, where she'd be safe. "What we're about to do might be considered treason, especially after the attack on the Order."

She scowled at him. "Why do you insist on treating me as if I were made of paper?"

He leaned back as if she'd slapped him, then ran a hand over his hair, letting out a weary sigh. "You've witnessed enough pain and bloodshed, princess. Digging any deeper could break you."

"It could break you too," she countered, her voice hoarse.

He almost chuckled. It would take a lot more than a bloodbath to break him.

"Liam, what we witnessed yesterday wasn't the Order, and it wasn't the In-Betweens. It was devilish work, unmerciful work." She raised her right hand and cupped his cheek. "We need to stop it."

He closed his eyes as he leaned against her palm, reeling in the feel of her touch. "I can't lose you."

"You won't." There was a ray of sunlight in her voice. "I'm here, and you're my charge."

For fuck's sake! Liam flinched and jerked away from her. "You mean your partner. I'm your *partner*, Ava."

Every time Ava called him a fucking charge, Liam wondered if she cared about him only because it was her duty. Plus, she'd had tons of charges throughout her angelic life. For all he knew, he was just a number to her.

Her befuddled stare looked stunning: rosy lips budded into a titillating pout, her delicate face frowning. Gods, Liam wanted to kiss her so hard he had to take a deep breath and focus.

"Yes," she said, assessing him. "I'm your partner. And I won't let you step into danger alone. Ever."

He gaped at her, realizing Ava might be simply too good for this world. *Too good for him.*

"Princess—"

She crossed her arms. "I'm going with you, and we're getting to the bottom of this. The Order, *my* Order, needs us to." Before he could argue, she turned and strolled toward the exit of the precinct.

Liam smiled wide at his fierce Guardian, his kind, unwavering force of nature, before catching up to her. He nudged Ava's shoulder with his elbow, shooting her a proud grin that was returned with one of her own.

His Princess. His Valkyrie.

"Where are you two going?" the Captain asked right when they reached the elevator.

Say what you will, but the woman had impeccable timing.

Liam turned around and walked to her, shoving his hands in his jeans pockets, trying to look as innocent as he could. "Just checking stuff, Cap."

"Checking *stuff?*" She narrowed her eyes at him, then pointed back to her office. "Inside. Now." She turned and entered the room.

Ava began to follow him, but the Captain shouted from inside, "Just Liam."

He sent Ava an apologetic shrug and entered the office, closing the door behind him.

Liam hated going into that office alone. It always

preceded the scolding of a lifetime. So he crossed his arms and waited for it.

"You're doing something bad, aren't you?" She went to her desk and dropped into the leather chair behind it. "Something so bad that you can't report it to me."

Hells. Sometimes Liam wondered if the Cap could read minds.

"Depends on the point of view," he said, then chided himself. This wasn't the moment to be snarky.

The Captain chuckled and shook her head. "I've known you since you were eight. I know when you're up to no good. I can feel it in my bones."

He straightened his stance but didn't say a word. The less the Captain knew, the better, especially so soon after the attack on the Order. Nerves were tense and sparks flew in the air, waiting to ignite and burn everything.

The Captain formed a triangle with her hands. "Have you noticed that demons have been awfully quiet? Possessions have dropped to almost nil, dealings in exchange for human souls haven't been recorded in the black market this week, and attacks on humans and angels have dropped. I haven't had to call for angelic support for three weeks now."

Whenever the Selfless uncovered second-tier demons wreaking havoc, they were ordered to call in Archangels, Dominions, or Virtues to handle the job. A Selfless, no matter how skilled, could never fight an ascended demon— or was it descended?—and survive to tell the tale.

"It's not just the high-level assholes," she continued. "Even lower demons who can't control their instincts are behaving —as far as demons can behave, that is."

He nodded. "Something's not right, and it has to do with the attack on the Order."

She leaned her elbows on the table. "What's your take on all of this, kid?"

He smiled. *Kid.* Only two people called him that: the Captain and Archie.

"Frankly, Cap, I think demons are forcing the In-Betweens to attack humans, which then forces the Order to smite them. They're making us kill each other, as we all saw by yesterday's attack. The weird thing is, I think they've got the help of someone in the Order." He shoved his hands in his jacket pockets. "My gut says this is why Archie died."

The Captain nodded, her lips pressed into a thin line. "So, a demon killed Archie to silence him." She shook her head. "It makes no sense. Why would Archie choose to become a demon, then?"

Liam studied his own feet, his tone weak as he said, "I'm guessing his heart was broken, Cap."

"Why?"

She still didn't get it.

"I don't think he was killed by a demon." The words hung in the air between them.

The Captain's eyes widened and she leaned back on her chair, her fingers digging deep into the leather of the armrests. "Impossible."

"I'm almost certain of it," Liam said. "A few nights ago, a Warrior killed a vampire without any reason. The blood-sucker wasn't attacking anyone. This entire thing stinks of a cover up that could destroy the entire Order and what it stands for."

Everything Ava so passionately defended, all that made her pure, kind, and perfect. The Hells he'd allow anyone to destroy that.

The Captain winced. "So they're weakening us from inside. Do you have a name in mind?"

"No," he lied.

Ezraphael was top on his list, but Liam couldn't be sure if this was because the Messenger might be guilty or because he just hated the guy. Better not to name someone so powerful without evidence.

"Well, then." The Captain fixed some papers on her desk. "Go find out who killed Archie and who's behind this mess." She bared her yellowing teeth at him. "And bring me their fucking head."

LIAM

*J*al had told Liam he would be at Club 23, a place located within the thirteenth sector, not far from where they had met Lilith—that fucking bloodsucker.

From outside, the building looked like an abandoned warehouse just like the others that peppered the wide street —big cement blocks with broken windows. But this one had a tilted display above the iron door that read "Club 2." The "3" was laying on the floor.

Liam pushed the rusting door. The hinges were cracked, so it should've been easy to break in. But the door didn't move. He tried again, pushing until blood thumped under his forehead.

"The place has been glamoured," Ava muttered as she watched the crumbling façade. "I can feel it thrumming against my essence."

"How can someone glamour an object?" Liam frowned at the decaying building. "As far as I know, glamour needs two people to work."

"Another mystery, then." Ava took the metallic cards from her jacket pocket and handed them to him.

"How are we supposed to use them?" Liam looked at the cards, studying their thin metallic surface.

He searched for a place to insert them, but the iron door looked like it had been built in the past century. Then again, this was glamour, and things might not look as they seemed.

"Here's to nothing." With a shrug, he slammed both cards on the door's surface.

Green light washed under the first card, then the second. With a click, the door opened.

"Holy shit, it worked." He scoffed as he put the cards in his pocket. "Whatever this glamour is hiding, it's hi-tech as fuck."

"The technology is quite interesting," Ava muttered. "Whatever this door is, it works like a barcode scanner."

"Have you seen anything like this outside the Order?"

She shook her head. "I suppose if anyone had the means to do this, it would be Jal. But that doesn't explain the glamour on the façade."

"Only one way to find out." Liam pushed the door open.

Ahead was a vast space drenched in sunlight—it poured through the giant glass roof. The floor was crowded with stretchers and medical staff dressed in gray who operated on injured werewolves. Holy wounds could be deadly to young In-Betweens, something to do with angelic light stopping their healing process. As a monster-slayer, Liam knew well how a holy blast from his gun, or a cut from a blessed blade, could end the life of a junior wolf or vamp.

A few of the doctors dressed in gray lifted their sleeves and allowed vampires to feed on them to regenerate. Most vamps endured daylight like someone endures a hot day without air conditioning. The newly turned, though, were more sensitive.

That's why they had gathered under a small squared cemented roof on the left, which created a safe penumbra.

From beside him, Ava watched the humans across the space, trying to decipher them. Their humble gray clothing was composed of large pants and shirts that resembled tunics. They didn't seem to be in distress, but Princess kept trying to find the hint of a threat.

He took her hand, and she looked down at their intertwined fingers with a soft smile.

"They're here to help, Ava," he whispered near her ear.

"They might've been glamoured," she stated, still looking for things that clearly weren't there.

Hells, sometimes his gut instinct could be better than her empathy. "Do they look like mindless robots to you?"

The humans smiled, their words kind to the patients who fed on them. In turn, the bloodsuckers controlled the hunger; even if they still starved, they jerked away from the humans the moment they sensed they might lose control.

"Who *are* these people?" Ava muttered to herself.

"They're the Gray," Jal's voice came from behind them. "Priests and priestesses of the Legion."

Jal looked different from when they last met. His playfulness had vanished, his amber skin had paled, and dark circles spread under his eyes. Right then, he was not a demon, only a man on the brink of exhaustion. Liam knew that look well.

"Legion?" Ava asked.

Jal gave her an enigmatic grin. "I believe you're here because of Archibald?"

Liam stepped forward. "Time for me to claim the favor you owe me."

"Consider this one on the house," he chuckled as if he'd remembered something funny. "Just keep in mind that some answers are not mine to give."

He showed them to a long wooden table near a window where they could talk in peace.

Liam sat beside Ava, both of them facing Jal across the table.

"The attack on the Order," Liam started. "Did Lilith and Lothar plan all of it? Were you involved?"

"Yes, they did, and no, I wasn't. The vampire queen and the werewolf lord were too impatient. I suppose noble creatures tend to die in stupid yet honorable ways." He gave them a sad smile. "Be that as it may, their attack almost jeopardized the entire operation."

"What operation?" Liam pushed.

"You'll soon find out. I've only been recently filled in. I might know more than you do, but not much."

He waved toward a vampire, who nodded and disappeared across the warehouse.

"Who killed Archie?" Liam pressed, sensing he was close to getting the answers he needed. *Finally.* "What does the attack on the Order have to do with his death?"

"Nothing and everything."

Blood rushed to Liam's head, and he slammed a hand on the wooden table. "Stop talking in riddles!"

"Easy, Selfless." Jal's eyes glinted in a feral manner, his sly grin widening across his face. Ah, there he was; the demon. The dragon. "You'll get answers soon enough."

The vampire interrupted them, bringing a tray with three glasses filled with malt whiskey. He laid the tray before them and left, half-bowing to Jal as he did.

Jal handed Ava and Liam their drinks, then took a sip of his own and closed his eyes, savoring the taste. "Ah, single malt, twenty years." He nodded to their glasses. "Drink, angels. You'll need it."

Liam didn't hesitate to take a long gulp. He slammed the glass on the table, but Ava kept glaring at her drink as if it was poison. So he took her glass and downed it too. Gods knew he needed it.

"Your number was on Archie's call log," Liam said to Jal. "He met with you before he died."

Jal bit his lip and looked down at his own glass. "He did."

"Why?" Liam asked, a certain desperation in his tone. "Who killed him and why did he choose to become a demon?"

Jal downed the rest of his drink and removed a crumpled envelope from his jacket. "Why don't you ask him?"

Liam's name was scribbled on the envelope. Blood vanished from his brain so quickly, he thought he might faint.

Ava squeezed his hand and leaned closer. "Are you okay?"

He swallowed as he took the envelope from Jal. "That's Archie's handwriting."

LIAM'S HEART pounded frantically in his chest. Did he really want to read the old man's last words? Where would this path take him? And why had Archie entrusted a demon with this?

He glanced at Ava, and she smiled softly at him, silently encouraging Liam to do what he felt was best.

"I'm here," she said.

He nodded, pulling the courage to go ahead from deep within and from his Guardian too. With a heavy breath, he opened the envelope, his fingers digging into the squared paper.

"*Kid,*" Liam read the words aloud but had to stop. Tears bubbled in the back of his throat.

He reminded himself he had to be strong now, so he swallowed back the mix of pain and sorrow that threatened to choke him and continued. *"If you're reading this, it's because Kevin has debugged my phone. Also, I might be dead, which means I'm a demon now.*

Son, I'm sorry for leaving like this, but I had to do what was best for you like I've always done since I found you starving in the streets. You're my kid, Liam. You always come first. One day, I hope you'll forgive me."

A small blotch stained the paper, a dry tearstain Archie left as he was writing this. Thorny agony pierced Liam from inside, but he sniffed and kept reading. He was Archibald Theodore Brennan's son and one of the Fury Boys. The Hells he'd back away now.

"Demons have left the In-Betweens alone for thousands of years, mostly because wolves and vamps brought a certain mayhem to mankind which kept the Order busy. But demons finally realized that when an In-Between turns a human, they take a potential soul from the dark. And despite the Order's efforts, the number of In-Betweens has been growing exponentially for centuries now.

Demons are done accepting those losses.

So they began withholding the vampire's food supplies and drugging the werewolves to force the Order to fall upon them. I guess they want the Order and the In-Betweens to kill each other."

Liam dropped the paper, his breathing ragged. He glared at Jal, his free hand atop his sword. "Why are demons doing this?"

Jal raised his hands. "Hey, I have no part in this. I gave you the letter, remember?" He hunched over the table. "I belong in the gray lines. Not every demon is evil, not every angel is a saint," he spoke through gritted teeth. "The light is too self-righteous and proud, the dark too mad and chaotic. What do you do when you no longer know where you stand?" He glared back at the vampires and werewolves across the warehouse. "You stand In-Between. Like them."

"A demon In-Between," Ava muttered to herself. She

opened her mouth to say something, but instead snapped her lips shut.

He returned his attention to Archie's letter.

"You see, kid, someone in the Order realized that when an In-Between turns someone, they also take away a potential angel, or a soul that would've gone to the Heavens. That's why the Order has been killing In-Betweens without asking questions. It's convenient —and kind of genius if you think about it.

Vampires feed on humans, and werewolves are half-human. If a war between light and dark would happen, the In-Betweens would side with their food supply and their half-brothers: humans. And by extension, angels. But the Order is clueless to this; they just want the potential souls they're losing. Whoever has betrayed us is a fucking moron."

"This is sacrilege," Ava muttered. "Angels would never," her voice faltered. "What he speaks of is genocide. The path of the Gods does not lead this way."

"You saw what happened at the Order, Ava." Liam peered at her, annoyed that even now she insisted on ignoring what was right in front of her.

She winced, her lips parted slightly, and her eyes glistened. Something cracked inside his Guardian; Liam could see it. Guilt slashed across him, but there was nothing he could do. Ava *had* to see the truth. All of it.

She stared at him for a long while before she nodded, a cue for him to continue reading.

"The In-Betweens are just the start. I'm certain humans are next, but I'll have to sacrifice everything to see how far this goes. There are only two things I trust in this world, son, and that's my faith and you. If I have one last lesson to give, it's this: don't be afraid of the dark. Jal is a demon and a good guy, though he'll deny this to the end of days. Things aren't black and white. Not anymore."

Jal snorted, a grin spreading on his lips.

Liam held the thin golden pendant hanging around his neck, a triangle within a circle, the symbol of the Gods. Somehow, he always felt closer to Archie when he did that.

"Liam, these are the answers you need. We've given so much to this fight ... it's time to rest, kiddo. I left enough money with Jal to help you start living on a small, secluded island. Be happy. You're better than all of this.

And don't worry, I'll make them pay for what they did. It's time for me to take care of you one last time. Please allow me to do so.

I love you, son."

"I ..." Liam wiped the tears that had accumulated in the corners of his eyes. He cleared his throat, steadying his breathing. Fuck it if he'd cry now, especially in front of Ava. "I don't know what to make of this."

"It's pretty obvious." Jal shrugged. "You're supposed to run away."

Liam frowned. "I can't."

He turned to Ava with an apology on the tip of his tongue. If he ran, her duty to him would be done, and she'd be safe. They both would.

Was he selfish by not doing what was best for her?

The words hurt as they left his throat. "I'm so sorry, princess."

She laid a hand at the back of his neck, bringing him closer. She gently pressed her forehead against his. "When darkness comes, angels do not run. And you, Liam Striker, are the best one of us all."

Her words were a slap to the face and a warm kiss at the same time. Ava was an angel. Not the standard Order angel, but the kind Catholic humans worshipped: a pure, caring, and devoted creature. Liam wasn't sure if he believed in the Gods, but he sure as Hells believed in her. Those damned tears bubbled again in the back of his throat, but he kept them in.

Jal rolled his eyes. "How cute."

The demon suddenly straightened as if he were a wolf catching a scent, his eyes wide. A stroke of darkness stretched behind him, then dissipated to reveal wings dark as night and red as blood.

"Motherfuckers," he grunted right before the doors and windows of the warehouse burst open, and Warriors crashed into Club 23.

AVA

*T*wo pitch-black spheres cracked by purple lightning grew from Jal's hands. His dragon wings spread wide, and with one boost he jolted toward the ceiling where an Archangel hovered over them, his blue and green wings setting him apart.

Gabriel. The only ascended angel in the attack as far as Ava could see.

Jal crashed against him with the fury of thunder while Warriors below cut and slashed through the warehouse without mercy.

"This can't be happening," Ava told herself as she watched Warriors ramming their blessed blades through vampires' chests, holy guns blasting werewolves' heads.

She stood there, frozen, witness to another massacre, this time against the injured and weak. There was no honor here, no kindness. This was retaliation, plain and simple. No matter how angels would justify it—and they would—this was *not* the work of the Gods.

"Stay behind me!" Liam shouted as he drew his sword, his

voice muffled by the screams and cries, the sounds of slashed meat and bone. *The sprays of blood.*

"Which side are we fighting on?" Ava mumbled, gaping at the battling bodies.

Liam pulled her closer to him, and when she looked into his green eyes, they washed away her shock and fear. "We're on *our* side, princess."

Ava nodded, and slammed her back against his, ignoring the sinking sensation in her gut. "We must protect the humans. They're the true innocents in all of this."

He nodded his approval; she could feel it through the shifts in his back muscles.

They went forward and into the crowd, trying to find those wearing gray, priests of something Jal had called the Legion. Ava had her sword in hand, ready to cut and punch with no mercy; anything to protect the innocent.

But the battle ignored them. Everywhere they went, the path cleared. No one, angel or In-Between, dared attack.

"What in all the Hells?" Liam halted and so did she.

"We're in-between," Ava muttered, the meaning of it sinking into her.

Right now, she and Liam were no one's enemies and no one's friends. They were angels, so the Warriors didn't attack them, but they had also been under Jal's protection, so the In-Betweens who fought back avoided them.

This was about to end, though, Ava could sense it thrumming within her bones. *The point of no return.*

Some humans gathered near the left end of the warehouse. Fear oozed from them in cold clouds, their bodies trembling. They crowded with the young vampires who were too weak to battle.

Not far from them, a group of humans was being punched and kicked, not by the vampires who fed upon them or the werewolves who'd love to taste their flesh, but by the angels who had sworn to protect them.

Ava's stomach lurched, and she swayed back. A red and thorny sensation filled her to the brim, and her teeth gritted so hard that the bite pricked into her jaw.

More out of instinct than anything else, Ava rushed toward the end of the room, and even though Liam screamed her name, she didn't stop.

She passed by an angel who gutted a werewolf, then another who'd split a vampire in half. They were *smiling* as they ended those who were too weak to fight, rejoicing in their massacre.

Tears dropped from the corner of her eyes as she ran.

She had to stop this. *This* was not the Order. *This* was not what she stood for.

A piercing scream caught Ava's ear. A woman dressed in gray crouched on the concrete floor, pleading for her life. Ava turned and went to her, only now noticing that behind the woman, a Warrior lifted his sword for a kill blow.

"Stop!" Ava cried. "For the love of the Gods, stop! She's human!"

The Warrior tilted his head to the right, observing Ava. His sword stopped halfway across the deadly swing, but his cold eyes revealed nothing. Like some of the Warriors, his black bodysuit was sleeveless, showcasing thick arms shaped to kill.

Ava was almost there, a few more steps ...

"If this human is helping them, then she's a traitor of the light, sister." His sword went down, severing the woman's head from her neck.

Ava's legs buckled midway; her kneecaps stung as they hit concrete. A void ate away her lungs, and warm tears flooded her cheeks. She tried to speak, but all that came out was a piercing shriek that shredded the walls of her throat.

The Warrior observed her with a sneer. "You're weak, sister."

He turned to pick out another human, this time a boy, not much younger than Kevin. The Warrior took him by his hair, and still the boy refused to let out the tears glistening in his eyes.

Something inside Ava snapped. She forced herself up, and her sword beat in unison with her heart, opening that familiar rift. It bled gold and warmth from her essence.

Her body's response to bloodshed.

"Enough!" Ava raised her sword toward the Warrior.

He stopped shaking the boy by his tuft of hair and watched her with annoyance. "Stand down, *Guardian*. You know nothing of battle. We're doing the Gods' work."

"This has nothing to do with the Gods," she said, sensing the sadness and rage inside the Warrior, the emotions that pulled him into the dark. After the slaughter in the Order, she could understand why he felt that way. Perhaps he could still be saved from himself. "You're angry," she added. "They attacked us, but you must fight the darkness. Killing innocents is not the way of—" Something flickered in the corner of her eye.

The Angel and Demon of Death appeared at a distance, near a group of fallen humans. Usually, they remained unseen, thoughts inside dying people's brains, but for some reason, the Angel of Death liked Ava and had revealed herself quite often to her.

The Powers were here and at the same time they weren't, and because they existed in non-existence, they weren't allowed to meddle in matters of Earth, Heavens, and Hells. Which meant that Death couldn't stop this madness, only handle the outcome.

The Angel of Death stared at Ava, and her ethereal voice

echoed in her mind like an old lost memory. *"Why do you think you're here?"*

Ava frowned, knowing the answer was on the tip of her tongue, and yet she couldn't reach it. The Angel of Death shrugged, then turned to the dead humans and began issuing their fate alongside her brother.

The Warrior watched Ava with a scowl, likely wondering where her words had gone. He looked around, glancing past the Powers, and shook his head when he saw nothing. "Are you having a meltdown, sister?"

The Warriors around him laughed and jeered.

"These humans are *not* innocent," he continued. "They were consorting with the damned." He walked to Ava, his sword in hand. "What were *you* doing here, sister? Were you also betraying the Order?"

No more.

The crack inside her shook. A waterfall of rumbling gold burst through the gaps, her hidden essence flooding into herself; she could *feel* it.

Ava's vision reddened, blood thumping against her veins. "You're the only damned here," she snarled through gritted teeth.

Without second thought, she boosted toward him, a war cry rushing from her throat.

The Warrior swiveled so quickly she barely saw him. The dry pain of a sword's hilt slamming against her back hit her at once, and she fell with her stomach on the floor.

Warriors were fast, and even with Liam's training, Ava knew she could never win against one.

"Little Guardian, you better stop." His playful tone mocked her. "Lay low, and I won't report you for treason."

Ava let in short, shallow breaths. "You're the one who should be reported." She crouched, pushing herself up, but the Warrior kicked her in her ribs, his movements a blur.

Piercing pain burst from her left side, and she fell with her back to the floor, groaning. Her bones poked at her own organs.

Up above the madness, near the ceiling, Gabriel smacked a punch on Jal that sent him crashing against a wall. They went in and out of focus, her vision blurring.

"Ava!" Liam's voice reached her ears.

He was being held by three bulky Warriors who watched her suffering with glee. The right side of Liam's head was coated in red, the left side of his face swollen. She stretched a shaky hand to him, and Liam growled something akin to a lion's roar as he twisted in the Warriors' grips. "Hellsdamned, let her go! Ava!"

He tried, but he couldn't break free.

Ava's failure to help him hurt more than the strikes she'd taken. So much more.

"Show her, brother," one of Liam's captors said, nodding to the Warrior. "Show them both the true path of the Gods."

Veins throbbed underneath Liam's skin. "Let her fucking go!" he spat, tears in his eyes as he thrashed under their grip. "I'll fucking kill you all!"

Ava smiled at him because inside all that pain and desperation, that turmoil of dark clouds exploding from him, she felt a tiny whisper of light, a gentle tug of love.

For her.

She strengthened her grasp on the hilt, and her sword pulsed repeatedly, almost as if it were knocking on a door, demanding to come inside.

Thump, thump, thump!

Thump!

Ava let it in.

The rush of power took over, her body feeling as light as air. All her wounds stopped hurting, and her broken ribs cracked back in place.

The Warrior licked his lips, watching her with interest. "Not so weak, are we?"

Ava jumped to her feet and charged at him, and this time, his blurred movements were clear as day. She dodged, swiveled, attacked, their swords ringing as they clashed. She stepped back, the Warrior forward, and his sword slammed against her blade.

She pushed it back, then swung hers in a half-circle that sent his weapon flying to the right. Ava could've struck a killing blow. Two steps forward, a blade into his heart and it'd be done. But she chose mercy instead.

"Repent!" she said as the Warrior picked up his weapon. "All of you!"

She felt silly saying it. Obviously, they wouldn't.

"We're not the ones who need to repent!" The Warrior charged with a fury and she blocked him, their blades screeching, but he was too strong and her arms were already shaking.

With one quick strike, he sent Ava's sword flying across the warehouse. Before she could recover, he punched her stomach, and she fell with her back to the ground. He dropped his sword and straddled her, then punched her face, once, twice, his knuckles crashing into her jaw bone.

"Ava!" Liam's strangled roar came from afar. She saw four shapes piling atop him, their forms blurred in a dream-like manner.

"Let him watch!" The Warrior atop her said, his eyes shining pure wickedness as they returned to her. Then came another crash into her right cheek, and Ava saw stars.

A tsunami of molten fire and light rumbled from the rift inside her. This was different from the force that had taken hold of her before. This was a gargantuan behemoth, roaring behind its cage.

Let me in.

All at once it slammed against the thin, cracked line, shattering the rift apart. Its furious waves of light wiped through Ava, pushing against the outskirts of all that made her who she was. The raging light bit into her, hungry, eager to burn *everything* in its path, even if it had to rip her apart to do so.

The innocent ...

They were all dead or had escaped—she could hope. The light that filled her to the brim *showed* her this like a radar: still hearts, unmoving bodies, apart from those that held blessed blades. And then there was Liam.

Up above, Jal punched Gabriel so hard that the Archangel slammed through the wall of the warehouse. The demon locked eyes with her, well, one eye, because the other was swollen and purple.

The light pushed against her, ready to explode and wipe everything in its path. *Not yet*, she told herself, pushing against the ravenous force that would end her today.

She shot Jal a pleading glare. *Save Liam.*

Somehow, he understood.

Jal dove like an arrow, piercing through the Warriors atop Liam, and when the demon emerged, he rose toward the cracked glass ceiling, carrying her charge, her *partner,* with him.

She smiled as Liam screamed her name, thrashing against Jal's grasp, helpless to break free. "Godsdamned! Go back, Jal!" he begged. "Go back!"

They would be safe.

The Warrior atop Ava punched her face so hard that she bit her own tongue. A bitter, coppery taste flooded her mouth.

"You'll die today, Guardian!"

He was right. And she would take all of them with her.

Ava's skin glowed like the sun. The furious waves of fire and light filled her, again and again, drowning her from inside out. Golden lightning cracked in the air around them, veins of light heralding the upcoming beast.

A flash of golden lightning struck a Warrior on the left, disintegrating him. One moment he was there, the next he was gone, nothing but ashes in his place.

The Warrior atop her gaped at the spot and then back at Ava. He wrapped his hands around her neck and squeezed. "Stop it!"

Smoke hissed from his hands, and he jumped to the side, shaking his scabbed palms.

"What in all the Heavens?" he asked with horror.

Her head felt fuzzy, halfway between consciousness and oblivion. She was going to die, of this she was certain. A thin agony spread inside Ava, but it was coated by overwhelming peace.

Liam was safe.

Her lightning cracked louder, whipping into a few Warriors and turning them to dust. But the light didn't threaten to rip her apart anymore. It flowed from her core easily, expanding in a dome around her as quick as a flash.

Ava thought she heard the start of screaming, voices cut off mid-way, and then the smell of burnt flesh, but she couldn't see the warehouse or the Warriors anymore, just white burning around her in golden flares. White and gold, swallowing her completely.

If stars could explode inside someone, this was it. Devoured by light and thunder, Ava drifted into oblivion.

25

AVA

*A*va woke to the sound of church bells.

She got up from her bed, then put on her cotton shirt and dark blue skirt. The cotton was rough to touch, worn from all the years she'd had it, but she couldn't afford new clothes, not anymore. She occasionally missed the soft touch of silk against her skin, but then she remembered the price of comfort, *of going back*, and the longing disappeared.

Ava had been born in high society, and as it was custom, she'd been married at the early age of eighteen.

Her life had been pleasant up until then, but the moment she said "I do" to her husband, her existence became a stream of gowns and balls in the ever-growing city, a bustling parade of golden chandeliers and evil intentions that felt wrong and dirty.

Her husband, Joseph, had been kind to her, and to a certain degree, she had loved him. But the poor begged for mercy and food on the streets, and rich men like him, with their top hats and golden watches, ignored their suffering. They even chortled at times, looking upon those in need with disgust and contempt.

Ava's life suffocated her, and people didn't notice, didn't care, so long as she put up a beautiful smile and a pleasant attitude. Those who claimed to love her didn't see her, like they didn't see the poor that piled up on the streets. She was a ghost to her own mother, to Joseph, and to all of the faces whose names she easily forgot.

When she asked her husband to leave it all behind, to come with her to the countryside and help children in need, he chortled. "They must learn to help themselves, dear." Joseph frowned, as if he thought she'd gone mad, when Ava was seeing clearly for the first time since their wedding. He fixed his cufflinks. "Now go on. We have a party to attend. Much business to be done today."

She left him that same day, and she never looked back. Joseph tried to contact her, but after his first letters went unanswered, he silenced.

And she was fine with that.

Her mother would visit every so often, but Ava knew she didn't tell any of her high society friends. After all, her daughter had become a castaway.

Not that Ava cared. She loved being a cook in the orphanage of the small town of Hergsby.

She had arrived with only the clothes on her body, feeling like it wasn't enough, that she should've taken some money to give to the children. But it had felt tainted somehow, and she wished none of that into her new life.

Sister Mary, who had opened the orphanage door for her, had chuckled at her excuses. "The children do not need your money, child. They need you."

Ava smiled at the memory as she stepped into her small living room, a construction of dark, creaking wood. The place had belonged to the orphanage's head cook, Mrs. Crawford, but she'd died last year and left Ava the little wooden cottage. It might be shabby and old, but it had been a gift from a gone friend. A friend who had *seen* her, and Ava treasured it.

The cold, though, Lord … she hated missing something from her old life, but this she truly did: proper heating.

She went to the kitchen and turned on the old gas oven, then placed a teakettle atop it.

A puffy white landscape stretched outside the window as far as the eye could see. Ava sighed as she pictured today's journey, the same journey she performed every day. She would cross the snow drenched fields, which usually took her thirty minutes, and then there would be another fifteen until she reached the orphanage, which bordered the outskirts of Hergsby.

During summer, the walk brought joy to her heart, but in winter, it was simply ghastly.

Ava hated the snow. It clung everywhere, and it drowned the world in thick silence. She never felt more alone than when she walked through those muted white oceans.

The cold bit into Ava's skin and all the way to her bones as she left the house. Her patched coat was not enough to endure the harsh winter, but she couldn't afford a new one. She could ask her mother for monetary aid, but every time the thought crossed her mind, Ava dismissed it.

'You're the most stubborn woman I've ever met,' her mother had once said. *'Did you truly come out of me?'*

Ava chuckled at the recollection, but her light mood soon vanished. Her steps sunk three inches down in the powdery snow, and the cold slipped through her boots. Her socks became soggy when ice reached her skin and turned into water.

"Lord, give me strength," she grunted.

Time seemed to last forever until the orphanage came to view, a small three-story construction with a gray, peeling façade.

Finally.

As soon as Ava stepped inside, shaking the snow off her clothes, something hugged her legs and didn't let go. She looked down at little boy Charlie, who smiled at her with one missing tooth, his chubby cheeks brushed with soot and dirt.

Ava smiled back, bent down, and took him in her arms.

"Can we have meatballs today, Miss Ava?" he begged with those big brown eyes, his tiny lips pouting. "Billy said he had meatballs once, but I never did."

The Lord might have not given Ava a child of her own, but instead he'd given her fifty who *were* hers, at least in her heart.

"It depends on what we have in the kitchen, sweetheart." She kissed his cheek and let him down. "Now go on." She pointed toward the main room where the younger children played. The older ones must be having classes upstairs. "Go play with your friends."

He nodded and ran to the main room.

Ava went to the kitchen, and then to the storage room outside, where they kept things that rotted quickly during winter. The cold preserved them, so that's where the meatballs would be. But all Ava found was a scarce assortment of smoked meat and chicken, a ridiculously limited amount that was supposed to last the entire month.

Heavens, the children would be close to starving this season.

Sister Mary was waiting for Ava when she returned to the kitchen. The nun's habit covered Sister Mary from top to bottom, which made her resemble a penguin. Her kind, round face wrinkled with a frown. "Everything all right, child?"

"I can't find meatballs." Ava placed both hands on her

waist and looked around. "I'll go quickly to the butcher; perhaps he has some left."

Sister Mary shrugged. "Funds are short, Ava. The children will be perfectly happy with bread and cheese."

"I know." She smiled. "But the butcher has a kind heart, and he's given us some meat in the past."

Sister Mary crossed her arms and raised one eyebrow at her. "I'm not sure if he gave you free food out of the kindness of his heart, dear."

Ava winked at her. "Well, if a bit of flirting gets us the food we need, then I'm sure the Lord will forgive me for this little deception. Don't you think, Sister?"

"I suppose." Sister Mary chuckled. "Go on, then. Do God's work." She drew the sign of the cross in the air, blessing Ava. "I'll see you when you get back."

There were no streets from the orphanage to town, just a path that cut through a thick pine forest. A small car or a carriage could drive the way, but the orphanage didn't have money to buy either. They relied on the kindness of the townspeople to give them rides.

Ava tracked the path until she stopped before Tearwinder Lake. The footway went up the left margin of the lake, and she let out a weary sigh. The right side of the path was open to cold wind gusts and there were no trees to protect Ava, just a nasty fall if she slipped.

Still, she went on. As predicted, the wind stung against her skin as powdery snow slammed on her face, making it numb.

Lord, she hated the cold so very much.

Thankfully, her journey was almost over. She could spot the beginning of town through the woods. Smoke went up from the chimneys, which meant heat. Her heart leaped at the sight.

Little Charlie had been through so much in his life, all the children had. Born in broken families or the result of torrid affairs, thrown to waste like garbage, Ava's children deserved any luxury she could afford them.

If she pushed her flirting skills up a notch, maybe the butcher would give her enough meat for two whole days at the orphanage. Now *that* would be truly grand.

A low whine caught her attention. Uphill, and deeper into the forest, a little fox had been caught in a metallic trap. It was so small, only a pup.

"Oh, you poor thing," Ava muttered.

She couldn't let it stay there. Harmed and cold, it would surely die.

Ava lifted the hem of her dress and climbed up the hill. "Don't worry. You'll be fine," she said to herself *and* the fox, her cheeks flushed and stinging because of the cold.

The little thing whined as she approached. She crouched and depressed the trap springs, setting the pup free, but in its agony, the scared animal jumped over her. Ava dodged just in time, yet lost her balance.

She tumbled backward and rolled down the hill, hitting her back against the snow that covered the path. She bounced like a ball, momentum throwing her off the cliff, and then there was only air beneath her.

She fell for what seemed like forever, horror stealing all the air she would've used to scream, until she hit the hard surface of the lake with a loud thud. Ice cracked underneath her.

Ava's skull snapped and she felt warm liquid bleed onto the cold behind her head, but the spot soon became numb.

Her mind felt fuzzy, and she couldn't move her body. She had to get up, go to town … Little Charlie asked for meat-balls today.

She laid there, freezing. She forced her body to move but

couldn't lift a finger. Soon enough, the cold stopped. Ava couldn't feel her body anymore.

She knew what the numbness meant. For the first time in her life, Ava missed the cold. Tears piled up in her eyes, but froze midway down her cheeks.

I haven't done enough, she thought to herself. *Please Lord, it's not my time yet. Not like this ...*

Slowly, darkness crept from the edges of her consciousness. Her heartbeat slowed, and Ava decided to sleep for a little while. Resting to save her strength made sense, and yet she knew she shouldn't. If she slept, she might never wake up again.

Her eyelids closed anyway.

When she woke, a woman with honey-colored hair and blank eyes was staring down at her. Her kind smile told Ava everything would be all right, even though Ava knew better.

"Can you help me?" Ava asked.

"In a way." The woman smiled at her. "But first, Ava, tell me why you think you're here."

She knitted her eyebrows. "I slipped."

The strange woman nodded but didn't say much, almost as if encouraging her to go on.

Ava swallowed, and her heart skipped a beat—the few she had left. "I'm dying, aren't I?"

"Yes."

Only now did Ava realize that the woman wore a sleeveless dress made of blinking stars. She should be freezing, but she seemed perfectly fine.

"Who are you?" Ava muttered.

"I'm the Angel of Death, and I'm here because you're ready. Your kindness to others has not gone unnoticed by the Gods."

"Gods?" she frowned.

Plural?

"Yes, but who knows if the Gods are three or one? Does it really matter?" She sighed. "Maybe they're light, maybe they're darkness, maybe both. To be perfectly honest, no member of the Order has ever seen them, not even the high angels." She giggled to herself, then crouched closer to Ava as if she was about to tell her a secret. "Did you know that in India they worship many Gods, and one of them is shaped like a blue elephant with many arms? Now, *that* would be exceptional, don't you think?"

Ava didn't know what to say. The Angel of Death made no sense.

"The Messenger might be the speaker of the Gods," the woman continued. "But he simply receives messages from the three Seraph kings in the Heavens, never directly from the Gods, you see. Even Brother and I have never seen them, only the Seraphs. Maybe they are the true Gods …" The Angel of Death watched Ava's confusion and waved a hand in the air as if she were whooshing a bug away. "You'll understand soon enough." She clapped her hands together. "Today you may choose to become an angel and carry out the Gods', well, your *Lord's*, work."

"Or you can become a demon." A man came into view, looking down at her, his long blonde hair nearing white. His eyes were two black beads. "Not that a do-gooder such as yourself ever would."

"Shush, brother," the Angel of Death said.

"She does have the choice." The man turned to Ava. "I'm the Demon of Death, and you should know you can also become a vampire or a werewolf if you don't wish to pick a side."

Vampires and werewolves? Like in the horror books she had read late at night as a child, when her mother was sleeping and the house was quiet?

Before Ava could utter a word, the Angel of Death

snapped, "She's not a neutral, brother." Annoyance coated her tone. "Let her essence speak to you, and you'll see. She has darkness and light, but she does not stand in-between."

"Fine." He crinkled his nose. "This one is so complacent, though. I doubt she'll ever—"

"I think she'll do just fine."

The Demon of Death shrugged, studying Ava. "What do you see in her?"

"Fire." The Angel of Death turned to her and smiled. "I see fire."

The Demon of Death squeezed his eyes at Ava. "Where?"

"I-I want to go back," Ava muttered. "The children need me."

The Angel of Death laid a hand on Ava's cold forehead, and it sent a jolt of warmth through her entire body. "The children will go on without you Ava, regardless of your choice. They'll follow their paths and they will die, like everything in this world does. Most will be reborn as humans again, while some might ascend to the Heavens or descend to the Hells. And few, very few, might be given the choice you have now. So let your essence speak to you."

Everything darkened. Ava couldn't keep her eyes open. "Choose what's inside your heart," the Angel of Death's voice boomed through the darkness.

Ava didn't need to scavenge for the answer. It came to her as easily as breathing. She wanted to help those in need, do good, and thus, she would. The words came out of her more like an instinct, something she couldn't quite control.

"I choose to be an angel," she muttered before giving herself into oblivion.

26

AVA

"*A*va!" Liam's voice came from a long distance. "Ava, wake up!"

His desperation slipped into her skin, a gnarling angst that made her want to scream. She tried to follow his voice but couldn't. Her eyelids were so heavy, she was so tired …

Drifting back into unconsciousness was easy, the darkness and quiet invited her like a warm bed after a hard day's work. Liam's voice was gone now, so Ava slept.

She wasn't sure how long she remained floating in that peaceful void. Perhaps days, perhaps years.

"Ava?" It was Justine's voice, coming from behind.

When Ava turned around, she spotted her friend floating in the darkness. Justine's hair and light-gray kilt flowed around her as if she were underwater.

"Oh thank the Gods!" Justine slammed both hands on her own chest. "You're alive!"

"Apparently." Ava studied the darkness around her. "Where am I?"

"You're unconscious, that's for sure, which isn't good at all. It's been two days since the explosion."

229

C.S. WILDE

"Explosion?"

It came to her as fast as lightning hitting the ground. A sun had burst from within Ava, shining and disintegrating everything in its path. *Except for its creator.*

She glanced at her arms and feet. They weren't gleaming, and she seemed to be in perfect shape. But then again, this wasn't her body, just a mental image of herself.

Or so she assumed.

"The Order and the precinct have gone Defcon one," Justine said. "I doubt the Captain has even slept, and poor Kevin ..." She studied her own feet. "I had to force him to eat; we were all so worried. We weren't sure if you and Liam were alive. The analysis from the clean-up teams didn't show your DNA in the wreckage, so we had hope." Justine's voice failed, and she sniffed back a tear. "I tried contacting you for so long."

Ava moved toward Justine, drifting in the darkness, and laid a hand on her shoulder. "What are they saying about the explosion?"

"It's being ruled by humans as a gas leak."

"And by the Order?"

Justine shrugged. "Ezraphael has admitted to giving you the sword of revelation. He said it was supposed to unlock your powers so you could stand beside him, but he also said you weren't ready. For that he blames himself, and Talahel is asking for proper punishment." Justine leaned her head left and shrugged. "Then again, it was the Sword's watch dog who led the attack on the warehouse without approval, so he isn't exactly free of guilt."

Ava's heart tightened. "You mean Talahel's trying to blame me and Ezra for killing his men?"

Justine knitted her brows and winced. "Kind of. Everyone understands why those Warriors attacked. The In-Betweens killed our brothers and sisters, Ava." She sighed.

"And so did you, because of Ezra. That sword is beyond powerful."

It hadn't been the sword. Ezra's blade had acted as a catalyst, yes, but the explosion, the lightning, all of it had sprouted from Ava's essence. She could *feel* the source of power ingrained within her, always there, always asleep.

Not so asleep anymore.

Ava's blood boiled, and she grasped Justine's shoulders. "Gabriel's Warriors killed innocent humans. They murdered the weak and the wounded, and then they beat me without mercy."

Her friend took a moment to acknowledge this, her eyes wide, her jaw hanging. Justine shook her head and chortled, as if Ava was telling her a joke. "Why would they—"

"Evil has infiltrated the Order," Ava said through gritted teeth. "It weakens us from inside, using excuses of revenge and anger. We must fight it."

Justine shook her head weakly. "All humans who died are claimed to have been victims of the In-Betweens or from your blast. Not that it's your fault," she added quickly. "It's on Ezra. He should've never given you the sword."

Ava glared at Justine, a mass of annoyance filling her from inside. *Was this what Liam felt when he'd tried to convince her?*

"Justine, *listen* to me," Ava commanded. "When did I ever hurt a human, intentionally or not?"

Justine blinked, as if the information was finally dawning on her. She opened her mouth, but the words disappeared midway. Finally, she managed, "I believe you. I'll *always* believe you, but this means we're in monumental trouble. Ezra is the only force against this madness, and he's losing the battle. Instead of punishing Gabriel for his insubordination, Talahel is claiming his actions bring up an important discussion."

"War against the In-Betweens," Ava muttered.

"Yes." Justine held Ava's hand. "Do you think Talahel has been tainted by evil?"

"Either him or Gabriel. There were no Erudites or Guardians in that warehouse, only Warriors. But we can't be sure if more are involved."

"Ava." Justine's voice quivered. "Archangels and Warriors are the *army* of the Order."

She took a deep breath. "I know."

Justine swallowed and straightened her stance. "All right. What do you need me to do?"

"Tell Ezraphael. Tell him what happened in the club; that the wounded and the innocent were murdered by angelic hands. Tell him that demons are tampering with the wolves' wolfsugar and stealing legal blood supplies from the In-Betweens. He must speak with the Gods or whoever sends him messages from the Heavens, and he must trust no one."

Justine nodded, this time avoiding her stare. Ava knew Justine long enough to know when she was hiding something. "What aren't you telling me?"

"The Captain was worried. You have to understand ..." Justine's voice failed. "She put a track on Liam's phone. It pinged back to the Order's servers, but she had no idea it would."

Ava inhaled sharply.

So that's how the Warriors had found them. She and Liam led them straight to Club 23. Before Ava could speak, Justine added, "I went into the Captain's mind when she was distracted." She increased her grip on Ava's hands. "When she lost Archie, it was as if a part of her died too. To her, Liam is what's left of him. I heard her agony, her fears ..." She blinked back tears. "You must understand."

"I do." She caressed Justine's cheek. "She only wanted to protect us."

Justine pressed her lips in a smile. "I'm at the precinct now, but I'll head to Ezraphael's office immediately." She looked to her left as if she were listening to someone, and then she nodded. "Kevin is asking if Liam is all right."

Ava's blood froze in her veins. *Liam.* The image of him being taken away by Jal sprung in her mind.

"I-I don't know where he is." The darkness, before so welcoming and peaceful, now chewed her essence at the borders. *Did they escape in time?*

The light within Ava, asleep beyond the rift, pulsed lazily. *Once, twice.* A violent stir rolled around the void.

"Heavens," Justine muttered, gaping at the trembling space.

In an eye-blink, her friend disappeared.

A loud cracking noise swam across the void, and then the darkness fell around Ava like shards of night. She opened her eyes, and a desperate gasp flooded her lungs as she shouted the most sacred word she could remember.

"Liam!"

AVA

*L*iam was watching her, his green eyes crystal clear, a three day stubble peppering his squared jaw. He smiled down at Ava with a beautiful grin that was half-boyish, half-man, and Ava's shattered world felt right again.

He's here. He's safe.

Relief washed through her, and her muscles relaxed.

"Welcome back, princess," he said as he caressed her forehead, the feel of his skin smooth on hers.

Ava opened her mouth to say she was so glad to see him, but her lips felt cracked and her throat made of sandpaper. Liam noticed her unspoken need. He grabbed a big water glass that stood on the bedside table and handed it to her.

She sat up and drank at once. When she looked down, she realized she was wearing the same flannel shirt and pants of the humans Jal had called priests of the Legion.

The sting of betrayal still hurt. Angels had murdered the innocent and the wounded. Those she'd once called brothers and sisters had behaved like demons. But Ava didn't want to think or remember, and because she tried nonetheless, her head spun. She slammed a hand on her forehead.

"Easy, princess." Liam took the empty glass from her hand and put it back on the bedside table. "You've been sleeping for two days now."

"So I heard." She noticed the question in his face and added, "Justine contacted me while I was unconscious."

Ava studied the room. Dark wooden walls filled with tapestry paintings surrounded them, pictures of heavenly wars and hellish damnation. The wooden furniture, carved to minimal details, belonged to a century or two before Ava had been born. The puffy, comfortable poster bed in which she laid on wasn't from recent centuries, either.

Ava had never been here, and yet the place felt oddly familiar. "Where are we?"

Liam sighed and rubbed the base of his palms along his eyebrows. "It's a long story."

His tanned skin looked unnaturally pale, and dark circles had formed under his eyes. Ava brushed his stubble with her thumb, assuring herself one more time that he was okay.

"When was the last time you slept?" she asked.

He gave her a careless shrug. "About a day ago. I've been dozing on the couch, though." He nodded to the tufted sofa on the opposite side of the room. It looked in worse shape than the one in his apartment.

Seeing Liam so exhausted brought a squeezing pain into her chest. She moved to the left side of the bed, a silent invitation for him to join her.

He scratched the back of his neck. "I'm not sleepy, princess. It's fine."

"It's not that," she said, a desperate plea in her tone.

Ava's world was crumbling around her, but it stopped when Liam was close. She didn't know how to tell him this, that he'd become the only safe and sure thing in her life, but he seemed to understand either way. He nodded to himself and laid beside her, his arms bringing Ava closer to him so that her head rested upon his chest and her body cupped the left side of his.

They stayed this way, in silence, Ava hearing the steady *ta-dum, ta-dum, ta-dum,* of his heart.

This, she figured, this was what the Heavens must be like.

"You wouldn't wake up," he said quietly. "I-I didn't know what desperation was until I shook you and you wouldn't wake up." He took her hand and interlaced his fingers with hers. "I had to lock myself in the bathroom yesterday because it was either that or showing Jal I was having a fucking panic attack." He bit his lip. "I thought I'd lost you, Ava."

"I'm here," she said. "But I don't think Jal would mind if you had a panic attack. He saved your life, after all."

Liam shrugged. "I guess the guy's all right for a demon."

She chuckled, pressing her face deeper against his chest. The sound of Liam's heart made for a soothing lullaby. Ava wished they could stay like this, together in this bed, until the end of days.

"I prayed," he added, his neck strained. "I worked as a Selfless my entire life, but I had never actually prayed. Too skeptical for that, which is ironic, since I'm an angel."

"You are first and foremost *Liam*. The angel part comes after that." Ava snickered. "I can't picture you praying, though."

"Yeah." His chest rumbled in a low snicker. "I prayed for hours, and still you wouldn't wake up. What does that say about the Gods?" He let out a deep sigh. "I saw you glow, and then this impulse burst from you like a nuclear bomb. I couldn't think, couldn't act, I just watched everything burn as Jal landed us on top of the nearest building." Liam stared at the wooden ceiling of the poster bed, his Adam's apple moving up and down. "I felt like I had died with you. It's strange, thinking you're dead when you're still breathing." He cleared his throat and took a deep breath. "Once everything settled, a rain of debris fell down, and Jal dove back into the warehouse to search for you. Half of his body was burned beyond recognition, his left wing pierced and scabbed, and Jal winced, Ava. Not because of the pain he felt, but because I was dead. *Seeing* me that way hurt *him,* the demon with half of his body destroyed. So he went back for you."

She pressed harder against his body, warmth flowing between their skin. Liam pulled her closer, if that was even possible. Right then, kissing him felt like an awfully good idea.

"When Jal came up with you, unconscious but alive, I lived again." He looked down at her with a curious frown. "How do you explain that?"

She couldn't, and she was done with it all. Memories, worries, Ava wanted nothing of that. This Heaven right here was hers and Liam's. It didn't belong to anyone or anything else.

She leaned upward and kissed him. His lips were warm, smooth, and their touch sent delirious tingles across her body, tingles that pooled below her waist.

"I'm here," she said, nudging his nose with hers. "Always."

Liam cupped her cheek, watching her. "I know." He pressed his lips against hers, his tongue venturing into her mouth, setting the fire inside Ava ablaze.

They kissed for so long that her lips felt numb, and Ava wondered once or twice if she had stopped breathing.

She kept giving herself to Liam, taking all of him in return. His tongue, his saliva, his skin, they were also hers. It was painful and delirious at the same time.

"Gods, Ava," he said between shallow breaths and hungry kisses. "I can't stop."

She couldn't either. She didn't want to.

Angelic power increases one's libido. This had been the explanation given to Ava when she'd asked why angels fornicated so often. *Fornicated, had relations, fucked.* Justine had once told her, "There's nothing wrong in saying we have sex or that we fuck, you prude. Geez, why do you have to be so proper all the time?"

Ava didn't know how to be improper; she had never even tried. She had always controlled her urges—often by herself, alone in her bed when it was dark and the world was asleep—knowing that bedding Ezra would be wrong, and that there were more important things than *sex* in an angel's life.

But Liam was a flood of sensation that drowned her. She wanted to be improper with him, so *very* improper. A fire had awakened inside Ava, a blazing madness she'd kept tightly controlled for an entire century. For the first time in her existence, she *wanted* this madness to swallow her.

Slowly, Ava's hand drifted down to Liam's pants, sliding underneath the rough fabric and then his boxers. Her fingers ran over his hardness, and she gasped. Heavens, Liam was big. It sounded cheap and wrong, but it was the truth.

Her hand closed around his flesh, and his body shuddered against hers. Liam looked down at her with hooded eyes, a certain desperation behind them. "Princess, if we start this—" His words vanished when she tightened her grip and stroked his length. He swallowed hard, flinging the back of his head against the pillow as she stroked again and again.

"Hmm, Ava," he grumbled. "As much as I love your hand, this isn't how this will go down."

The fire in her roared furiously, demanding Liam's pleasure. Her partner had been through so much. He deserved *everything*. But he was right. This wasn't how she'd take his release.

Ava raised herself and sat astride him, studying the fierce male under her. She memorized his tousled black hair, his sharp jaw, and those green eyes, usually so sad, now filled with surprise and lust. Oh, they *burned* with lust and she'd claim all of it. They would have sex, make love, fuck, she didn't care; they would have it all.

She leaned down and kissed him slowly, nibbling at his lips. Ava wanted to tease him, draw him to the same edge where she stood.

Liam groaned and sat up, leaning his back on the headboard of the bed. His fingers dug deep into Ava's waist, then her behind, bringing her closer to him. His other hand clawed the back of her neck, pulling her face down and trapping her there, so close. Their lips merged again.

"There she is," he whispered between kisses that left her breathless. "My Valkyrie."

The roughness in his voice was a release all on its own, but when he cupped her right breast with his firm hand, sending delirious shivers down her spine, she realized he was teasing her as much as she did him.

Oh, he would pay for this.

The need, the hunger, the *fire*, took over, and Ava could barely think straight. She yanked off his black shirt, tossed it away, and then fumbled with the buttons on his pants. Liam took off her large gray shirt while she worked on his zipper, and when Ava dragged his pants and boxers down, quickly shoving them off the bed, she had to stop and admire what she had freed.

Liam gave her a naughty grin, clasping his muscular arms behind his neck. He flexed his hips up, highlighting his abs — and *that* exquisite part of him. He knew what he offered; he knew it very well. But his playful manner vanished when his attention locked on her breasts. With a finger, he called her to him, an entranced look tattooed on his face.

Ava wanted to taste his length first, but she would obey him.

For now.

She removed her pants and crawled back to him, pinning Liam once again between her legs. She drowned him in wet, passionate kisses that threatened to destroy her.

His hardness pressed into her entrance. Ava moved her hips up, then down, taking all of him in one starving move.

"Heavens!" she cried as she adjusted to him, her insides adapting to the fullness of his flesh.

Slowly, she began to move.

Liam leaned his head back, inhaling sharply. "Fuck, Ava," he breathed, then drowned at the curve of her neck, cupping her breast, her nipple between his fingers.

Her rhythm increased. *Fuck, fornicate, make love.* This was all of that and more.

She pulled at the short hairs on the back of his head as she hammered against him, forcing them to lock eyes. Ava moved harshly, watching the pleasure beyond his irises burn him as it burned her.

His face crumpled in a mix of pain and rapture that sent her mind spinning, the ecstasy she gave him fueling her own.

"Too good, princess," he growled before wrapping one arm around her. He turned, taking her with him as he slammed Ava's back onto the mattress.

His body crushed hers in powerful moves that felt close to impalement. Liam thrusted with the strength of punches, but oh, she welcomed those thrusts, those movements that lifted her higher and higher until her world spun. Ava's head thumped, and she moaned so loudly that her throat hurt.

The bed creaked with their savage lovemaking—maybe it would break—but Ava didn't care. Her mind seemed out of reach, and when Liam softly bit the skin at the curve of her neck, she couldn't help but rise and explode again, so hard and fast that she couldn't feel her body anymore. She thought she heard herself scream his name, but she couldn't be certain.

"When you come, princess," he said roughly, sweat beading on his forehead as he kept thrusting, "Oh, that's a fucking prayer."

Her intimacy might be crying with joyful tears that slid down her thighs. Wet noises came from below, following their rhythm. She received Liam, again and again, their connection so strong that Ava *felt* the bond they shared for the first time. It was a string of light and warmth, a path into Liam, a path of love and care connecting their hearts.

It might not be thunder striking, but it was *a* bond, and a fine one at that.

She closed her legs tighter around him, clenching muscles she didn't know she had around his throbbing length.

Liam hissed through his teeth, and Ava wondered if she'd hurt him.

"Hells, woman!" he bellowed before bursting inside her in one shattering release.

Ava couldn't help but follow, feasting on his pleasure, taking it as her own. She could feel a part of him spurting into her womb, even after his initial cries and thrusts, and it only fueled her own release.

Once they were done, Liam slumped, still fastened to her. He breathed heavily against her neck.

For the first time since she could remember, Ava was happy. So completely happy. And relaxed. Gods, *so* relaxed.

There was no world outside this room, no threats, no faith, and no damnation. No Ezraphael, either. There was just her and Liam, and the path of love that connected them.

He dropped by her side, taking her in his arms, so that once again she heard the frantic beating of his heart.

"Princess," he said as his breathing steadied. A low laugh rumbled in his chest. "We're pretty good at this."

She kissed the spot below his collarbone, his sweat salty against the tip of her tongue. "We are."

She couldn't remember *sex* being like this, not by a mile. She did have relations with the husband she'd never really loved, over a hundred years ago, but it hadn't come close to her experience with Liam. Relations, intercourse, sure, but it hadn't been a flurry of sensation and emotion that flooded through her. She doubted that if she'd given herself to Ezra, it would have been the same.

This lovemaking was hers and Liam's and only theirs.

They stayed in bed for a while, their breathing the only sound between them. Ava hoped the world had frozen, and that she could stay here forever.

She couldn't believe how close she'd come to losing Liam. If it hadn't been for Jal, her partner would be dead, and she'd be responsible for it. The mere thought stole her breath.

"Is Jal going to be okay?" she blurted.

"Yeah, his healing is just taking longer," Liam said. "Apparently something to do with the light you created. Do you know what it was?"

Ava shook her head, then pressed her cheek onto his chest. "It was me. A part of me, I guess."

"We'll figure it out." He drew soft patterns on her arm with his fingers. "The fact that every demon is evil has been hammered into us since when? The beginning of time?"

Ava frowned. "Your point?"

"Jal is a demon, and he saved us." He stilled for a second, his bands of muscles tightening. "Those Warriors made me *watch*, Ava."

"I know," she muttered.

He sniffed the top of her head before kissing it. "I destroyed the mood, didn't I?"

She giggled. "It was bound to happen eventually." She

looked up at him and bit his chin gently, his prickly stubble tickling the inside of her bottom lip.

Liam groaned deep within his throat, something akin to a lion's purr. "Princess, if you start this fire, we'll have to put it out again."

Ava smiled at him, but as soon as a thought sneaked into her mind, her spirits dimmed, and agony squeezed her heart. "Jal was right. An angel could've killed Archibald. After what we saw ..." Her voice failed.

Liam's heartbeats quickened, and he spoke through gritted teeth. "I need a fucking name."

"When Justine came to me, she told me Ezraphael might be punished for what happened, and that Gabriel and Talahel are trying to pin the whole disaster on him." Her fingers closed into a fist over Liam's chest. "Gabriel was responsible for the attack on Club 23, so I think he might be the one behind *all* of it. Perhaps even the Sword himself is aiding him, but I can't be sure."

Liam was silent for a long while. "It's hard to reach conclusions when we have no proof. Are you sure the Messenger is innocent?"

"He's not involved. I *know* him, Liam." She sighed deeply. "Ezra needs me. I can feel it."

Liam's heart broke. Ava could swear she heard it.

He untangled from her and left the bed, grabbing his clothes from the floor and throwing hers onto the mattress. Then he picked up Ezra's sword from a wooden table on the far end of the room and handed it to her.

The blade felt cool upon her touch and eerily quiet, as if it were sleeping. A brand new brown leather belt followed.

"I don't know how your sword survived the blast," he said mindlessly. "Everything else was vaporized."

"Liam, I didn't mean—"

"We have a lot of work ahead of us if we're to help your

boyfriend, Ava." He avoided looking at her as he put on his clothes.

"He's not my boyfriend." She got out of bed and dressed. "Evil is circling Ezra, trying to crush him. It's clear to me now. I *saw* it when the In-Betweens attacked the Order, and after what Justine told me—"

"Then go to your fucking mate." He threw his arms in the air. "That's what you were going to do once we finished this, isn't it? Go ahead! No one's stopping you. I can finish this investigation on my own."

She stepped toward him, trying to touch his arm but he jerked away. The distance between them stung her chest and left a bitter taste in her mouth.

"Right now, Ezra isn't the Messenger or my mate," she said. "He's a charge that needs my assistance, and you should see him as such."

"A charge? Just like me, then." He shook his head and looked out of the window.

Damned the Hells, her partner could be exasperating at times. "Of course not! It's different."

Her feelings for Ezra remained in the past, and Liam was her present, her future. If only her partner could see that! But nothing she said would convince him. As a Guardian, she knew that well enough.

Time. Liam needed time to understand.

They stood in silence, words needing to be spoken but swallowed back.

"I'm your charge and you care for me." He shoved his hands in his jeans pockets and stared at his own feet. "You confused that with whatever happened ..." He nodded to the bed. "We both did."

"No," she started, but he shook his head, silencing her.

"It's okay, Ava. No hard feelings. We had fun."

She stepped toward him, cupping his cheeks between her

hands. This time he didn't move away, he just peered at her with those sad green eyes. "It meant so much more than that. But Ezra needs me, Liam."

"I need you too," he countered, his voice a whisper.

A knock came from the door, and an old man with ebony skin and a white beard walked in; the same old man who had followed Ava. This time he wore a black shirt that said "Linkin Park" and light gray jeans.

He frowned at Ava and then Liam, clearly sensing the tension between them. Instead of taking the cue to leave, he chose to ignore it.

The old man clapped his hands and turned to Ava. "Well, then. I see you're up."

AVA

*A*va and Liam followed the old man through wooden corridors that reeked of pine and decay.

They had been walking for a while, which meant that they were either in a mansion or a palace. Probably the latter. Ava sent Liam worried glances, but he ignored her. He had done that since they left the room, and Ava hated the invisible wall that had risen between them.

Time, she told herself. Liam needed time.

The old man took them to an inner balcony that showcased a big entrance hall. A golden chandelier lit up the room, and a wine colored carpet rested on the floor below with the golden symbol of the Gods—the triangle within the circle—woven into the tapestry.

The old man led them down a row of stairs, soon arriving at the ground floor. He turned to a door below the inner balcony which opened into yet another corridor. This time, their path was packed with rushing In-Betweens who paced from one room to the next, their voices a mix of exhaustion and anger.

As the old man went on, Ava tried to observe what

happened inside the rooms. In the first to her left, a vampire threw papers up in the air in a frustrated fit. Inside another room, a werewolf snarled and then slammed his paw on a table.

A few humans peppered the madness, wearing the same gray flannel clothing of those who had perished in Club 23. The same flannel Ava wore.

She grabbed Liam's hand and squeezed it. He interlaced his fingers with hers, as if he had forgotten about their fight.

"It's confusing, but they're on our side," he muttered before letting go.

A vacuum birthed within Ava, but she kept a composed demeanor. "And what *is* our side?"

"I'm not sure yet." He gave her a mellow grin. "But at least they're not trying to kill us."

Someone pushed Liam against the corridor's wooden wall, and the surface creaked with the impact. It hadn't been a harsh blow, but Liam stood there, his attention fully on the culprit.

One bulky man with white hair and dark skin snarled at him, his hands balled into fists. *Werewolf.* The stench of wet fur was unmistakable. He had pushed Liam, clearly looking for a fight with a Selfless.

A thorny and angry mass swirled inside her partner; Ava could feel it. The sensation mingled with a red, velvety cloud that hinted at delight. Liam wanted a fight. Ever since they left the room he'd needed to blow off steam. This random werewolf had just given him the chance.

"Liam," she tried, but he didn't listen. Instead, he shot the werewolf a ferocious grin, the muscles on his shoulders and arms clenching.

Before this could turn into a disaster, the old man swiveled around and watched the werewolf with both hands clasped behind his back.

The wolf man immediately bowed to him. "Forgive me. It's been a hard couple of days."

The elder nodded. "Focus on the true enemy, child, not on those who bear no fault. We've had enough of that lately." His tone was eerily similar to that of a Guardian speaking to a charge.

The old man turned and kept walking.

Ava and Liam exchanged a confused glance before following after him. She narrowed her eyes at the man, shooting her Guardian powers forward, hoping they could tell her something about the mysterious elder.

The only response Ava got was a warm tug that playfully tickled the back of her neck, a mischievous smile imprinted on it.

"He's different," she whispered to Liam.

"Different how?"

"I can't feel him." She frowned. "My Guardian instincts can go through any creature, sometimes even through the high angels, but he's just a blank. I think he's blocking me."

If the old man had heard her, she couldn't say.

He suddenly stopped before a big wooden door and turned to them. "Here lies the truth. Once you enter this room, you cannot go back. Will you come in?"

Liam and Ava looked at each other, then nodded. They didn't have much of a choice anyway.

The old man opened the door to a gigantic library at least five stories high. A round glass ceiling showed the blue sky above, the walls piled with books and scrolls of all shapes and colors. And in the center of this cathedral of knowledge, atop a wooden table, sat a woman wearing a moss colored Victorian dress.

Ava saw red, and her fists closed so hard that her nails bit her palms. The light beast inside her snarled, pulsing beyond the rift in her essence, and it wanted blood. *Vampire queen blood.* She glanced down at her sword. It didn't beat to the rhythm, remaining fast asleep within its sheath.

Had it turned into a normal weapon after freeing what it had intended to free?

Lilith ignored Ava's anger as she smoked a slim cigarette propped in a golden cigarette holder. Her red curls graced her plump cleavage. "Well, well." She tapped the tip of her cigar on a glass ashtray. "Took you long enough."

"Behave, child," the old man said as he walked toward Lilith, the irony of him calling an ancient vampire a child not going amiss.

The vampire queen shrugged. "They're not ready."

"It's not about that anymore. The Legion has suffered severe casualties, especially after what you and Lothar did." Ava sensed a bite in his tone.

"Sorry if we grew tired of being murdered," Lilith snapped. She focused on Liam, her neon-blue eyes shifting to ruby red. "In any case, I can *make* him ready."

A cold sting slashed through Ava's chest, and the furious words left all on their own. "If you come near him, I'll kill you."

And she would. She really would. The harmless Guardian, daughter of the Goddess of Love and Life, she would end that godsdamned vampire right here.

And she would enjoy it.

"It's hard to glamour a Selfless, you know." Lilith looked at her own red nails, snubbing the threat in Ava's words. "We need to find their deepest desires to make it work, which isn't easy. Their resilience is stronger than a human's, and boy-toy here is *mighty* strong." She licked her lips. "His key was you, angel girl, and I can use that key whenever I want."

Ava blushed, then quickly glanced at Liam, but he refused to look at her, his face as red as hers might've been.

"I," he croaked, then closed his eyes. "I couldn't get out, I …"

The hurt in his voice clawed at Ava. She glared at the voluptuous woman and fury took over. Lilith had hurt Liam, *defiled* him, and Ava would make her pay.

"Gods forgive me," she muttered as she stepped toward the vampire with a hand over the hilt of her sword.

"Enough!" the old man's voice boomed.

Ava blinked, centering herself. The wrath which had blinded her dissipated, but only enough to allow common sense to take over.

Lilith rolled her eyes, her irises returning to blue. She made a face at the old man. "Darling, why do you have to be such a party pooper?"

Ava returned to Liam's side and took his hand, pressing it against her heart. "Are you okay?"

He gave her a weak smile and brushed her chin with his thumb. "Yeah." Then he straightened his stance and let her go, the soft care in his manner replaced by harsh indifference. He turned to the elder. "You promised me answers when Ava woke."

"Indeed." The old man frowned and paced in circles, as if he were thinking of a way to explain something incredibly complex to them. Finally, he stopped and let out a frustrated sigh. "I'm Seraph Jophiel, King of the first Heaven." He glanced down at his own arms. "Or at least I used to be."

The high-pitched laugh burst from Ava's throat, and all too late she slammed a hand on her mouth. Still, laughter coursed through her body, and she took a deep breath to center herself.

"I'm sorry, that's impossible." She cleared her throat, controlling the remaining chuckles that threatened to slip out. "If a Seraph steps on Earth, he will shine like a thousand suns and engulf the world in light."

The old man watched her with a hint of amusement. "Oh, really?"

Ava nodded. "Also, a Seraph has never stepped on Earth. It's physically impossible because they live in another realm."

"Hmm, such blind conviction." He made a swirl with his hand. "And I suppose you've read this in the book of revelations?"

"Indeed."

"Very well." The elder raised an eyebrow at her. "Ah, you mentioned that I should burn with the light of a thousand suns. Does that sound familiar to you?"

Ava stepped back, her legs weakening as she remembered the light bursting from her core and destroying *everything*. "W-what do you mean?"

Jophiel raised his hands as if in surrender. "I don't know yet. I have come to learn that the Gods keep too much from me, even though I rule the mightiest of their Heavens. It may not be fair, but I do not question them." He nodded at her sword. "None of this changes the fact that you're carrying my blade, young Ava." Before she could utter a word, he raised his palm. "Do not worry; you may keep it."

She glared down at her weapon. *The sword of revelation.* Nothing in the scriptures said it had once belonged to Seraph Jophiel, who probably still ruled the first Heaven while this charlatan used his name in vain.

The old man locked eyes with her, and Ava knew he had read her thoughts.

Heatwaves oozed from him, smashing against her in burning tsunamis that sent her a few steps back. She gritted her teeth as heat burned and swallowed her entirely.

"Ava?" Liam cried, his voice muffled by the thundering roars of light that pushed against her essence. "Ava!"

The sun flares pierced into her core, but soon they stopped hurting. Peace and understanding wrapped Ava at once, and a relieved smile bloomed on her face. Her breathing stopped, so did her heart, and perhaps time itself.

This must be what heavenly light felt like.

"Look further," Jophiel's voice boomed in her mind, and when she glared at him, she felt a mountain of firestorm rumbling beyond what he allowed her to see, the tip of his gargantuan power circling all of her essence. The sheer preview of his light made her legs buckle, but strong hands quickly wrapped around her.

Liam.

"Are you all right?" Concern, pure and true, gleamed in his emerald eyes.

"Can you feel it?" she mumbled, still catching her breath.

Liam frowned, his attention shifting from her to the man. "Feel what?"

"His human body can't cope with my power," Jophiel explained. "I've protected him from it."

Liam raised an eyebrow. "Gee, *thanks.*"

Nothing made sense. According to the holy books, there were three Heavens led by three Seraph kings. Jophiel was the wisest, a creature older than time itself, closer to the Gods than any other being in the Heavens or Earth. The books depicted him as having a long beard of snow, eyes of fire, his skin made of dirt and rain, and when he flapped his golden wings, he created hurricanes.

The elder before them might have white hair and dark skin, but he missed everything else.

"How?" Ava mumbled. "Why?"

"Because his Gods have forsaken him," Lilith said with a wicked grin. "Just like they have forsaken us."

"Lilith, the Gods did not abandon the In-Betweens," Jophiel countered with annoyance. "They simply test you like they do all of us."

She scoffed. "Must they be so cruel? They gave us immortality, but they also allowed the Devils to curse us with blood thirst, turning us into monsters."

"That's because the Gods hoped the In-Betweens would overcome the weaknesses gifted by the Devils, child!" Jophiel's tone was sharp with exasperation.

"Time out," Liam said, forming a T with his hands. "Let's say this is true, that you *are* a Seraph. Why the fuck did you create this *Legion* of yours," he motioned to the room around them, "and why are werewolves and vamps siding with you?"

Jophiel gave him a knowing grin as if he was proud that Liam had questioned him.

"Evil is rising, and the Order can't beat it on its own." He clasped his hands behind his back. "The notion that every angel is incorruptible and every In-Between evil is flawed. It's not that easy, never has been, but the Order refuses to acknowledge this. It has spent millennia ignoring one simple truth: the Gods love *all* their children. Pride can be a dangerous sin." Jophiel clicked his tongue, then turned toward the arched window. "Even a demon can reach redemption if he has good in him. Nothing is black and white."

Ava observed the Seraph who wore a rock band's T-shirt and faded jeans. Appearances could certainly be deceiving.

His back heaved with a chuckle. "I'm a Seraph, child, but I can still appreciate good music. As the King of the first Heaven, I watched most of what happened down here and caught a certain taste for human music."

Well, the King of the first Heaven could definitely read minds; that was certain.

"Why did the Gods send you here?" Ava asked. "Why not send you directly to the Order? If you reveal your light to them—"

"The blind cannot see, Ava. I'm here to prove that most of

the Order's beliefs are wrong. It's not an easy take-over, and it shouldn't be a hostile one, either."

She skipped a breath. Jophiel had spoken like a true Seraph and a worthy king.

"Nothing is simple when it comes to the Gods." He kept watching the day outside, his back to them. "They didn't explain *how* they wanted me to save the Order; they simply sent me here. And they trapped my essence in this body so I could step among you without destroying the entire place." She caught frustration in his tone. "If they wanted a reckless takeover, they would have sent my younger brother, Uriel. Now, *he* has a temper." He shrugged. Daylight created a halo that outlined Jophiel's figure. "See, there's only the Gods' choices and how I interpret them. I could be angry, or I could do what I was sent here to do."

"That's mighty of you," Liam said from behind, his arms crossed. Ava couldn't decide whether his remark had been ironic. "How do the Gods communicate with you?"

"Hard to say. It's light and feeling, mostly." Jophiel turned to them. "I didn't know how to complete my mission when I first arrived here, but now I do. It becomes clearer every day. That's how the Gods work."

Liam chuckled to himself. "What if the Gods are just full of shit?"

Jophiel shot him an amused grin. "What if they are?"

Ava never imagined she'd see her partner speechless, but there he was.

"The way I see it," Jophiel continued. "The Order has to acknowledge its flawed ways before accepting the truth. Only by exposing what's been rotting it from inside will I be successful in my mission. But I can't do it alone." He glanced left and observed Lilith the way a father would. The vampire either ignored him or didn't care. "Besides, the In-Betweens need light and guidance. I believe that's another reason why I was sent here."

Lilith scoffed. "You try to help us, Jophiel, but so far you fail."

His smile didn't meet his eyes. "Then why are you still standing here, child?"

The vampire queen didn't answer.

Liam rubbed the bridge of his nose. "All right, then. How do we solve this mess with the In-Betweens and the Order?"

"Always ready to do the Gods' work." Jophiel studied him. "So much has been taken from you, and yet here you stand."

Liam's shoulders clenched. "How do you know about what I lost, *King of the first Heaven?*" A taste of his fury swam down Ava's essence.

"You used to pray for me, long before you became Liam." Jophiel's gaze seemed lost for a moment. "These attacks couldn't have come at a worse time." He glared at Lilith, and she shrunk slightly under his reproach. Even if she didn't stare directly at him, it was clear she could sense his disappointment. "The Order isn't ready for the Legion and the changes it will bring, especially after the massacres both sides have cast upon the other." He pointed to Ava and Liam. "You however, are already a part of the Order. You must show them the way, and stop the rising evil from within."

Ava's mind spun, bile rising in the back of her throat. The information overload hit her with an unmerciful punch. Her Order, the Order she had dedicated her entire existence to, the principles she lived by, they were *wrong*. And *she* would have to fix them. A powerless, meek Guardian.

It was too much. She needed to get out of here, to be alone. She bent over, grasping for air.

"I need to leave," she said through rushed breaths.

Jophiel approached and took her hand. A jolt of peace

flooded through Ava, and the need to vomit waned. Slowly, her breathing steadied.

"Your principles are pure," he said in a soothing, Guardian-like tone. "You're not what's wrong with the Order. You're its very best, Ava, and yes, you *can* save it."

Tears stung her eyes, her lips quivering. "I-I need to go."

He nodded and turned to Liam. "Jal is looking for you. Go to him. Ava will be fine."

Liam looked at Jophiel and then at Ava, as if he doubted the Seraph's word. Ava observed the elder, sensing there was a reason why he wished to send Liam away.

"I'll be fine," she said, her tone cracked and powerless. *Like herself.*

"I'll show you where Jal is," Lilith said with a chipper tune, resting her cigarette atop the ashtray on the table.

The rift inside Ava rumbled, and warmth spread beneath her skin. She didn't glow, even though she felt as if she were burning. The power, the light, it was inside her, pulsing, ready.

Awake.

Lilith must've sensed it because she stepped back, her mouth shaping an 'O.' Her clear blue eyes glinted with fear, and Ava rejoiced.

"No funny business. I promise," Lilith said, trying to feign nonchalance. But Ava was a Guardian, and she'd tasted the vampire's fear.

It was delicious.

"Keep that promise if you know what's good for you," Ava snarled through gritted teeth, surprised at how fury had changed her manner, and yet pleased at the effect it had on Lilith.

The vampire queen nodded and quickly left the room.

Liam followed her without paying Ava much attention.

The anger that had consumed her vanished, replaced by grey, cold anguish.

He didn't look back. He simply left.

Jophiel laid a hand on her arm, a sympathetic look stamped on his face. "Come, child. The trials of your path have only just begun."

LIAM

*L*ilith led Liam through lush greens peppered by purple and yellow flowers. The mansion formed a square around the garden, shielding it from the outside. The façade was freshly painted, but the architecture had to be at least two hundred years old, like an old French castle put through a renewal.

Scattered butterflies flew gently from one leaf to the next as Lilith led him through a stone pathway lined by thick bushes and exotic flowers.

Soon they walked out into an open field, passing an apple tree on the left which provided shade to a couple of priests. Then came a willow on the right, sheltering a group of young vamps.

Liam couldn't recall the day being so sunny, the sky so perfectly blue. The tingling scent of fresh-watered plants whirled in the air. It almost felt like a dream.

Did Jophiel's Heaven look like this? And if it did, would Liam ever belong there, or even here?

They moved toward a metal gazebo made by thin rococo

decorations that swirled atop one another, the entire frame painted white. Almost like a giant bird cage.

Jal sat inside, at a round garden table that matched the gazebo in shape and color.

Before stepping in, Liam glanced back at the two skyscrapers that towered over the sides of the mansion. With the sun out of view, one of those towers should be casting a gigantic shadow over the garden, and yet the bright sunny day brought all colors of the place to life. In fact, Liam heard zero city noises. No car honks, engines whirring, or people talking.

Nothing.

Perhaps the Legion was shielded from the outside, or perhaps it existed in a parallel dimension—something straight out of the *Doctor Who* episodes he used to watch with Archie on Wednesday nights.

As soon as they entered the gazebo, Jal turned to the vampire queen. "Well, if it isn't my favorite bloodsucker."

Lilith rolled her eyes. "Good to see you too, *demon*."

Thick scabs covered the left side of Jal's face, including his eye. His arm rested in a sling, his grey flannel shirt and pants hiding the burns that covered the left side of his body.

Jal's wings were tattered like a leaf ripped in several pieces, but they looked better than they had when he'd brought Liam to this place. A couple of days ago, the demon had been nothing but ripped, burnt flesh and snapped bones.

"I assumed demons only showed their wings when they wanted to fly, fuck, or show off," Liam said.

Jal shot Lilith a playful grin. "Well—"

"His wings are too damaged to be kept in the darkness," the vampire explained as she watched a butterfly dance over the gazebo's railings.

The demon angled his head and peered at Liam through his good eye. "You know Lilith likes you, right?"

The vamp huffed with annoyance. "I do not *like* anyone." She curled her lips, showcasing her fangs at Liam. "Especially when said someone is an angel."

Jal raised his eyebrows at him as if his point had been made.

"She's not a favorite of mine either," Liam said, disgust oozing from his tone.

His words hurt Lilith; he could see it by the scowl she shot at him.

Good that she was hurt. She *deserved* it. Back at the warehouse, Lilith had almost raped him in front of Ava. And he would have *let* her because he thought he was kissing his Guardian, not the dirty bloodsucker. The simple memory of the vamp's touch irked him.

Jal showed Liam the one free chair across the table, then turned to Lilith and grinned. "Sorry love, but we're out of chairs."

She gave him a fake grin. "I didn't want to stay anyway, *Jal of Jaipur.*"

Lilith turned to Liam, her lips parting into what felt like an upcoming apology. Instead, she snapped her mouth shut and left.

"You must forgive her," Jal said as Liam sat. "It's hard standing In-Between. Sometimes we tend to one side, sometimes the other. I'm sure she wouldn't have gone through with it when she glamoured you."

Liam smirked. "You'd bet on it?"

Jal's grin showcased perfectly white teeth. He had never looked more like a dragon than right then, especially with the black scabs on the left side of his face. "No, I wouldn't bet on it. Vampires tend to be lustful, so maybe she would've fucked your brains out, my friend."

"Are we? Friends?"

"I saved your ass, so yes." A laugh rumbled in his chest. "Besides, Archie has always been good to my people, and I have a feeling so will you."

"Your people?" Liam snorted. "You're a demon, Jal. Don't forget that."

"I prefer seeing myself as an honorary In-Between." He wiggled his brow at Liam.

"Why?"

"History," Jal's voice was a murmur, his playfulness suddenly gone as he watched the path Lilith had taken to leave, almost as if he could still see her in the air.

Liam knew when a subject had to be changed. There was a time for everything and this was not the time to prod about the demon's past. He rested both hands atop the table, intertwining his fingers, then nodded to Jal's wounds. "You look better."

"Don't lie." He glanced down at his broken and scabbed arm. "Gabriel did a number on me, but Ava finished the job gloriously. I've never seen light like hers. Your partner is something else, isn't she?"

Liam smiled to himself, remembering her silky hair sliding through his fingers, her smooth lips, and her delirious moans as she reached her apex beneath him. *Three times.* Princess was insanely responsive. And Gods, that thing she did with her hips ...

A brooding sensation pierced his chest. Even after all they'd been through, after being so deeply connected with her, Ava had decided to stand beside the Messenger. And sure, maybe Ava's Guardian instincts forced her to help someone in need, especially someone she considered a friend —Gods knew why. Or maybe Liam simply wasn't enough for her. Perhaps he was just one of her charges while Ezraphael was the end game.

He blinked and cleared his throat. "She certainly is."

Jal tapped the table the way a judge pounds a gavel, indicating the end of a subject. The demon was more perceptive than he led on.

"I assume you talked to Jophiel?" Jal asked.

"I did." Liam observed him. "Why are you here, Jal?"

"I guessed that was obvious? Being a demon isn't what defines me." He shrugged. "Yes, I was once evil, but if you live as long as I have, the lines become blurred. I mean, it's not like I'm as good as an angel, but I'm less angry than I used to be." He leaned forward. "See, angels need to abide by the Order, but demons live in scattered factions. We rarely unite like you do. Which means we're free in ways you can't comprehend, and yet, we lack purpose, something beyond wreaking havoc upon angels and mankind."

"So that's what you're after. Purpose."

"Aren't we all?"

"Hmm." Liam watched the beautiful gardens as he leaned back on his chair. "So you became a part of the Legion." He motioned to the construction surrounding them.

Jal blew air through his lips. "I did. Though Jophiel is extremely cautious, which unnerves some of the members."

"Like Lilith and Lothar."

Jal dropped his gaze to the floor. After a mournful moment, he said, "The wolf man wasn't all that bad."

"I know." He gave Jal a weary sigh. "Did you at least get what you wanted from the necklace we stole from him?"

"The vision? Yes." Jal scratched the back of his neck and accidentally pulled off a piece of scab. He tossed it on the ground with a flick of his finger. "The psychic saw the Order falling everywhere in the world, all of its branches burning with the main headquarters. A mess of war and blood, coated by shrieks of pain and sorrow. Really nasty stuff."

Fucking demon. He'd spoken as if the vision had been nothing more than a bad dream.

"You seem pretty calm about it."

"I have the Legion. So do you and Ava." After a quick silence, Jal tapped the table. "I still owe you a favor."

"You saved our lives," Liam said. "We're even."

Jal rolled his shoulders. "That was on the house."

"You do a lot of favors 'on the house.' Someone might think you're going soft, demon."

"Oh, but I'm still a creature of the Hells." Jal growled behind his playful grin, a gurgling sound fitting of a beast. He watched the garden for a while, then took a deep breath. "Archie's away right now, but he's also with the Legion."

Liam stared at Jal, his mouth half-open. "What?"

"He is or so I've heard." Jal watched his own fingers. "I haven't seen him yet. He's away on a super-secret mission."

Liam gulped, his heart beating in his ears. "Then you *know* who killed him."

"All I know is what I told you before: a blessed blade killed Archie—this one I heard through the grapevine, and you're welcome, by the way." Liam rolled his eyes, but Jal continued. "I don't think anyone else knows he's with the Legion, not even Lilith. Maybe Jophiel knows who Archie's murderer is, but then again, that Seraph has a tendency for knowing *everything.*"

Liam's fist slammed against the table, making it shake. "Then why the fuck doesn't he do something about it?"

"Isn't it obvious?" Jal frowned. "If he did, he would start a war. The Legion can't fight the Order, not yet. Nor do we want to. We're here to *save* it."

Liam growled in frustration, a sound that resembled Jal's own draconian grumbles. "Then Jophiel should've told me who did it."

Jal frowned at him as if Liam had said something really

fucking stupid. "I assumed you knew your partner better than anyone else?"

Realization dawned on him, and it was a sucker-punch to his gut. "Archie *asked* Jophiel not to tell me."

Jal nodded. "As a demon, Archie's testimony is worthless to the Order, which means you'd have no base for punishment. Killing Archie's murderer would likely get you a death sentence, you know, a very real and *final* one."

"I don't care." Liam bit his own teeth. "I'll kill whoever murdered Archie. Then I'll run, maybe go to that island he wanted me to live on."

He wondered if Ava would join him, but he knew better.

Jal leaned back in his chair, a pleased grin spreading on his face. "Sounds like a good plan. Make sure to jab your blade twice across their chest for me, will you?"

"Hells, yes."

Liam closed his eyes, inhaling the sharp scent of leaves and flowers, enjoying the absence of car horns and any sounds typical to a city. His heartbeat slowed. He could get used to this. Perhaps in another world, another life, this peace would last.

"I feel like I should tell you ..." Jal's voice made him open his eyes. The demon took a deep breath, barely looking at Liam as he spoke. "My psychic saw something else through the necklace."

"What?"

Jal parted his lips but no sound came out, as if he had lost the courage to speak. He cleared his throat. "She saw Ava walking toward the sunset with the Messenger by her side."

Invisible needles jabbed Liam's lungs, but he knew Ava would do what she needed to do regardless of how he felt about it. Hells, that determination of hers, that undying will to help others no matter the cost, it's what had drawn Liam to her in the first place.

He rubbed his forehead, then dropped his arms on the table. "Yeah, I know. Her duty always comes first, and her duty is to help those who need her. It's why I …" He trailed off.

"It seems to me that Ava follows her faith." He pointed to Liam's heart. "It's time you follow yours."

AVA

*A*va bent over her knees on the sidewalk, catching her breath. The mansion before her—a palace, really—was massive at three stories high and at least a football field wide. It had an old, crumbling façade, a missing roof, and a dying garden of dried leaves and dark gray earth. Two skyscrapers stood on each side of the mansion, but something seemed off about them. It was almost as if they weren't there, even though Ava could see them.

Anyone passing by would dismiss the mansion as abandoned, but a tingling sensation thrummed under Ava's fingertips. She could feel the rift inside her pushing against the façade and the towers, the molten gold of the light beast trickling into her.

Jophiel stood behind Ava, waiting for her to regain the ability to form words.

"You've glamoured the place," she finally said, then looked at the skyscrapers that cast no shade. "The entire block, actually."

"It's not exactly glamour." He shrugged. "You know how

angels can mask their essence so humans won't pay attention to them?"

"Being there but not really?"

Jophiel nodded. "Humans can't see the entire block. What you're witnessing is a failsafe because your perception is much stronger than a human's. The Order does the same to its headquarters, by the way. Haven't you ever asked yourself why a hundred story-high building passes unnoticed in the middle of town?"

She turned back to the palace of decay and broken windows before her. "So what does your Legion really look like?"

The elder chortled. "Perhaps after a few lessons, you'll be able to break through the illusion."

She glanced at him from over her shoulder. "Lessons?"

Jophiel nodded. "Come with me."

They crossed the mansion's dead garden and entered the main hallway, going straight to the corridor beneath the inner balcony.

The pathway led them to a round room that split into four dimly lit corridors, each going underground as far as Ava could see.

They took the second path on the right and went down for what felt like an eternity. Soon the path stopped descending, and gray plaster peppered by cold LED lights replaced the dark wooden walls. The corridor's ceiling went up, expanding until it reached at least two-stories high, perhaps more.

An underground facility.

"Why were you following me?" Ava asked, her voice echoing throughout the cavernous space.

He didn't turn back to her. "I could sense how wayward your light became with each passing day. I needed to make sure you were safe."

"Then why weren't you at Club 23?" Poison oozed from her words, fueled by a petty need to hurt Jophiel. Ava chided herself, but the words were already out.

"It happened too fast," he said as they went on, a heavy weight in his tone. "I also couldn't stop the attack on the Order. I should've seen the signs, but I …" He halted, lowering his head. "I wish Lothar and Lilith had been more patient."

She felt his sorrow, boulders pressing on his shoulders. Ava cleared her throat. "You should've told me and Liam about all of this." She motioned to the gray walls. "Maybe we could've helped."

He angled his head, peering at her. "Your devotion to the Order blinded you, and Liam was too angry. Still is, actually." He gave her a small shrug, then walked on.

Big windows showcasing padded training rooms lined the corridor on both sides. This must be where the soldiers of Jophiel's Legion trained.

"So, we're ready now?"

"Not at all," he said. "But life tends to make choices in spite of one's will."

Ava pretended the sting didn't hurt.

"You instructed Lilith to show Liam his memories as Michael," she said. "Why?"

As they followed the corridor, Ava's attention slid toward the enormous training rooms. Duels raged inside most of them, the sounds of battle muted by the thick glass. *Human versus vampire, vampire versus werewolf, werewolf versus human.*

"Lilith was meant to trigger some of his memories as Michael, the ones his body could endure." Jophiel stopped before a training room with padded dark green walls and floor. "It could've been done in a more subtle way, I'll admit." He opened the glass door beside the window-wall.

Ava chortled as she entered the room. "Yes, it could." She paused and then said, "Is he really my soulmate?"

Jophiel winced and clicked his tongue. "Hard to say. Lilith saw the affinity between your essences and likely misinterpreted it. If Liam were your soulmate, the bond would've snapped into place by now. And it hasn't, correct?"

It pained her to say yes.

He gave her a cocky grin. "What you should be asking yourself is: does it matter?"

A smile bloomed on her face as Ava realized that no, it didn't. Liam was still her partner, her friend, her lover. Soulmates were fables and fog; Liam was real, and he loved her. Gods save her, she loved him too.

Jophiel closed the door behind them and knocked on the thick window-wall. "It's been blessed by me. It should hold for our future trainings."

She frowned. "What *are* we training for, by the way?"

"I won't lie to you, child. I have no clue why you have a Seraph's light. The fact you are standing before me is baffling." He intertwined his fingers and tapped his hands softly on his chin. "You're untrained, young, and take no offense, but you're also weak. The light should've consumed you completely."

Flashes of the bloodshed at the warehouse burst in her mind, and then light, flooding everywhere, ripping flesh and bone apart. The only reason innocents hadn't died was because Warriors had killed them before Ava. And the fact that she survived puzzled her as much as it must puzzle Jophiel.

"I feel much better now, thank you." She crossed her arms, uncaring about the irony in her tone.

Jophiel patted the air with his palm. "I have faith in you, Ava, but you cannot control the light or use it to your advantage if you're a lower angel."

She swallowed, her throat closing in on itself. "You mean I need to ascend to Dominion?"

"High angel would be preferable, but I'll take what I can get. It shouldn't be hard. You're almost there. You simply need to acquire one more ability." He lifted his index finger and gave her a mischievous grin.

She shook her head. "I don't want to."

Forcing emotions onto someone felt wrong, even if it was accepted by the Order.

Jophiel straightened his stance and clasped both hands behind his back. His glare was a storm and a placid lake at the same time, and Ava caught a glimpse of the King of the first Heaven, the ravenous force of nature from the books, who now stood mightily before her in a human shell. "Forgive me if I gave you the impression that you had a choice."

Ava looked down at her sword as if looking for answers, or support, knowing fully how silly that sounded.

"I dropped this sword into your plane of existence when the Earth was still young and the Order new," he said, reading her thoughts. "This weapon is precious to me, and now to you as well, but it has freed what it was meant to free. Its purpose has been met."

"The blade is still sharp," she countered.

He gave her a knowing grin, then began strolling around the room, hands behind his back. "Your essence can tap into the powers of Erudites and Warriors. In time, we'll practice such abilities, but today, we'll focus on bringing you to Dominion level." Jophiel motioned for her to sit on the padded floor. "Close your eyes."

She followed his command, hating the fact she'd have to force emotions onto someone. But Ava had to ensure that the disaster at Club 23 never happened again, no matter the cost. In the end, Jophiel was right: she had no choice.

"Take a deep breath," he ordered.

She did. Once, twice. The room fell utterly silent, and Ava had the sensation of floating within herself.

"You have many types of light within you, Ava. We all do. Today, you will search for the light that burned and consumed everything in its path."

"I'm afraid. What happened at Club 23—"

"—can happen again if you fail to gain control." Ava felt his weight dropping on the padded surface in front of her. "We all fear, child. It's the mastering of fear that gives us power. Now find your light. You know where it is."

She took a deep breath and sank within herself. After a while, she found it in the darkness of her consciousness: the pulsing rift that spewed molten gold coated by golden lightning. And inside it, shining like a sun through the crack, lived the light beast.

"Good," said Jophiel's soothing tone. "Let it speak to you."

Ava touched the outskirts of the rift. Golden lightning wrapped around her arms, and she nearly jerked away but Jophiel ordered, "Do not fear."

So she didn't, or at least tried not to. The cracking lightning danced atop her skin, as if it were a puppy begging for her to throw a ball. Beyond the rift, the light pulsed something that felt like a pleased purr.

"It adapts so quickly," Jophiel muttered, wonder in his tone. "Let the light soak into you."

As if it had listened to the Seraph's commands, the lightning dove into her skin, sending a warm, giddy sensation through Ava's core.

"Is it working?" she asked.

"We're about to find out. Use the light to push your emotions toward me."

Ava loved her empathy. It soothed her charges and helped with their pain, but it only worked if they were open to it. Never did she force the words, never did she take over.

"Isn't free will a gift of the Gods?" she asked, trying to steady her quickening heartbeats.

"You're not interfering with free will, child," Jophiel's voice ran with a hint of annoyance. "You're merely projecting your emotions onto someone else."

"It still feels wrong."

He let out an exasperated sigh. "Look for a good memory and push it toward me. That should make it easier for you, yes?"

Somehow, the light knew what to do. It guided her to a well of darkness, diving with Ava down the empty void. After a long while, they hit a black-glassed surface that reflected Ava's glowing figure.

She watched herself floating in the darkness, her body enveloped by a halo of light while lightning cracked around her. Her skin was golden and so was her hair, which floated as if Ava were underwater.

She raised one hand. Her reflection did the same, if only a little slower.

A deep darkness stared at her from beyond the glassed surface. It reminded her of Jal's demonic energy. It oozed cold and desperation as it moved inside its cage. Ava couldn't see it, but she could feel it, a tiger eager to break free.

The lightning around her whipped at the obsidian glass, pushing Ava forward, but she stood her ground.

From an unknown distance, the light beast roared something that felt like a demand. It hit her all of a sudden: the light *wanted* what was behind that glass.

She narrowed her eyes, trying to see beyond the obsidian surface. Darkness, pure and consuming, stared back at her. A jolt of fear swam across Ava's skin.

"Not today," Jophiel warned, his words sharp and on edge. "Force your emotions onto me."

Ava focused, and her light pushed her upward, away from

the darkness. Memories and sensations flooded into her. She saw flashes of her mother caressing her cheek, and Ezra telling her he was so proud. Then little Charlie's hugs, and Sister Mary's soft smile, followed by Justine's fierce loyalty, and then the faces of all her human charges, all the people Ava had helped since she had become a Guardian. And then Liam, kissing her, looking at Ava the way one would look at the Gods.

Tears of joy rolled down her cheeks. "Are you feeling this?"

"No," Jophiel said with a hint of frustration.

The lightning that cracked around her turned to Jophiel in the way of a dog catching a scent. She couldn't see him in the darkness, but somehow her light tracked him. It spread in a pulse, scanning the entire room, including Jophiel's body. Ava could see him even with her eyes closed. He sat with his legs crossed, facing her, his shape made of glittering sparkles against the darkness.

"Spectacular." His voice was embedded with a smile. "Try to shoot your emotions toward me using your light. That should work."

Ava nodded, and her light plunged toward him, slamming into Jophiel. It trailed a path into his consciousness until it reached a massive iron wall that stretched beyond her vision. Ava couldn't actually *see* the wall, but she could *feel* it, endless and indestructible amidst a desert with roaring skies.

The golden lighting that cracked around her sucked her happy memories and then pushed them against the wall. The lightning struck the surface with a fury, but nothing happened.

"I can't break through," she said.

He let out a busty laugh that felt unnatural to a human. "Of course not. Try to make the feelings slip through it. Like a sponge."

That sounded absurd. The wall was massive and impenetrable. It would take some sort of mental drill to even make a scratch.

Still, Ava pushed her light forward, and it swam atop the wall's surface, looking for a soft spot.

Glimpses of a giant old man sitting on a golden throne flashed in her mind. His white beard was bushier, his face made of sharper, merciless lines, his skin the color of bark, but his blue eyes were kind and welcoming. His golden wings must be the span of an airplane, and they shone behind him with such intensity that it seemed the sun was eternally rising behind him.

"Is that you?" she asked.

Jophiel nodded, his form imprinted in her light. "Somehow, your empathy has morphed into telepathy." A certain awe peppered his words. "Follow your essence, it wants to show you something."

By now, Ava's bones should feel like they were rusting, and a monumental headache should spread beneath her skull, just like it did whenever she used Erudite abilities. But Ava couldn't remember the last time she'd felt so good.

Suddenly the wall disappeared, and she was looking down on an Archangel—she could tell because of his wings and his black bodysuit. Ava floated near the ceiling of his dark room. *Like a ghost.*

She had never seen wings like those, with feathers the color of snow. The Archangel crouched by his bed, his hands intertwined as he muttered prayers. She sank toward him, watching the angel from the opposite side of the bed.

His skin was tanned, and his black hair reached his shoulders. She couldn't see his face, hidden behind his fisted hands, but he was shaking and crying.

"Mighty Jophiel, King of the first Heaven, hear my plea," the Archangel said, his deep tone familiar and yet so foreign.

"I must be punished for I've lost my way. Evil is coming, and I can't fight it alone. Mankind cannot fight it alone. Help the Order, oh holy one closest to Earth, leader of the first Heaven. Give me strength for what I'm about to do."

His voice was filled with pain and sorrow. Ava wished to wrap her arms around him and mutter the words of the Gods in his ear.

The Archangel repeated his prayer non-stop until he got tired and leaned back. His face was made of sharp cuts and squared lines that felt familiar, but it was his clear green eyes, kind and sad, that broke Ava.

She gasped. "Liam!"

Her lightning whipped, boomed and cracked, the snarling beast ready to attack and destroy everything.

He's hurt!

"Control it, Ava," Jophiel demanded.

The lightning growled at Jophiel, refusing to obey. It charged the air around them with electricity, gaining momentum for the inevitable blast.

The release of the beast.

"You won't burst again, Ava," Jophiel said calmly. "Believe this."

She didn't. That storm of light raged inside her; Gods, she would explode and take out the entire Legion.

"Help me," she croaked, her body shaking.

"Do. Not. Fear." His voice boomed around her, digging into her bones.

Liam was in the Legion, and if she went off, she would kill him. She would kill *everyone*. So Ava focused on his smile, and then on his thumb brushing her cheek. The kisses that had trailed blazing paths across her skin only a few hours ago.

A sense of peace flooded her, soothing her fears *and* the beast at the same time.

Slowly the lightning calmed, and then all at once it snapped back into the rift inside her, leaving Ava feeling empty and alone.

"Wonderful!" Jophiel clapped. "We made great progress today."

"Did we?" Ava opened her eyes and glanced sideways at her shoulders.

No wings.

He blew air through his lips. "You didn't expect to become a Dominion after your first lesson, did you?"

"Are you guys meditating or something?" Jal's voice came from the door.

Ava turned around to see him and Liam entering the room. She wanted to run to her partner, trap him in her arms and never let go, but Liam didn't even glance at her.

"I called the Cap," he said, hands shoved in his pockets, eyes on the floor. "I'm heading back to the precinct. I gave Kev the lead on Gabriel and Talahel, so let's see what he comes up with."

"Don't worry, pretty angel," Jal added. "I'll make sure your partner doesn't get into trouble."

Ava frowned at Liam. "You're taking a demon to the Nine-five?"

"Not *to* the precinct, only to the vicinities." He tapped Jal's good shoulder.

"The truth is I need fresh air," Jal said. "Our garden gets boring after a while."

Watching Jal's body was hard. Half of it was covered in scabs, his wings tattered and burnt. Surely, not all of this was her fault, but Ava's light had wounded him so much more than Gabriel's attacks.

"I'm so sorry," she said, her voice a whisper.

"Don't be." He shrugged. "I'm fine, angel girl."

She stood up and stepped toward them. "Well, let me join you. I'll be glad to help in any way I can."

"He's been praying to me," Jophiel said as he stood from the padded ground. "He's praying right now, but he's not ready to listen. Not to me, at least."

"Who?" she asked, but deep down, she knew who he meant.

Ezraphael.

"The Messenger is drowning in the darkness around him, Ava. I know you can also feel it. It has already begun taking over. You must do what feels right to you." Jophiel pressed a hand against his heart. "But without you, Ezrapahel *will* succumb to the darkness."

She turned to Liam. Her Guardian instincts told her that the veil of nonchalance behind his eyes only masked a world of hurt.

"I have to," she said, her legs suddenly weak.

He raised his head and stared at her. *Into* her. "I know."

"I'll meet you at the precinct once I talk to Ezra, I promise." She shot him a supportive grin.

"It's fine, Ava. You wouldn't be who you are if you didn't help someone in need. Focus on that." He scratched the back of his neck. "But you're not stepping inside the Order. Not until we know who in there killed Archie. It's not safe."

Jophiel closed his eyes and silenced, as if he were listening to a song no one else could hear. Finally, he opened his eyes. "Ezraphael isn't at the Order."

AVA

*E*zra stood on the ledge of a building's roof. He watched the city below, clearly ignoring Ava's presence behind him. A soft wind tousled his long silver hair, which was odd. Ezra rarely let his hair loose, and if anything, the Messenger was a creature of habit.

The feeling that something wasn't right thrummed in Ava's bones.

She stepped forward, and he slowly turned to her. At first, he watched her as if he couldn't believe she was here. Like Ava was a dream. A cloud of anguish swirled inside him and prickled against her essence.

"Ezra," she started, but the moment he heard her voice, something snapped inside him.

He rushed toward her without warning, closing Ava in a tight hug, his fingers digging into her skin.

"I'm so sorry," he said, his voice muffled against her hair. "I shouldn't have given you the sword of revelation."

Ava didn't know what to do. Her hands remained frozen midway, uncertain if she should hug him back or not. She settled with, "You should've told me the truth, Ezra."

He let her go and stared at her, hurt wrinkling his forehead.

Only now did she realize how Ezra had changed. His sky-blue eyes had turned opaque, his cheeks were sunken, and his skin was paler than usual. His once lustrous silver hair had lost its shine, the strands oily and glued together.

The Messenger was a shell of the mighty angel he'd once been, and still that fierce beauty remained, even if faded under a stale, worn façade.

Heavens, what had happened to him?

"My intentions were good," he whimpered. "I only wanted to boost your light. I needed you to be strong so you could stand by my side."

She held back a contemptuous snort. "The path to the Hells is paved with good intentions, Ezra."

"So goes the saying, but …" He blinked, then shook his head. "I needed *you*, Ava. So much. I've been the Messenger for an eternity, sometimes I …" He lowered his head. "Sometimes I forget things that should've been ingrained within my essence. Things that come so naturally to you." He took her hand and pressed it against his chest. "Ava, you remind me of the Guardian I used to be. I hope you'll still consider becoming my mate."

She jerked her hand away and stepped back. "How could I possibly—"

His pain burst from him and slashed Ava in a thousand pieces. Ezra didn't deserve her anger or her despise. Not long ago, she had looked up to the Messenger, trusted him with her life. *Her heart too.*

The kind man she once loved was still there, inside this broken and frail angel. Ava simply needed to bring him to surface.

It might doom her someday, this indestructible need she

had to help others. But she couldn't leave Ezra, not when he needed her the most.

"You need help," she said. "I won't deny that to you."

"Thank you." Ezra gave her a brief smile, then noticed her gray clothing. "What happened to your uniform?"

"It doesn't matter." She stepped closer. "Did Justine come to you?"

His throat bobbed, and he turned away.

A flash of despair flicked through Ava. "Ezra, what did you do?"

"The words Justine spoke are sacrilege," he said through gritted teeth. "The Order, *my* Order, has not been tainted by evil. Those humans weren't innocent. They were siding with the In-Betweens like Gabriel said. It was a blessing you killed them all with your light."

"The Warriors killed them, not me!" Her voice broke. "How can you say that a *massacre* was a blessing? You're the Messenger, the most merciful and loving angel in the Order!"

Had Ezra been brainwashed? Gods, was he so far gone?

Maybe she couldn't save him. The bitter tang of failure made her stomach clench, and cold sweat beaded on her forehead.

Ava bit her teeth, and closed her hands into fists. She was a Guardian, the best in all the Order. She had never given up on a charge, and she wasn't about to start now.

Ava took a deep breath and focused on the matter at hand. "What did you do to Justine?"

"I put her in detention, of course." He avoided Ava's furious glare. "It was a merciful decision. The sacrilege she spoke of demanded her head."

Ava gasped and stepped back. "There's evil in your words. Madness too."

"Ava, please ..." His eyes glistened with tears. "Can't you

see our faith is being tested? This is the moment we need to remain strong."

Ava nudged her own heart. "My faith is just fine. *Yours* is the problem."

He threw his arms up in an exasperated manner. "Those creatures killed our brothers and sisters! They painted the hall red with their blood! I wished to forgive them, to think they didn't know better, but Talahel helped me see." His tone wavered. "Sometimes, we must be ruthless."

She slapped him with all her strength. It didn't affect him much; his face barely moved. But he stood there, frozen, his eyes wide as if he couldn't believe she had just done it.

"Who are you?" she spat.

Ezra blinked, his eyes glistening. He turned to Ava and ran a hand through his hair, his chest heaving up and down. He tried to speak but no words came out, so he crouched down and interspersed both hands, pressing them against his forehead in prayer.

"I don't know what to believe anymore." He held a sob, his body trembling. "I feel like I'm choking on air."

A bitter sensation crawled up Ava's throat, regret for slapping him when he was already so weak. "You're the Messenger. Leader of all Guardians, the strongest child of the Goddess of Love and Life. The best angel in the entire Order. Do not forget who you are, Ezra."

He rocked on his heels, back and forth, and Ava doubted he had listened. So she knelt beside him and laid a hand on his back. She summoned the light from her rift. If she was to soothe a high angel, she would need a lot of it.

"The Gods are with you," she muttered as she pulled the light. Golden wisps sparkled around her palm before merging into his skin. "And you're with the Gods."

He closed his eyes, taking what she offered. Slowly, his body relaxed.

"Your touch is a blessing," he whispered.

But something inside Ezra caught her light's attention. The cracking lightning that lived inside her flowed through their connection, diving deep into his consciousness until it found an ivory wall weaker than Jophiel's. The lightning whipped and cracked against the surface.

Ava ordered the light to return, but it ignored her command. It scanned the wall through its unending length until a scene burst into Ava's mind.

Ezra paced around a big room made of ebony marbled walls that resembled the night sky.

Talahel observed him through predatory hazel eyes. The Sword's orange hair was tied in a long braid behind his head, the sides of his temples shaved, making him resemble a Viking warrior from history books. Swirling tribal tattoos decorated his skin on both sides of his head.

"I'm going to the hospital to heal that Selfless," Ezra said.

Talahel leaned on a wooden table with a big fruit basket atop it, his entire body wrapped in a wine colored bodysuit that neared black, almost mingling with his obsidian kilt. His orange wings lazily stretched behind him, and Ava gasped.

Angels only showed their wings if they wanted to fly, fuck, show off, or *fight*. And by Talahel's weary stare, he was preparing to do the latter.

"Then you'll need to heal every Selfless who falls in the line of duty until the day you stop being the Messenger." Talahel shrugged. "How long was Cassiel the Messenger before he gave his place to you and went into his long sleep?"

"Two thousand years, give or take."

"That's a long time healing an endless stream of angels. You won't be able to keep up with your normal, and much more important, tasks, brother."

"It's not fair, Talahel! The Selfless fight with us in the battle against evil. We can't let them die just because it's convenient for us," Ezra said, anger all over him. "Archibald Brennan was horribly injured. He did not deserve such a fate."

"Their deaths are always cruel," Talahel countered matter-of-factly. "Your mercy is admirable, but remember that Archibald will be reborn as the Archangel he used to be, and he'll become more useful to us." He took a grape from the fruit basket and popped it into his mouth. "As has always been the way."

"I never liked *the way*," Ezra grumbled, but Talahel's words seemed to poison him. Eventually, the Messenger's shoulders slumped. "I suppose you're right."

"Do not worry. I will watch over his sacramented body until he wakens as one of us." Talahel's eyes glinted with something calculating and cold that sent chills down Ava's spine. "We'll find whoever did this to him. I have a name in mind, a demon who stands with the In-Betweens."

"Jal." Ezra sighed. "Find proof and then act. In the meantime, I'll assign my best Guardian to help Archibald's partner. It's the least we can do."

Talahel bowed at him, a mockery in the way he did it. His wings disappeared in a flash of light, which meant he didn't see Ezra as a threat anymore. "Your mercy knows no boundaries, brother."

Ava blinked, returning to the roof and the crouching angel before her. She looked around and noticed that Ezra's wings had spread around them, forming that familiar cocoon.

A part of him must've sensed the menace of Talahel, if only too late. *His first instinct is always to protect*, she realized with a certain pride.

Ezra opened his eyes and looked up at her. "Thank you, Ava." The smile he gave her oozed with adoration. "I feel better now."

C.S. WILDE

Ezra hadn't seen what she'd seen, or else he would be glaring at her the same way she glared at him. He didn't know about Talahel, or maybe he wasn't ready to know yet.

Ava understood Jophiel's intentions now. The Messenger, through his kindness and mercy, could pave the way for the Legion. The peaceful transition the Seraph had mentioned.

Ava simply needed to remind Ezra of who he was. But right now, he balanced on a thin line, and any small blow could turn into a fall that would doom him.

Her chest prickled when she took in the full meaning of this. If she refused to become Ezra's mate, she would send him down a path that could end him. *And the Order.*

"You need to free Justine," she said, her throat dry and her heart aching. "She merely spoke the words I told her, the words you need to understand before I'm to side with you."

He nodded. "Consider it done."

Ava wanted to run into Liam's arms, go back to that bedroom in the Legion where only they existed. Her eyes stung with tears she couldn't shed, not here, not in front of Ezra.

She had a duty, not to the Gods, not to the Order or the Legion, but to everything she fought for, everything that she was.

A friend. A Guardian. His savior.

Ezra leaned forward and kissed her forehead in that kind, warm way that had always soothed her before, but now Ava didn't know what to feel.

"I believe you, Ava. But if there's evil within the Order, I'll need all the help I can get. Will you stand with me?" he asked softly, watching her with a plea.

The words hurt as they left Ava's throat. "Yes, I will."

LIAM

*L*iam and Jal followed the sidewalk toward the precinct. The demon rambled about great feats of his past—he'd once spent seven days shoved inside a brothel in Amsterdam learning the arts of the flesh with Madame Daan, and he'd also sailed the Andaman sea, surely Liam, you should try that once—but never did he address why he helped the In-Betweens.

Liam was glad that Jal felt well enough to babble, but his mind simply wasn't there. So he murmured absent "Hmms" as they went, only half-listening to what the demon said.

He did notice the girls, though. Almost every woman they passed shot them smiles of pure lust, especially at Jal.

Demon appeal, he guessed.

Liam narrowed his eyes at the scabs covering half of Jal's body. "Did you turn into some Hollywood star when you masked your essence?"

"No, they just see my unscarred, gorgeous self." Jal grinned at two passing brunettes. "The heart doesn't feel what the eyes don't see, my friend."

The demon fixed his hair and puffed up his chest. The

brunettes blushed and giggled, their hips moving in sensuous waves on purpose. Jal spun around to watch them go, his gaze lingering on their waists.

Liam was no stranger to flirting. If this was a normal day, and his entire world hadn't been turned upside down, he would have removed his leather jacket and hung it over his shoulder, showcasing his biceps and tight frame. *The perks of years of training and fighting for the damn Gods.* It did the trick most of the time, and it had gotten him some fine one-night stands.

But everything had changed. He didn't need random women; he needed his fierce, kind Guardian, the angel who had shown him a happiness unlike any other. A smile spread on his lips at the memory of his Ava, her soft lavender scent, her kind smile, and the smoothness of her curves, the softness of her skin ...

His Ava?

She was meeting with the Messenger, and she would be by *his* side now. Liam's fists clenched and so did his jaw.

"If it helps," Jal said, drawing Liam from the angry mass that clouded his thoughts, "I don't think they're having sex."

Liam snapped his head at the demon, his nostrils flared. "I didn't think they were until now!"

"My bad." Jal showed him his palms. "You should be prepared for the worst, though. I mean, he's a handsome guy, that's all I'm saying."

"Stop with the dumb-ass comments, asshole," he grumbled. "Fucking demon."

Jal gave him an amused chuckle and patted his back.

They soon neared the block of the Nine-five, and relief washed through Liam. He already needed a break from Jal. Maybe the demon was trying to make him feel better in his own, twisted, demonic way, but he was failing spectacularly.

"All right." Liam turned to him. "You stay here. I can't waltz in there with you."

"Oh, come on. I can mask my essence like I'm doing right now. They wouldn't know."

"We can smell a demon from a mile away." Liam chortled. "You all stink of sulfur."

Jal craned his neck and peeked at the precinct's entrance. "Seems fine to me."

Liam followed his gaze to the empty sidewalk before the precinct. *Odd.* Usually, Danton and Wheeler would be having their four o'clock smoke by now. But there was no sign of them at the entrance and no inflow of Selfless carrying In-Betweens in special cuffs, either.

Liam shook his head. The boys had probably left early, lazy bastards that they were.

"Look, the Captain will be breathing down my neck as it is," Liam said. "And I don't want to piss her off any more than I have to. So you stay right here, you hear?"

"Aha, so that's why." The demon laughed. "You're scared of *mommy.*"

Liam punched Jal's broken arm. The demon growled in pain, cursing him in a bunch of ancient languages.

Who knew punching Jal could be so liberating?

Liam's chest rumbled with chuckles as he left the demon behind.

He stopped by the stone stairs that led into the building, hoping to find the butt of a cigarette or at least a trace of ashes, any indication that Danton and Wheeler had been there. But the floor was spotlessly clean.

It made no sense. Those two smoked like chimneys.

He took the elevator up to the precinct, warning bells echoing in his head. His hand went to the hilt of his sword.

The doors opened to a deserted office space. Well, it

wasn't exactly deserted. Kevin sat on a chair in the middle of the room, his head hanging low.

Relief washed over him. "Kev, what in the Hells?"

Liam stepped forward, and his feet slipped on something slick. If he hadn't leaned over a nearby table, he would've smacked his butt to the ground. He regained his balance only to spot a pool of blood below his boots.

Something inside him cracked.

He glared at Kevin, who had raised his head to watch him. A purple blotch marred half of the boy's face, and his chest heaved up and down in the way of a scared deer. His entire body shook as a stream of blood flowed down his left temple.

Liam didn't know who'd done this, but he would fucking kill them. He grunted a curse and unsheathed his sword, then walked toward Kevin, every step a meticulous move.

Once he got close enough, he whispered, "What happened?"

"H-he tapped the Cap's phone. He knew you were coming." Kevin nodded left but didn't look. "He stacked the bodies inside the cell."

A void ate Liam from inside as he found a pile of corpses inside the bars. The people he had trained with, the brothers and sisters in arms he'd greeted every morning … they were gone.

The entire precinct. He had slipped on their blood.

"He said—" Kevin's voice broke, "he said they'd be more useful to the Order as angels. That humans were weak." His breathing sped up and hitched at the same time. "He made me watch, Liam."

"Where is he?" Liam growled, his teeth clenched.

Whoever *he* was, *he* would die a horrible death today.

"With the Captain," Kevin whimpered. "Waiting for you." He grabbed the fabric of Liam's jacket, tears tracing thin rivers on his blood-splattered cheeks. "Don't go. He'll kill you too."

"Kevin, listen to me," Liam whispered. "I need you to stand up and run. Now."

"He said they were starting with the main trunk of the Order, and then they would spread their way across the other branches, across the world." He swallowed. "We have to stop them, mate."

"We will." He snapped his fingers before Kevin, hoping this would grab his focus. "But right now, you need to run."

The boy shook his head. "I won't leave you alone with him."

"Kevin," Liam said patiently but with enough edge to show him this wasn't a discussion. "Now."

It took his friend a moment to center himself, then nod and stand. Kevin got up and rushed toward the elevator, limping on his left leg. Liam guessed whoever had done this had twisted Kevin's ankle to slow him down, to make him powerless enough to watch all his friends die before him.

The level of cruelty here was the same Archie had faced. Whoever stood inside the Captain's office had murdered his partner, of this Liam was certain.

He held his sword so tight his knuckles turned white. *Time for reckoning.*

He heard the elevator door close behind him and sighed in relief. Kevin was safe.

Liam stalked toward the half-open door of the Captain's office, his entire body shaking with anger.

He pushed it open to find the Captain sitting on her chair, her lips pressed into a line. Darkness instead of eyes gaped at him, her empty eye sockets crying blood. The right side of the Cap's face was almost black from being punched too hard.

His stance dropped as furious tears threatened to come

out. The Captain's voice snapped in his mind, a memory from when he'd first started as a Selfless. *"Keep your guard up! Distractions can cost your life, kid."*

Sure thing, Cap.

He tightened the grip on his sword and closed his stance.

Beside her stood Gabriel, holding an empty whiskey glass. Lava burned within Liam, hissing and hungry. This bastard had killed his precinct, and he'd taken out the Cap's eyes.

"It took you long enough, brother." Gabriel set the glass on the table, next to the Captain, then picked a whiskey bottle from Cap's stash and poured. He took the glass and dropped himself on the leather sofa near the wall.

Even so injured, the Cap didn't scream. Her breathing was calm and steady, but her bloodstained fingers clawed at her wooden desk.

A mountain against an unending storm.

She frowned at Liam and then shook her head. "You shouldn't have come, kid," she said, her voice a shuddering whisper.

"Let her go, Gabriel," he demanded. "She has nothing to do with this."

"I'm not leaving you alone with this *demon*," the Captain snarled.

An annoyed frown creased Gabriel's forehead as he sipped his whiskey. "You're blind, Selfless. Do tell me how you can save your precious *boy?*"

The Cap bit back a remark because the truth was, she couldn't. No one could help Liam now.

"Stubborn and stupid, just like that lover of hers." Gabriel grinned at her empty eye sockets. "Archibald, wasn't it? Utterly useless, the both of them."

Liam's lips curled into a snarl. "You fucking—"

"Spare me the rough linguistics of the Selfless. You

brought this upon yourself, brother," he said. "All because you had to grow a conscience, you pathetic fool."

Liam gulped. Even though his anger demanded Gabriel's blood, he knew that defeating an Archangel, even with a lot of luck, was pretty fucking impossible. Which meant he would have to be smart, especially if he wanted to save the Captain.

He sheathed his sword. "I see it now," Liam said, not knowing exactly what *it* was.

Gabriel's eyes gleamed with hope. "You do?"

Liam nodded. "Humans are weak. This world should belong to angels."

Gabriel slapped his own leg. "You saw the truth once. I knew you'd see it again!" He swallowed the rest of his drink, leaned forward, and slammed the glass on the Cap's table. "Prove it."

Liam looked from him to the glass. "I don't understand."

"Prove to me that you see the truth." He nodded toward the Captain. "Kill her."

"She will die in her own time. She doesn't matter to us," he inhaled and added, "*brother.*"

Gabriel peered at him, variables running behind his cruel eyes. "I can still hear your partner's screams, you know. Such beautiful symphony."

Liam's blood boiled and froze at the same time. The urge to rip Gabriel's head from his neck flooded him, but Liam kept a composed stance. This was a test, and he had to pass.

Gabriel leaned back on the leather cushion. "Archibald had an air-tight case linking me to a couple of human murders. A few unauthorized In-Between takedowns too." His eyes darkened. "The Throne would cut my head off for that. She's not on our side, not yet."

"I'm sure Talahel would've saved your ass," Liam countered.

"He would've tried. But the proof was right there, and the Order is still, well, blinded. Too many don't see the way, but that will change in time." He chuckled at that, nodding to the Captain. "Archibald was going to the Messenger and the Throne to expose me. I couldn't let him."

"So you murdered him." Liam's nails bit into his palms. "Why did you torture him? You didn't have to, you sick fuck."

He shrugged. "Well, it was just so much fun."

Gabriel stood, patting his black Archangel's bodysuit. He only had one belt around his waist, a holy gun and his sword hanging from it. Usually Archangels were packed with weapons. If Gabriel carried only two, it meant he didn't consider any of this a challenge.

An entire precinct ...

"When I came back to finish the job," he added, "Archibald's sacramented body was gone. But I'll find him, I promise you."

"You know the demons are using you, right?" Liam said, ignoring Gabriel's threat. "They're starving vampires and drugging werewolves to increase attacks on humans, making the Order strike the In-Betweens without mercy." He shook his head and slammed both hands on his waist. "Can't you see? The dark is making half of the opposing army annihilate itself without lifting so much as a finger. And you're *helping* them, you idiot."

"What *I* want is a world without In-Betweens and humans, brother. Eventually, without demons as well." He rolled his shoulders. "One step at a time. Sure, a few angels might fall in the process, but the strongest will remain."

"Gabriel, please, you—"

"I'll make this easy for you." He pulled the Captain's chair and grabbed her arm, forcing her up. "If you want to save this precious human, follow us to Dock 5."

Gabriel withdrew his holy gun and shot five times at the

window. The sounds of the blasts mingled with the shrieks of glass cracking and the hollow thud of crumbling concrete. When the Archangel was done, blue smoke crowded the spot, soon revealing a gaping hole in the wall where the window used to be.

"If you see the truth behind my cause, don't come," Gabriel said. "Let her die. It's easy, you know. I'll do all the heavy lifting."

The Cap turned a little too much to Liam's left. "Don't come, kid. I'll be fine."

"She won't, of course," Gabriel chortled. "I won't lose hold of another sacramented body. I'll kill her, and then I'll give her the final death once she wakes as an angel." His brown eyes glinted with insanity. "Time to prove yourself, brother."

"You fucking monster," Liam spat, his every muscle clenched, a void biting at his gut.

"Your *papa* called me worse things," Gabriel sneered. "Try to keep up, will you?"

A flash of light revealed his sea-green wings, and then Gabriel boosted out of the precinct with the Captain in his grip.

33

LIAM

*L*iam's breathing echoed in his eardrums as he rushed through the empty streets that led to the docks. He smelled seawater, and soon enough, the harbor came to view.

He patted the two holy guns hidden beneath his jacket, then his sword, and the two sun daggers on his belt. Before he'd left the precinct, he'd made sure to pack enough heat. This might have given Gabriel a few minutes of advantage, but if Liam was going down—and he knew he would—he'd go down with a bang.

He had run into Jal and Kevin on the way, but he'd wasted enough time getting his weapons. As Liam ran past them, he'd shouted, "Dock 5, get help!" and that was it. He didn't stop, even when they begged him to, and soon enough, their pleading voices faded in the distance.

Now here he was, ready to face his end.

The place was eerily empty. Seagulls' caws rung in the distance, and a soft breeze caressed his skin. Fading sunlight drenched Dock 5 in dim orange.

"Gabriel!" Liam shouted as he threaded the space, his

sword in hand.

No reply. He turned left near a container and found him.

Gabriel watched the canal and the city that stretched beyond it, his sea-green wings folded behind him. Not far from the Archangel, pinned to a red container, was the Captain, her hands and feet nailed to metal, shaping a cross.

She hung there, lifeless, her mouth hanging open, her empty eye sockets staring back at him.

Blood rushed to his head and he gasped, sniffing back the tears. "Fuck!" He looked away, but the scream still burst from his throat, a mix between a sob and a howl.

If only he hadn't stopped to grab the weapons ...

"Then we'd both be dead," the memory of the Captain's voice echoed in his mind.

She would have also told him to run from here as fast as he could, but that, Cap, he couldn't do.

Liam swallowed back the tears and focused.

"Why do you feel her death so?" Gabriel asked without turning to face him. "At least she'll be reborn as a Virtue. I believe that's what she used to be. The Powers have likely already blessed her deep in her mind. She'll enjoy a few moments as an angel before I finish her off. Now *that's* true angelic mercy, brother."

Liam raised his sword. "You'll be dead by then. I won't let you kill her twice."

"You saw the path once." Gabriel turned to him, hands behind his back. He clearly didn't see Liam as a threat. "You were one of us, but you betrayed me."

"I'm *nothing* like you."

Gabriel smiled and walked to him. Liam didn't step back, his grip firm on his sword.

The Archangel stopped only a few inches from him and leaned forward. "Kill. Them. All. Does that ring a bell?"

The words made Liam dizzy, his mind fuzzy, and he closed his eyes, trying to center himself.

Screams burst in his ears, flashes of people running from him, fire in the background. When he looked down at his hand, he was holding a man's head by his hair. He shouted and dropped it.

Was this the Hells?

Liam fell to his knees and bellowed, the agony in his cries also shattering him inside. His body now acted on its own will, as if he was trapped inside a marionette.

"Make them pay, Michael!" Gabriel stood before him, his image wavering like a TV with a bad reception. "Humans murdered one of ours, and what did the Gods do? Nothing!" Gabriel held a weeping woman by her long dark hair. "We'll bring doomsday upon them ourselves." His blade slashed across her throat, and blood spattered on Liam's face. "Kill their precious and their brave. Kill their weak and useless." Gabriel licked his lips. "Kill them all!"

Liam glared at his own blood-soaked hands. "What have I done?" It was Liam's voice, but he hadn't meant to say it.

He looked up at Gabriel but he had disappeared, along with the screams and the fire, leaving Liam alone in a freezing dark.

Remorse slammed against him, a cold flood that slashed across all his senses. "I-I didn't mean to! I was so angry!" he told himself, not understanding his own words.

The choking grip of agony released him, and Liam glared down at his now perfectly clean hands. He moved his fingers, and they obeyed his command.

An image wavered in the darkness. A tall Archangel walked toward him, his black uniform ripped and cut by blades. Long dark hair curtained the sides of his face, and sweat plastered a few strands to his forehead. It struck Liam then that the Archangel's wings were white as snow.

296

His chin had a dimple, his nose was too flat, and a scar cut across his left eyebrow. He didn't resemble Liam much, but the Archangel *was* Liam. He couldn't say why or how he knew, but he did.

Michael.

Gabriel materialized in the Archangel's way, both their images flickering holograms in the darkness.

"Raphael went in peace," Michael said, raising his silver and blue sword. *Liam's blade.* "He chose to perish rather than to kill the humans who threatened him. He was better than all of us. We should aspire to be like our fallen brother."

"We'll never *be* like him, Michael," Gabriel snapped. "Darkness lives inside us now. There's no coming back."

"The Gods forgive, brother," Michael countered, a certain pity in his tone. "There's a difference between having darkness within and letting it consume you."

Gabriel bared his teeth. "Raphael was a fool, and so are you!" He boosted forward, his sword in hand.

Their bodies clashed, their blades clanging loudly. But Michael was winning, and with one strike he flung Gabriel's sword away. He pressed the tip of the blade softly against Gabriel's chest. "We must pay for our sins."

"Why do you deny the darkness in you?" Gabriel spat. "Embrace it!"

"Not like this."

A sphere of red lightning hit Michael from behind, throwing him on the floor.

Liam blinked, and now he was lying on his back, on the same spot Michael had fallen.

He stared at Gabriel and Talahel, who looked down upon him. Once again, he couldn't move his body. He was trapped inside Michael's memories.

"We should kill him," Talahel said with contempt, his cold eyes assessing Liam—well, *Michael.*

"Give him time." Gabriel turned to the Sword. "As a high angel, you can sign off on his Selfless reincarnation. No one will know."

Darkness crept from the edges of Liam's vision. He tried to force himself awake, but his eyelids were so heavy ...

"He'll remember what happened once he dies and becomes Michael again." Talahel raised an eyebrow. "Easier to kill him now."

Gabriel grabbed his shoulder. "He's my brother-in-arms like Raphael once was. Give him a chance, and if he still doesn't join our cause, I'll end him myself."

Dizziness took over, and when Liam opened his eyes, he was standing on the pier. He inhaled deeply, feeling as if he had been underwater for a long time.

Gabriel frowned. "Daydreaming, brother?"

"Y-you made me kill people," Liam stammered as he patted his chest and arms, making sure he was really here. "We lost someone we loved, and we killed the humans who hurt him. An entire village, Gabriel. We killed them all."

"Someone *we* loved?" Gabriel snarled, his nostrils flared. "I lost much more than a brother when Raphael died, Michael!" He fixed a flock of his lemon-colored hair back, straightening his stance. "Besides, I didn't *make* you do anything. We both wanted revenge for what they did to him, and we got it."

Liam raised his sword and shifted into a battle stance. "I won't let you walk away."

Gabriel snorted at the blade. "Do you truly believe you can beat me?"

"No." With his free hand, Liam withdrew the gun from the holster and shot Gabriel in the heart, point blank.

The Archangel had been focusing on his blade and failed to dodge the blast. It pushed Gabriel several feet back, but Liam knew it wouldn't kill him, not when he had the strength of Archangels and the healing inherent of second-tiers.

Gabriel put a hand over his wound, which had already started to heal through his ripped black uniform. "Pathetic."

He jolted at Liam, his movements a blur, but Liam dodged the attack by an inch. Before the Archangel could turn around, he aimed the gun at Gabriel's head and fired.

Luck was definitely on Liam's side.

The blast flung Gabriel into a container, making a huge dent on the metal, and Liam heard the Archangel's wings crack between his body and the harsh surface. Blood poured from Gabriel's forehead, but considering how close he had been to the blast, his head should've been blown to pieces.

The Archangel's limp body slumped against the container.

Liam couldn't wait; Gabriel's healing had already started. He aimed and ran toward him, and as he did, Liam thanked Archie for teaching him how to get a good shot while moving. He focused on Gabriel's head and fired.

The bullet hit metal.

Fuck, Archangels were fast.

He felt Gabriel's presence looming from behind, his breath brushing Liam's neck. He turned back to look straight into Gabriel's furious eyes. Half of the Archangel's face was painted with fresh blood, and the spot where the bullet had hit him showed the white surface of a cracked skull.

"Nice try, brother." His breath stank of mint and blood.

Liam tried to step back, but Gabriel grabbed both his wrists, his grip like iron. They stood there, the pressure of Gabriel's hold increasing, but Liam refused to drop his sword and gun, even though pain swarmed up his bones.

Gabriel laughed. In a few minutes, his head would be completely healed. "Your stubbornness is admirable."

The Archangel pressed harder, and Liam's hands opened.

He bit back the yelp of pain that scratched his throat. His sword and gun clanked on the ground, and pain pierced through his tendons, but Liam didn't scream. He wouldn't give Gabriel the pleasure.

"Time to die, Michael," Gabriel said with a sneer, but all joy suddenly vanished from his face.

"Let him go!" Ava's voice came from behind the Archangel.

The tip of her blade pressed the back of Gabriel's neck.

Liam lost his footing, and he couldn't breathe. *No, no, no!* His princess would die with him today.

Gabriel turned slowly, pulling Liam with him. As he moved, Ava's blade drew a thin line of blood on his neck that quickly healed. She didn't flinch or move back, she merely glared at Gabriel with an unmerciful fury that belonged to the Valkyrie inside her.

The Archangel smiled and licked his lips. "Oh, this will be so much fun."

"Don't touch her!" Liam pushed against Gabriel, trying to set himself free, but one twist of Gabriel's hand sent Liam down to his knees.

The screams burst inside his throat, but Liam kept his lips closed, trapping them there.

Fuck. The asshole had broken his left wrist.

"Let him go!" In one swift move, Ava pressed the tip of her sword against Gabriel's trachea. "Now!"

"Or else what?" Gabriel laughed. "You'll kill me, *Guardian?*"

"Ava, run!" Liam managed between hushed breaths. Seeing her so close to that sadistic fuck hurt more than his broken wrist. "Just run!"

"I'm not leaving you," she said, her attention fully on Gabriel.

"Cute." The Archangel shrugged, never letting go of Liam. "You'll die together. How tragically beautiful." A jealous glint flashed in his eyes. "It's an honor, really. Not everyone gets the same chance."

He let go of Liam, swiveled out of the blade's reach, and jabbed a punch on Ava's stomach. She stepped back and bent over, her sword clanking on the ground as she gasped for air.

Liam's head thumped with rage and pain, but his movements felt detached and calculated.

He had to save Ava.

He crouched over his elbow so Gabriel couldn't see him pulling the second holy gun from the holster. But the Archangel's attention snapped at him. The fucker grinned all too widely, like monsters in movies.

Shit.

Liam pressed the trigger, but Gabriel became a blur once again. He missed the shot, and then something slammed against his chest, a fist or a foot, he couldn't say. His back slammed on the ground, and then Gabriel was looking down at him with a hint of curiosity.

Liam fired, once, twice, but the Archangel dodged the blasts and kicked the holy gun away—snapping a bone or several in Liam's right hand.

He held his screams once again. He was getting good at this.

The Archangel pressed his foot on Liam's chest, and it weighted like a fucking concrete wall.

"You need a diet," Liam gasped, blood thumping in his head as he tried to push free of him.

"You've developed an interesting sense of humor. It's funny how you're Michael and, at the same time, not like him at all." Gabriel smirked and removed his foot while raising Liam's sword—how he'd gotten to it, Liam didn't know.

The asshole was way too fast.

"Goodbye, brother." He shoved the blade into Liam's chest.

34

AVA

The crush of despair cracked Ava's essence into a million pieces. She stood there, breathless, broken beyond repair. A piercing wail stung her ears, and she realized it had come from her own throat.

Gabriel yanked the blade from Liam's chest with a wet, sharp sound that destroyed her.

It was silent now, painfully so. Ava's breaths rung in her ears as she watched the blade drip red on the floor.

Liam's red.

The bastard gave her a victorious grin before stepping aside, showing her the way to Liam. "I'm not wholly devoid of mercy, Guardian. I know how important your charges are to you."

Ava shouldn't trust Gabriel, but she had no choice. Her legs carried her forward.

Her knees scraped the cement floor as she knelt by Liam's side. The pain of her wounds was nothing.

"Stay with me," she begged.

Liam tried to speak but choked on blood instead.

The beast roared inside Ava, shooting golden light from

the rift into her body. Warmth flooded through her arms, quickly reaching her hands, which glowed like tiny suns.

She pressed them atop Liam's wound.

His organs and flesh began to mend underneath her palm. The light weaved them together. She could feel every tendon connecting, the walls of slashed muscle closing over the cuts.

Ava could save him. There was still hope!

"Not so fast." Gabriel whacked her away with a bone-cracking punch, which flung Ava against a container's wall.

Her body slammed into the hard surface, the back of her head crashing on metal. Her legs became butter beneath her, and then she dropped on the floor, dazed and bordering on unconsciousness.

As Ava tried to focus her blurred vision, she spotted the Captain's body pinned against a red container to her left.

Her eyes were missing.

Ava's head spun, and she tried to center her thoughts. She was too hurt and weak to stand, so she crawled on her knees.

"Liam," she muttered, stretching a hand to him, painfully aware that he was too far.

Gabriel approached Liam's body, raised his sword and sunk the blade into her partner's flesh.

Twice.

A new scream ripped through Ava, shattering everything on its way out; her soul, her thoughts, her reason. And then she couldn't scream anymore, only sob.

Liam's body stopped moving.

Gabriel turned to her with a grin. The sword was still shoved in her partner's chest.

"Your turn, pretty Guardian."

Ava couldn't speak, despair trapped her where she was, her body numb. Liam was her charge, her partner, *hers*, and she had failed him as a Guardian, as a lover, as a friend.

Amidst the sobs that tried to choke her, she bellowed,

"Why?"

Gabriel yanked the sword from Liam's body and strolled to her. "Isn't it obvious? He had to die."

A thick layer of Liam's blood painted the blade, and bile rose up Ava's throat.

She had lost a part of her, one that had crept up inside without being noticed, making itself vital. *Her partner.*

Liam was gone, his voice silenced, and the quiet *killed* her.

"No hard feelings." Gabriel put his hand on his heart as he approached. "But I can't let you walk away, either. I'm sure you understand."

She didn't. She didn't understand any of it. The Order was falling, Liam was dead, and her world was burning. The man who had become her safe haven now laid lifeless on the ground.

Gabriel stopped beside her, holding Liam's sword high. He observed her with fake pity. "I would say prepare to meet your makers, but it's not like you'll go to the Heavens, is it? Your next stop is oblivion." His smile showcased madness. A flock of his yellow hair brushed on his forehead. "Farewell, weak little Guardian."

Weak. Little. Guardian.

Golden lava gushed from Ava's rift, enveloping her body. She saw the sword coming down in slow motion and closed her eyes.

Let it be done with.

The blade slammed down on her neck, and the sound of metal hitting metal clanged loudly. Her head remained in place.

Her shield's molten gold had swept over her skin, cold and tingling. Gabriel's blade had scratched its surface, but it'd felt like a papercut.

She took advantage of his surprise and jumped up, sucker-punching him miles into the water.

She glared at her golden wrist with a mix of shock and awe. A Dominion or a Virtue couldn't punch like this. She doubted a Warrior could, either—Ava would know. She had faced a Warrior's knuckles back at Club 23.

This ... this had been an Archangel's punch.

She waited for her head to hurt, knowing she had used a power that wasn't hers. But Ava felt nothing.

Liam!

She rushed to him and quickly dropped by his side. She pressed her heavy, gold-coated hands on his chest, shoving the beast's light, *her* light, into him.

"Please, please ..."

If it weren't for the gaping wound on his chest and his blood-soaked chin, Liam could very well be sleeping.

His cold body didn't react to her light. There was no life there to be saved.

"I'm sorry, Ava," the Angel of Death's soft voice rung in her ears.

"No," she whined, caressing his cheek. "I swore I'd protect you." Her voice cracked into a sob. "I'm so sorry."

Miles ahead, Gabriel broke through the water, rising up like a rocket. He landed before them, dripping wet, his cruel grin showcasing white teeth.

Ava leaned down and kissed Liam's forehead. "I'll finish this. I promise."

All she wanted was to curl up and cry by her fallen partner's side, but instead Ava stood, her hands balled into fists.

She was perfectly aware she should try to escape and warn the Order or the Legion. But she wouldn't. Not until she had Gabriel's head.

Her light beast purred in agreement.

"You're an interesting nuisance." Gabriel pointed Liam's sword at her. "I haven't had a challenge in a while."

Ava picked up the sword of revelation, which lay on the

ground not far from them. Gabriel didn't try to stop her; he just watched. He must know he couldn't hurt Ava if her golden shield was up, or at least that it would take a great effort for him to break through—an effort he clearly wasn't willing to make.

A rumbling calm took over her, a serenity filled with rage. *The calm before the storm.*

"Why can't any of you see?" Gabriel showed her the city beyond the water line. "This world must end so a better one can rise. One with no demons, no In-Betweens, and no humans. Just us, the Gods' truest servants. We can make Earth the fourth Heaven!" He laughed loudly and ran a hand through his blond curls. "Why must you be so stubborn?"

"You forget one thing." She raised her sword. "You stand no longer with the Gods."

Ava shot forward, remembering Liam's lessons. *Attack, dodge, charge.* Her blade clanged against Liam's sword. *Unworthy,* she thought. Gabriel had no right to wield that weapon, and she'd make him pay.

The Archangel's attacks, however, easily pierced her defenses. Gabriel was a powerful second-tier with many centuries of experience, and Ava was a simple Guardian. Her golden shield spared her life, but it also pressed upon her body. It slowed her down and sucked all her energy.

Her breaths came in chunks now. Keeping the shield up took more effort than she could afford.

Just as the golden surface swept down her face, Gabriel snatched a punch that made her spin twice. Then he kicked her unprotected stomach, sending her several steps back. Her sword fell on the ground, all too far from her.

Pain stabbed inside Ava, and she bent down. Her entire shield sunk into her core the way water goes down a drain.

Hells!

She couldn't win against Gabriel, not like this. So she

forced the rift open, drawing power from the light beast. It roared, shaking her essence. Golden lightning shot from Ava's rift and whipped in the air around her.

A storm of gold.

"Marvelous," Gabriel muttered.

The lightning snapped toward him, and he took the attack with open arms.

Back at Club 23, her lightning had disintegrated Warriors because of the boost provided by the sword of revelation. Now the sword was dormant, and the lighting didn't feel as ravenous and chaotic as before. So when the jolts of electricity hit Gabriel, he only shook slightly.

Heavens, her attack should've caused him at least some degree of pain.

Was she so powerless?

"I'm not a weak lower angel, little Guardian," he said with an eager grin.

Perhaps she was using the wrong approach. The beast inside the rift growled, and the crackling electricity slammed farther, penetrating into Gabriel's conscience. It only stopped once it found the borders to his mind, a long wall that felt like it was made of bone.

Breakable bone.

Gabriel chuckled as he stepped toward her. "You can't force your emotions into me. You're only a third-tier."

She shoved her power into his wall regardless.

It didn't work.

Gabriel was approaching fast and soon he would be here, ready to cut off her head.

A rumbling sound caught her attention, a mix of thunder snapping and waves crashing.

At first, Ava thought it had come from a distance, but no, it came from *inside* her. The beast beyond the rift demanded to free something, and Ava knew exactly what.

The sound of glass cracking echoed in her ears.

Obsidian glass. The darkness was free.

A pitch-black mass shot from her depths like a geyser, and her rift discharged golden light forward. Both forces mingled, forming a swirling mass of light and dark inside her.

Gabriel frowned. "You all right, little Guardian?"

They were almost face-to-face now.

Ava barely heard him through the frenzy of light and darkness that raged under her skin, like water flowing downriver, possessing, consuming, and at the same time, *freeing.*

Cold and foggy, the darkness fed on the anger of Liam's loss, on the heartache she had felt as he bled before her, and on the deep sadness that took over when he was gone. Her warm light countered with the joy of helping others, and how wonderful it had felt to spend a fraction of her existence with her partner.

Serenity to balance the rage. Joy to balance the sorrow.

Her hands closed into fists, and she shot her lightning forward once more. It smacked into Gabriel's wall, cracking the surface as easily as an eggshell.

The Archangel stopped midway, glaring at the black and golden lightning crossing through his chest. He slammed a hand on his head, trying to push her away from his essence, but he was only an Archangel. The children of the God of War couldn't raise powerful mental walls.

Ava smiled. Or maybe it was her darkness, or her light, she couldn't be sure. They were all the same now.

"Stop!" he barked, an angry scowl forming on his face.

Ava shot forward the despair of seeing the sword plunge into Liam, how she had died if only for a second. Gabriel dropped to his knees and bellowed the same cries she'd bellowed.

Ava added musings of what she thought the Hells were like. Lakes of lava, sulfur hanging heavily in the air, and then there was Gabriel, tied to a wooden log that sank into the magma, his skin hissing and smoking as his wings burned behind him. She snuck all of it into the golden and black lightning that shattered his wall to pieces, injecting raw, maddening pain into every crevice that made Gabriel who he was.

The Archangel howled louder, clawing at his lungs because they burned from inside, even if only in his head.

Once, Ava would've stopped.

Not today.

Guilt for what she was about to do birthed from the light and fueled the dark. She shot it at Gabriel, through the golden lightning, the corroding sensation a piercing blade.

Gabriel grasped for air. "Stop!"

Images burst into Ava's mind. An Archangel with hazel hair smiled at Gabriel as he kissed a trail down his naked chest. The scene then shifted to Gabriel, holding on to the Archangel's lifeless body, and howling the same screeches Ava had bellowed when she lost Liam.

She pushed that gnawing despair into Gabriel ten times over, hammering his greatest hurt into him. The dead angel's face was ingrained within the lightning that possessed Gabriel's mind over and over again.

"Raphael!" He screamed so hard he soiled himself.

Once, Ava would've felt mercy.

Not today.

Gabriel didn't notice her approaching. She grabbed Liam's sword from the ground and stopped behind the Archangel.

What Ava was about to do went against everything that had guided her this far. Perhaps killing Gabriel would end the best part of her. But this monster had murdered Liam, and if the cost for his punishment was her soul, so be it.

She raised her sword swiftly and shot Gabriel one last image of his dead lover. He stretched his hand toward the canal and the city beyond.

"My Raphael," he whispered.

Her sword went down in a circle, slashing Gabriel's neck. His head hit the floor with the harshness of a ripe coconut, and his body slumped forward, blood squirting from his neck and pooling on the ground.

Once, this gruesome death would have appalled her. Once, Ava doubted her hands could inflict such horrors. Today, her shoulders slumped and she inhaled deeply, leaning her head back.

Ava closed her eyes to the sky and felt—felt the wind brushing her skin, heard the waves crashing to shore, and the seagulls cawing in the distance. Every sensation seemed sharper, clearer. Failing Liam destroyed her, but her cracked pieces glued back together, only in a different order, making her anew. Even if the pieces were still the same.

"Ava?"

She turned to Ezra, who stood behind her. He glared shock and disappointment all at once. "What have you done?" His tone was weak, much like the owner.

The storm of light and dark inside her faded. The two beasts slowly went to sleep but not before snarling a threat at Ezra.

Easy, Ava told them, well, herself. They were one in the end.

"I did what I had to do," she said.

He shook his head. "No, you didn't."

Without meaning to, she bared her teeth at him. Let Ezra try and punish her for killing that monster. See how well that would fare for him.

Ezra stepped back, and a shivering cloud of splinters and jagged pieces brushed against Ava's essence.

Fear. The Messenger was *afraid* of her. Perhaps she should fear herself too.

Ezra swallowed, then surveyed the scene around him. "Gabriel lost his mind. Yes, that's what we'll tell the Order. We'll tell them I killed him."

"No, Ezra, I—"

"They already want to punish you for blowing up an army of Warriors." He pressed his lips together, assurance flowing from him. "Let me handle this, Ava. It's the least I can do."

The sensation was a prickle on her back at first, a scratch that escalated into whipping pain. Blades of bone cut through her skin from inside out. It felt as if a tree was growing from her spine, and Ava screamed as she fell to her knees.

Bones that hadn't been there a moment ago kept cracking into place, and it all sounded awfully like wood snapping. The structure behind her cracked some more, and then it stopped. The flesh on her back burned as it spread over her newly formed bones, pulled in a thousand different directions.

Ava stored the pain in tight-lipped screams that made tears flow from her eyes.

Just when she thought she couldn't take it anymore, the pain waned. A soft breeze caressed the brand new and aching limbs that sprouted from her back.

A white feather tipped in blood swung gracefully in the air before Ava, dropping the way snow falls.

Ava caught it, then looked up. "Heavens ..."

Majestic blood-soaked wings enclosed her in a cocoon. White wings.

Her wings.

She took a deep breath and stood on shaky legs, still

entranced by her brand new feathers. Her back was sore, her muscles still ached. She tried to flap her wings, but they bent awkwardly behind her.

"I'll teach you how to use them." Ezra watched her with awe. "They're such a pure white."

Ironic. Those pure white wings had been acquired through bloodthirst and fury.

Far back on the street, Ava spotted Jophiel and Jal. The grief on their faces asked her for forgiveness; she didn't need to sense their emotions to feel their mourning.

Jophiel gave her a supporting nod, then left. But Jal stood there, his hands balled into fists as he watched Liam's body.

Ava remembered meeting Jal and Kevin as she headed to the precinct, both of them wounded in different ways. Kevin couldn't run, and Jal couldn't fly. They had said, "Liam" and "Dock 5," and that's all she needed to run after him.

The Angel of Death materialized through thin air, standing beside Ezra and blocking Ava's view of Jal.

"It's time," she said.

Ava nodded and walked to Liam. Her wings refused to gather behind her, bending at uncomfortable angles.

She knelt on the floor and propped Liam's head on her thighs, caressing his cheek as he blinked back into consciousness.

"Hey there, princess." He gave her that charming half-manly and half-boyish grin.

"Hey." She sniffed back tears. "I'm so sorry I couldn't protect you, I—"

"You're one hell of a Guardian, Ava. Don't ever doubt that." He frowned at her wings. "Got a promotion?"

She chuckled. "Kind of."

His playful grin vanished and fear crumpled his face. "Gabriel?"

"Gone." She brushed her thumb on his temple. "Don't

worry. Everything is fine."

Ava wished she could keep him here with her for just a little longer.

The Demon of Death materialized beside them. He crossed his arms and rolled his eyes, as if he considered his job a complete nuisance. "Let's get this over with, shall we?"

The Angel of Death stood on Liam's right, the Demon of Death on his left. Together, they said in unison, "Liam Striker, as it is told, as it is said, the Selfless are granted a choice at their time of death. Like the humans they swore to protect, like the flesh and bone they chose to become. Be reborn as a human, an angel, or a demon. If you refuse, be cursed to the In-Between. The Gods and Devils require your decision."

"It's time to come home," Ezra said with a soothing tone that reminded Ava of the Messenger who had taken her in, the man who taught her all about kindness and compassion. The man who had defied the Order in his own way.

Yes, Ezra was still there. He could still be saved. The Order too.

Liam looked at Ava, and tears slid down his cheek. "There's a difference between having darkness within and letting it consume you."

His words hit her like a speeding car. "No, Liam," she mumbled.

"I'm not ready to be Michael again," he said. "I think I'm not *supposed* to be."

Ava's breath hitched, and she squeezed his hand. "I will always stand by you, no matter what."

He smiled weakly and raised his shaky hands to nudge her heart. "This is the only faith you should follow, princess." He took off his pendant with the symbols of the Gods. He didn't turn to the Angel and Demon of Death; his gaze remained locked on Ava's. "I choose to become a demon."

"Heavens!" Ezra stepped back, his mouth half open and about to ask Liam why he'd made such a choice. But Liam's hand had slumped on the floor, showing the pendant, the symbol of the Gods, in his lifeless palm.

The Demon of Death leaned over and touched Liam's forehead, sacramenting his body. He then gave Ava a supportive nod before fading away.

Ava kissed Liam's forehead one last time, then laid his head gently on the floor.

She stood wearily, feeling old and broken.

And alone. So alone.

Ezra wrapped her in his arms. Ava didn't want *his* arms around her or the beating of *his* heart against her ears. But she was too tired, and pushing Ezra away might as well push him into Talahel's side.

The sirens of the clean-up teams wailed from the distance. Soon they'd be here.

Ezra let her go. "We'll transport him to the Order and find a way to help him when he wakes."

"Forgive me for not trusting the Order with one of mine." Jal stepped out from behind a container. He shot Ava a look that seemed to say, *"Not until you've cleaned up your house."*

She nodded.

Jal took Liam's body, wincing at the weight inflicted on his half-broken arm, but he didn't let go.

Ava stepped forward and pressed her forehead against Liam's. "Always," she muttered. "I'll always be with you."

Ezra put an arm around her and pulled her gently away from her partner. "Ava, I know he was important to you, but if he's not taken to the Order, then we'll have to kill him once he wakes." He glared at Jal. "Release him at once, demon."

Jal's expression was unmoving lines. "Make me."

"Let him go, Ezra," Ava more demanded than asked. "He's not safe in the Order."

He blinked. "B-but we're bound to the Gods, Ava."

Bound to the Gods?

She smirked. Ava was bound to nothing but herself, to the faith inside her.

She observed Liam one last time, already feeling the pang of longing that would only grow stronger.

"Keep him safe," she told Jal.

"Will do." He smirked, clearly enjoying the outrage that flashed in Ezra's face.

The demon turned and walked away, soon disappearing beyond the containers.

Ezra gave her a desperate sigh but soon took her hand. "Come. I believe we have much to discuss."

They certainly did.

As they walked off the dock, Ava nudged her heart and smiled. Helping others was her faith, but there was something else now, a hunger for justice, to set things right, no matter the cost.

Light and darkness balancing within.

She would rid the Order from evil, and to do so she would sneak right under a devil's nose. Perhaps she would have to become a devil herself.

Ava turned back and locked eyes with the Angel of Death, who was still standing where Liam had fallen. Her empty, glowing stare cast a question, one that had always been with Ava since she'd been reborn as an angel.

Why do you think you're here?

A soft smile creased her lips. Ava knew her purpose now.

She was here to start a war.

∾

Pre-order *Cursed Darkness: Angels of Fate Book 2*

Thanks for reading!

Choose which book you want next!

Ratings help me determine which series I'll prioritize, so if you can't wait for the next book in this series, leave a review and show your love. The sequel to BLESSED FURY is almost done, but production on the third instalment only begins once we reach thirty reviews on this book.

That's right: YOU get to choose which books come next by leaving a review.

Yay!

Keep up to date with the latest news and release dates by joining C.S. Wilde's mailing list at www.cswilde.com

ACKNOWLEDGMENTS

A huge thanks to my designer Mirella Santana, and my brilliant editors Christina Walker at Supernatural Editing and Sara Mack at Red Ribbon Editing.

Another huge thanks to my husband, which comes as no surprise to him since I thank him in each and every one of my books. Without him, none of these stories would ever see the light of day.

ABOUT THE AUTHOR

C. S. Wilde wrote her first Fantasy novel when she was eight. That book was absolutely terrible, but her mother told her it was awesome, so she kept writing.

Now a grown up (though many will beg to differ), C. S. Wilde writes about fantastic worlds, love stories larger than life and epic battles.

She also, quite obviously, sucks at writing an author bio. She finds it awkward that she must write this in the third person and hopes you won't notice.

For up to date promotions and release dates of upcoming books, sign up for the latest news at www.cswilde.com. You can also connect on twitter via @thatcswilde or on facebook at C.S. Wilde. You can also join the Wildlings, C.S. Wilde's exclusive Facebook group.

31040734R00197

Printed in Poland
by Amazon Fulfillment
Poland Sp. z o.o., Wrocław